FOOL FOR LOVE

Kelly made her way to the bathroom. She smiled at her reflection in the mirror, an intriguing thought taking shape in her mind. This trip would be quite interesting. She was no longer a shy, awkward teenager. In fact, she had blossomed into a confident woman. If Ashton was anything like she remembered—and she'd bet her last dollar that he was—he'd be sure to notice her feminine appeal. The dress she planned to wear flattered her womanly curves and would certainly make it clear to Ashton that he had been a fool to treat her the way he had all those years ago. And if, by any remote chance, he showed any interest in her, she would enjoy the power that would come from rejecting him the way he had rejected her. Not that it really mattered to her, but as far as she was concerned, that would be poetic justice at its best.

"Ashton Hunter," she announced to her reflection, a devious sparkle in her bright brown eyes, "you are in for a big surprise."

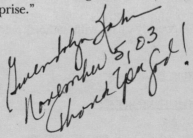

FOOL FOR LOVE

Kayla Perrin

ARABESQUE

BET BOOKS

BET Publications, LLC
http://www.bet.com
http://www.arabesquebooks.com

ARABESQUE BOOKS are published by

BET Publications, LLC
c/o BET BOOKS
One BET Plaza
1900 W Place NE
Washington, DC 20018-1211

All Kensington Titles, Imprints, and Distributed Lines are available at special quantity discounts for bulk purchases for sales promotions, premiums, fund-raising, and educational or institutional use. Special book excerpts or customized printings can also be created to fit specific needs. For details, write or phone the office of the Kensington special sales manager: Kensington Publishing Corp., 850 Third Avenue, New York, NY 10022, attn: Special Sales Department, Phone: 1-800-221-2647.

First Printing: November 2003
10 9 8 7 6 5 4 3 2 1

Printed in the United States of America

This one's for my new love,
my darling little girl.
You've enriched my life in ways
I never thought possible.
Your mama loves you,
always.

Prologue

Ten years earlier

Hotter than sin.

Bracing her hands on the edges of the pedestal sink, Kelly Robbins giggled as she stared at her reflection in the bathroom mirror. *Sinfully hot. Hot, hot, hot.* She giggled again. Though relatively inexperienced in the love department, she knew that something as explosive and pleasurable as what she had enjoyed last night could only be described with those words. Last night's event was, quite simply, the best experience of her life. Now she truly knew the meaning of "out of this world."

Closing her eyes, she licked her bottom lip, remembering—experiencing again the delightful sensations as last night played in her mind. She hadn't known what to expect, whether reality would live up to fantasy. For months, she had dreamt about it, and last night her dreams came true. Finally, she had made love with Ashton Hunter, and it had been wilder than any of her most secret fantasies!

She opened her eyes, let her gaze roam over her forehead, down the length of her face to her chin, down to the base of her neck, finally resting on the fullness of her breasts. No doubt about it, she was a different person now than twenty-four hours ago. Even her reflection was different. Her lips were fuller, sexier. Her eyes were brighter, her face more mature. She was vibrant. Her reflection said she was no longer a child. Now, she was a woman.

Ashton's woman.

Her breasts tingled at the thought, remembering the way Ashton's hands and mouth had caressed every inch of her body, bringing her to a height of ecstasy she had never dreamt possible.

With a fingertip, Kelly traced the outline of her lips, lips that were still swollen from Ashton's kisses. Her eyes grew serious. Yes, last night had been incredible, but there was so much more to what she and Ashton had shared than the physical enjoyment. Last night, through the ultimate physical intimacy, their emotional connection deepened. With each drugging kiss, with each heated caress, Ashton had shown her the depth of his love in a way he had never been able to verbally express.

And Kelly was lost. Head over heels in love.

The shrill ring of the telephone interrupted her thoughts, and, excitement washing over, she darted from the bathroom into her bedroom. Ashton said he would call today, but she hadn't expected him to call before noon. Not after getting to bed so late last night. . . .

But maybe, like her, he had found it hard to concentrate on sleep.

Though her heart danced with anticipation, she let the phone ring three times, not wanting to appear too anxious. She lifted the receiver just before the machine picked up and in her sexiest voice said, "Hello."

"Don't tell me you were still sleeping? Whoa, that must have been *some* night."

Her excitement faded at the sound of her best friend's

voice, not Ashton's. "Karen, hi." She sat on the bed. "What's up?"

"You're asking *me* what's up? Come on, Kelly. Don't keep me in suspense. The last I saw of you at the grad party, you were sneaking out with Mr. Drop Dead Gorgeous himself. Inquiring minds want to know!"

"Hmm . . . You mean . . . Ashton?" Kelly asked slyly, knowing exactly who her friend meant.

"Of course I mean Ashton! Ashton Hunter—the most wanted guy in the senior class. The one *you* left with. And let me tell you, almost every other girl at the party was green with envy! Especially Taleesha Harper. I promise not to hate you as long as you tell me every last detail. So come on. Tell me what happened!"

Smiling, Kelly lay back onto the pillows. To think she had once worried that Ashton might not be attracted to her because she wasn't as slim as some of the other girls in their high school. But he was more than attracted to her; he was hers, and everybody knew it. She pinched herself to make sure she wasn't dreaming. "What can I say, Karen?" She paused for effect. "Last night was . . . the best damn night of my life!"

Karen's high-pitched squeal nearly deafened Kelly. "I knew it! Girl, I'm *so* happy for you!"

"I still can't believe it. I mean, I knew our relationship was getting more serious, but when Ashton asked me to leave with him last night . . ." Kelly sighed, contented. "Karen, he loves me. He really does."

"I am *so* jealous."

"What about you? How did your night go?"

"Malcolm got drunk and forgot I existed. But that's okay. I still had a great time."

"There'll be other men in college," Kelly assured her. "Tons of gorgeous men who will be lining up to go out with you."

Karen chuckled. "I certainly hope so, 'cause I am through worrying about Malcolm." She paused. "But what happens now? With you and Ashton, I mean. You're moving any day . . ."

Kelly frowned, then rolled over onto her stomach. She didn't want to think about her pending move. Last month, her father had surprised the family with the news that his job required he move to Fort Lauderdale, Florida—half a world away. It would have been hard enough leaving Karen, but after what she had shared with Ashton she knew she couldn't leave. Not now, when she was happier than she'd ever been.

"I don't think my father will mind if I stay here for college," Kelly finally said, hoping she was right. "At the very least, I have the rest of the summer with Ashton. And if necessary, we can always visit each other."

"I guess you're right," Karen said.

Kelly glanced at the digital clock radio, noting that she had been on the phone with Karen for over five minutes. "Karen, let me call you later. I'm expecting Ashton's call."

Four hours later, Kelly was still waiting for that call. Her stomach was a ball of knots as she sat cross-legged on her bed, chewing on a fingernail. With each minute that passed, she grew more uneasy. Why wasn't the phone ringing? Had Ashton forgotten his promise to her? How could he, after what they had shared? No, he must be sleeping, exhausted from their night together. Either that or extremely busy.

An hour and a half later, Kelly could wait no longer and decided to call Ashton. Maybe they could get together tonight, experience once again what they had last night.

"Hello, Mr. Hunter," Kelly said when Ashton's father answered the phone. "It's Kelly. Can I speak with Ashton, please?"

"Ashton . . . ?" If Kelly wasn't mistaken, he sounded puzzled. "Um, Ashton's not here, Kelly."

Something's wrong. "Do you know when he'll be home?"

Silence. Then, "Didn't Ashton tell you?"

The skin on the back of her neck prickled as a sickening feeling spread through her body. "Tell me what?"

"Ashton's gone, Kelly."

Mr. Hunter made "gone" sound final, like forever. But that couldn't be true. "Gone? I don't understand."

"I can't believe he didn't tell you. Ashton left this morning. He got a job out west for the summer, and after that I'm not sure he's even coming back."

The room spun. Her ears rang, drowning out the sound of Mr. Hunter's voice.

Gone. For the summer. Maybe not coming back.

It couldn't be true. Ashton wouldn't leave her like this, not after what they shared last night. He wanted to be with her as much as she wanted to be with him.

And even if he did have a job out west, surely he wouldn't leave without saying good-bye.

This had to be some kind of mistake.

". . . tell him you called if I hear from him," Kelly heard Mr. Hunter say.

She couldn't speak. Quickly, she replaced the receiver, Mr. Hunter's words playing in her mind over and over again.

Her brain searched to make sense of the words, to explain what was clearly inexplicable. But as Kelly collapsed onto the bed, her body finally going numb, she knew that Mr. Hunter couldn't be mistaken.

Ashton had left her. Without looking back.

Chapter 1

"At last," Kelly muttered as she stepped into her air-conditioned home and out of the blazing heat. Leaning her back against the door, she reveled in the cool, refreshing air. As much as she loved the heat, jogging for charity in ninety-degree weather was absolutely insane. Which made her certifiable. Yet she couldn't resist Fort Lauderdale's annual run to raise funds for breast cancer research.

It was the one cause that would always be near and dear to her heart, after a close friend and colleague at the school where she worked had died of breast cancer at the age of thirty-one. Rebecca's sickness had been a horrible shock, her death devastating. That had been three years ago, and Kelly still felt the pain of her loss.

At least the run had gone well. She had gotten close to four hundred dollars in sponsorship money. Every bit helped, and she prayed each day that the cure for cancer would soon be found.

Kelly pushed herself off the door, determined to put negative thoughts out of her mind and relax. A shower was the first order of business. Make that a cool bath, she decided—one filled with lots of bubbles. She de-

served it after the day she'd had. Then, she would spend
the rest of the day chilling out and reading the romantic suspense she had picked up a few weeks earlier.

Turning to the right in her apartment, Kelly headed
straight for the large bathroom with its grand oval tub
that she had hardly had the opportunity to use during
the school year. But now that the school year had ended
a few days ago, she planned to enjoy many a summer
day in this tub, relaxing and recuperating. All so that
she could be rejuvenated and prepared to teach another hectic fourth-grade class in the fall.

The bubble bath hit the spot, cooling her heated
skin and soothing her tense muscles. Sufficiently relaxed,
Kelly dried off and walked naked to her bedroom. She
was about to throw herself on the bed when the flashing
green light on the answering machine caught her eye.
Extending a finger, she pressed the Play button.

The tape rewound, then began to play. "Hi. This is a
message for Kelly Robbins. Kelly, this is—"

With lightning speed, Kelly reached out and pressed
the Pause button on the answering machine, staring
down at the small black box in stupefied horror. No. It
couldn't be . . .

Her mind fought to deny the truth her heart knew.
Ten years had passed since she'd last seen him, since
she'd last heard his cool, sultry voice. Yet she knew without a doubt that the voice recorded on her answering
machine belonged to him.

To Ashton Hunter.

Ashton Hunter!

A weird tingling sensation coursed through her veins
as an image of his wickedly sexy smile invaded her mind.
She shook her head, trying to toss the image aside. But
it only grew clearer, taunting her. Damn him! Ten years
of trying to forget her worst nightmare, eradicated with
one phone call!

Why, after not hearing from him since high school, was Mr. Heartbreaker calling her now? And how on earth did he get her telephone number? After all, she lived in Fort Lauderdale now, and the last place she had seen him was Toronto, Canada.

Her emotions mixing somewhere between confusion and anticipation, Kelly expelled a flood of warm breath, feeling as though someone had knocked the air out of her lungs. She never expected to see or hear from Ashton again, yet here he was, contacting her. Why, Kelly wondered. Why was he calling her after all this time?

The answer wasn't going to come from her standing around wondering about it. There was only one way to find out. Slowly, she extended a quivering finger and pressed the Pause button again, and the tape began rolling.

". . . Ashton. Ashton Hunter. Uh, it's been a long time. . . ." Pause. "Uh, I'm calling about Karen Stewart. Actually, I got your number from her phone book. Anyway, in case you don't already know, Karen has landed a part in a musical. She'll be leaving for a tour of Canada next week. And I'm planning a surprise party for her. I know you two were best friends in high school, and that you're still in touch, and I think it would be great if you could come to Toronto right away to surprise her. Maybe even help me plan the party. Give me a call at 416-555-2391 to let me know if you can make it."

There was a quick pause before his smooth-as-velvet voice dominated the answering machine once again. "I really hope you can make it, Kelly. I look forward to hearing from you."

The machine came to a stop and gave out a series of quick, loud beeps, indicating that there were no more messages.

Finally blinking, Kelly let out a slow, deliberate breath. Ashton Hunter had just called her? This couldn't be real. She had to be dreaming. Someone must have zapped her into the twilight zone.

She rewound the message. Played it again.

It was the same message, Ashton's voice as devastatingly sexy as she'd always remembered. And despite the time that had passed, the memory of the crush she had had on Ashton Hunter was suddenly as fresh and new as when she'd first laid eyes on him.

It was totally irrational, but Kelly's heart was beating faster than when she'd run twenty miles earlier. Turning, she moved to the window and shoved it open. The warm summer air mixed with the honeyed scent of wisteria did nothing to calm her frazzled nerves.

Utter and complete shock over hearing Ashton's voice quickly turned to downright anger as she remembered his words. "It's been a long time," she said aloud, then curled her fist into a ball. It sure as hell had been. Ten years too long!

Despite her anger, Ashton's sexy image filled her mind. Golden brown skin, powerful muscular physique, and the most remarkable hazel eyes she had ever seen. Eyes she had once believed regarded her with love, but what a fool she had been.

All the painful memories she had long ago buried now resurged with overwhelming clarity. Ashton's sweet words, his warm smiles. And her stupid, naive trust. He'd preyed on her weakness, on her affection for him, and in the process had trampled her heart. For a brief period of her life she'd been silly enough to believe that the school playboy actually cared for her. God, she really had been a fool. Ashton Hunter didn't care about anybody but himself. And he had the notches on his bedpost to prove it, she was sure.

Hers was one of them.

Kelly closed the window with more force than necessary, then quickly dressed. She would have erased that damn message and burned it from her memory, if it weren't for the fact that it had to do with Karen, one of her dearest friends. If Karen had a part in a musical, she wanted to be there to help her celebrate.

A jarring pang of guilt hit Kelly as she thought of Karen Stewart, her best friend through grade school and high school. They had shared every secret, every special moment in each other's lives during those years. When, after high school, Kelly and her family had moved to Fort Lauderdale, she'd been devastated. Not only had she left Ashton and those silly dreams behind, she'd left Karen, the one person who had been as close as a sister. During their frequent phone calls after Kelly's move, Karen had confessed to her that Toronto just wasn't the same without her favorite sidekick.

It had been several months since Kelly last corresponded with Karen. The responsibilities of adult life left little time to write, and the longer friends were separated, Kelly acknowledged sadly, the less often they tended to write or call. But she would be there for Karen now. She had to be.

Kelly made her way to the kitchen, enjoying the feel of the cool tiled floor beneath her feet. It was the end of June, and if Karen was leaving next week, she had to make arrangements to go to Toronto right away. Opening the cupboard where she kept the yellow pages, she took the heavy book into her arms and strolled into the living room, then sank into the comfort of her plush beige sofa.

Starting with the most popular, she called all the airlines listed, but to her dismay, the prices for travel the next day were outrageous. Every airline had told her the same thing—that for the best price, she would need a two-week advance purchase.

Maybe she would have better luck calling a travel agent. Goodness, how could she have forgotten? Her brother's cousin-in-law was a travel agent!

Her brother, Michael, had met and fallen for Diamond Montgomery months earlier. Kelly had met Diamond's cousin, Tara, at her brother's wedding two months ago. Kelly had liked her, and promised to utilize her services should she ever plan on traveling.

Kelly dialed Michael's number. He answered on the first ring.

"Michael, hi."

"Uh oh. What's going on now?"

"Is that any way to greet your only sister?"

"You can hardly blame me, Kelly. You've always got some drama going on in your life."

Touché. Her last call to her brother had been about Glenn Ritter, a coworker—and a man who wanted her hand in marriage. Over the past weeks, he had been giving her notes or cards practically every day. "I love a sexy, confident black woman," one of his notes had read. "I miss you," read another card. Kelly didn't know how he could miss her when they had seen each other the day before.

Finally, on the last day of school, he had asked her out to dinner. She had accepted—only to be stunned by his proposal of marriage over sweet and sour chicken balls. Kelly had promptly called her brother, asking his advice about Glenn and whether or not Michael thought he could be a stalker.

"You and the crazy men you deal with," was all Michael had told her after she had spilled her guts to him.

"So I should stay away from him?" Kelly had asked.

"You said he's a friend, right?"

"Yeah. Well, I always thought he was, anyway."

"Maybe he's a nice guy."

"So I should *marry* him?"

"Oh, Kelly. Nothing is ever easy with you, is it? It's always drama."

Kelly had gone on to talk to Diamond about Glenn. If anyone would know what to do, it was Diamond. She gave advice for a living on her radio show *The Love Chronicles*.

Diamond hadn't seen Glenn as a stalker—and she knew plenty about the subject as she had been stalked by a deranged fan. Earlier this year that horrifying ordeal had come to an end when Clay had been shot to death by police while he was trying once again to abduct Diamond.

"You'll be happy to know I'm not calling about any drama now," Kelly said into the phone, though the truth was, hearing from Ashton was *major* drama. She couldn't wait to speak with Diamond about it.

"You mean you're not calling to tell me you and Glenn eloped?"

"Shut up!" But Kelly laughed. "I need Tara's phone number."

"Ah, already planning your honeymoon."

Kelly continued to giggle. It was good to see her brother back to his normal self. After he had lost his baby girl to Sudden Infant Death syndrome and his first wife had walked out on him, Kelly wasn't sure she would ever see him smile again—much less happily married to another woman. But Diamond was good to him, and falling in love with her had been the best thing for Michael.

"No, I'm not planning my honeymoon. Remember Karen Stewart? My best friend during high school?"

"Of course I remember her."

"Well, I just found out that she's landed a pretty big role in a musical, and I . . . I figured I'd take a trip up to Toronto to visit her."

"She called? I didn't know you were still in touch."

"Uh . . ." Kelly paused, not sure if she should tell her brother the truth. "Actually, I heard from Ashton Hunter. I'm not sure if you remember—"

"Ashton Hunter! Whoa. Now that's a surprise."

Michael knew all about how Ashton had broken her heart. "For me, too," Kelly said. "He called out of the blue to tell me about Karen."

"And you thought you'd hop on the first plane out of here?"

Kelly couldn't help feeling annoyed. "This is about Karen, not Ashton."

"Hey, you don't have to explain anything to me. But maybe Glenn might be concerned." There was a smile in Michael's voice.

"Can you give me Tara's number? I'd like to give her a call as soon as possible." She didn't want to talk about Ashton with her brother. He wouldn't understand. Because he had known how much Kelly had been in love with Ashton in high school, he naturally assumed she still had a thing for him.

Which she didn't.

"All right. One sec."

Michael was gone for about a minute before coming back onto the line. He recited Tara's work and home numbers.

"Thanks, Michael."

"No problem."

"Tell Diamond I'll talk to her later."

They ended the call. Kelly started to dial Tara's number, then stopped. Her brother's teasing words were making her think twice about this.

What was she doing? Because Ashton Hunter had said to jump, she was asking, "How high?" She didn't have to do a damn thing that man wanted, especially not go to Toronto at a moment's notice. If he thought she was the same lovesick teenager who would do any-thing he demanded, he had another think coming.

She had learned her lesson the first time. Blindly, she had surrendered her body—and her heart—to him. And what had that gotten her? One wildly passionate night, but years of heartache.

Kelly ran a hand through her long, thin braids. The memories were bittersweet. Ashton had been a tremen-dous lover. After he'd abandoned her, Kelly had figured that the experience had been so special simply because Ashton had been her first. But as the years had passed, she had found no other man equal to Ashton in that re-gard.

Even now, she could still remember vividly Ashton's hands on her body, his thrilling kisses, his mouth on her breasts. . . .

Kelly steeled herself against the memory. What was wrong with her? She was a fool, indeed.

Forget Ashton. She was going to Toronto for one rea-son: to see her dear friend Karen whom she hadn't seen since high school. To miss this opportunity simply be-cause Ashton had invited her would be asinine . . . and immature. Already, Kelly couldn't wait to pull Karen into her arms and squeeze the life out of her.

That decided, she picked up the phone and dialed Tara's work number.

"I'm looking for Tara," she said when the reception-ist answered.

"Hold, please."

It took about a minute for Tara to pick up. "Tara Burkeen."

"Hi, Tara. This is Kelly Robbins. I don't know if you remember me—"

"Of course I remember you. How are you?"

"Pretty good."

"I've been meaning to call you. Darren and I are having a huge family get together in two weeks, and of course you're invited."

"Oh. That sounds great, but I'm not sure I can make it. I'm actually going to be heading up to Canada. That's why I was calling you."

"Where exactly do you need to go?"

"Toronto."

"When?"

"As soon as possible."

Kelly could hear the clicking of a computer keyboard. "Let's see what I can find."

Several minutes later, Tara groaned. "All the commercial airline prices are extremely high. Wait a second. Are you willing to fly into Buffalo? It's not too far of a drive to Toronto from there."

"Whatever's cheaper."

"Have you heard of Jet Blue?"

"No."

"It's a great airline with great prices. They fly out of Fort Lauderdale into Buffalo, and you don't need a two-week advance in order to get the best price." More clicking. "Ah, here we go. This is much more reasonable. Do you know when you want to come back?"

"Not really."

"No need to worry. You can easily book a flight back when you're ready. But, you can fly out the day after tomorrow for under two hundred, including taxes."

"Excellent," Kelly said, relieved. "Book it."

Kelly spent the next several minutes giving Tara a credit card number and all her billing information.

"That's it," Tara said when she was done. "You're booked. The flight leaves at 2:45 P.M., stops at JFK airport for a short layover, then you'll continue on to Buffalo, arriving there at 8:05 P.M. You have an electronic ticket. Just bring your ID to the ticket counter. If you have a passport, that's best for traveling to Canada."

"Okay."

"You're all set."

"Thanks so much, Tara."

"No problem. And if you're around in two weeks, please remember the get together. We'd love to have you."

"If I'm in town, I'll be there."

Kelly ended the call. She had written down all the information Tara had given her. Now all she had to do was call Ashton and let him know when she would be arriving.

A simple phone call, a quick exchange. . . . She was an adult. She could do this. Yet her stomach twisted painfully as she walked to her bedroom. The thought of actually speaking to him. . . .

She rewound Ashton's message, jotted down his phone number, then stared at the phone for what seemed like hours. "This is ridiculous," she finally said, then reached for the phone and dialed Ashton's number. Yet her hands were sweaty and jittery as she listened to his phone ring, praying that the answering machine picked up. If he answered the phone . . .

"The cellular subscriber you are trying to reach is currently unavailable. Please leave a message after the tone."

A cell phone, Kelly thought, both relieved and irritated at the same time. He hadn't even given her his home number. An oversight, or was he so used to giving women his cell number because of the life he led?

Kelly frowned. The guy was still a playboy, no doubt leading a wild and crazy lifestyle, breaking countless hearts in the process.

Just like he had broken her heart several years ago.

Kelly left a simple message explaining when she would be arriving at the Buffalo airport in two days. She suddenly realized it might not be easy for him to get to her there, but renting a car for two weeks was hardly necessary. She added, "I hope it won't be a problem to pick me up. But if it is, please call me and let me know. Otherwise, I'll expect to see you around eight P.M. I'll be the one wearing the bright red sundress and carrying designer luggage—in case you have trouble spotting me," she added with a touch of sarcasm.

If she had to deal with seeing him, she may as well look good. Make him realize what a big mistake he had made in letting her go.

Hours later, Kelly lay in bed, deep in thought.

She was nervous now. Nervous about seeing Ashton and what it would mean.

"Oh, for goodness sake. It's not gonna mean a thing. You're over Ashton."

And she was. Had been for years. But that didn't mean it would be easy to see him.

Sighing, Kelly wondered what she should do about Glenn. Should she call him before she left? She wasn't exactly ready to hear any more talk of his proposal. Even though he had told her that she could take as long as she wanted to think about it—within reason, he'd told her, with a laugh—she would feel pressure to give him an answer just by talking to him.

Glenn was a sweetheart, and as out of the blue as his proposal had been, Kelly had actually given it some serious thought. She was twenty-eight. Hardly over the hill, but she didn't want to be too old before she got married and started a family.

And she had to admit, she liked the fact that Glenn appreciated her fuller figure. She wasn't fat, or even overweight as far as she was concerned, but people often called her "thick" or described her as being "big-boned."

The problem with Glenn was that she wasn't in love

with him. "You'll grow to love me," he had told her as they'd eaten dessert. "I was married once, and I can tell you firsthand that love is overrated. What matters most is that there is mutual appreciation and respect."

Kelly didn't exactly have a ton of other offers. Over the years, she had met her share of losers, but no real prospects. It was the main reason she hadn't dismissed Glenn's suggestion.

No, it wouldn't be right to leave town and not call him. If nothing else, he was her friend. If she didn't reach him, she would leave him a message explaining what was going on.

And maybe going away would help her gain perspective so that she could make a decision and give him an answer soon.

Kelly sat up. For some reason, she was too wired to sleep.

Ashton. He was the reason she couldn't get any rest.

It was the shock of hearing his voice that had caused her unease, and the unwanted memories that had followed. And, she couldn't deny, fear over seeing him again.

But she was a different person today than she had been in high school, one who had long gotten over Ashton Hunter. She had to remember that. There was no need to be intimidated by him now.

Kelly made her way to the bathroom. She smiled at her reflection in the mirror, an intriguing thought taking shape in her mind. This trip could be quite interesting. She was no longer a shy, awkward teenager. In fact, she had blossomed into a confident woman. If Ashton was anything like she remembered—and she'd bet her last dollar that he was—he'd be sure to notice her feminine appeal. The dress she planned to wear flattered her womanly curves and would certainly make it clear to Ashton that he had been a fool to treat her the way he had all those years ago. And if, by any remote chance, he showed any interest in her, she would enjoy the power that would come from rejecting him, the way he had rejected her. Not that it really mattered to her, but as far as she was concerned, that would be poetic justice at its best.

"Ashton Hunter," she announced to her reflection, a devious sparkle in her bright brown eyes, "you are in for a big surprise."

Chapter 2

"Damn!" Ashton said, slamming his palm against the steering wheel. The horn blared in protest, alerting the driver in the car before him. The driver, obviously as frustrated as he, raised his hands as if to say, "What can I do?"

"Sorry, man. That wasn't meant for you. It was meant for me. For forgetting my brain at home." If he'd remembered his brain, he would have known better than to take the Don Valley Parkway, or rather, the Don Valley Parking Lot, as it was affectionately called by those who lived in Toronto. On a good day, this highway was a nightmare, but when there was an accident—like there was today—traffic virtually went nowhere.

At this rate, he would no doubt be late picking up Kelly from the airport.

Yesterday, he had returned her call but hadn't reached her. So he had left a message telling her that he would be able to pick her up at the Buffalo airport.

But because he'd had to make an appearance at today's studio session with his band members, he was already running late. He glanced at the car's digital clock. Eleven minutes after six.

Yeah, he'd definitely be late. He hoped she wouldn't be too upset with him.

Kelly . . . Man, it had been a long time. Ten years. Ten long years since he had made the decision he knew she probably hated him for.

Coward.

That, he had been. In hindsight, he probably should have trusted Kelly with his fears. Even though they couldn't have a relationship, she would have at least understood. Instead, he had run because it had been much easier to do so.

He detected the note of sarcasm in the message she'd left. She was still angry with him. Hell, she had a right to be. He'd been a jerk ten years ago, leaving without even a good-bye.

He couldn't help wondering, when he made it to the airport, would she even be happy to see him?

Kelly sat on a varnished oak bench a stone's throw from the baggage claim area, her two Louis Vuitton suitcases at her feet. An excited buzz filled the air as loved ones reunited and as arriving passengers chatted around the baggage claim belts.

Frowning, Kelly flicked a wrist forward and looked down at her small silver watch. It was ten minutes to nine, and since collecting her luggage, she had been tensely awaiting Ashton's arrival for well over thirty minutes. Waiting, like she had waited for his call ten years ago. She only hoped he had the decency not to stand her up. More than irritated, she picked up the fashion magazine she had purchased upstairs and began flipping through it.

After another ten minutes ticked by, Kelly plopped the magazine down beside her, then stood and stretched. Where on earth was Ashton? He had called her back, had confirmed the time he was to pick her up. So why wasn't he here?

Maybe she ought to head back upstairs and book a flight back home. How could Ashton be so irresponsible?

Unless he'd been in an accident.

Dear Lord, Kelly hoped that wasn't the case.

Sighing, she scanned the crowd, then sat back down, hoping Ashton made an appearance soon.

Ashton jammed his car into park outside the arrivals section of the airport. He quickly scanned the area.

He saw several people, but no one in a red sundress.

Man, he prayed she was there.

He prayed she wasn't too upset.

He got out of the car and made his way inside. It was a small airport, much smaller than Toronto's. Still, it seemed like there were a million people milling about.

Just what he needed.

He didn't see her. Placing his hands on his hips, he took a few steps to the right. Several feet away, a woman in a red dress caught his eye. Kelly said she'd be in a red dress. But this couldn't be Kelly, he decided as his eyes roamed over the back of her body. This woman had curves—round, soft curves that a man could get lost in. While the Kelly he remembered hadn't been thin, she also hadn't been curvaceous. This woman's hair was in long, thin braids. Kelly hadn't worn braids in high school. Of course, that didn't mean she couldn't have her hair braided now.

Like a magnet, Ashton was drawn to her. He supposed with a body like the one she possessed, a lot of men were drawn to her. Men who appreciated a woman with a fuller figure.

Slowly, he found himself moving toward her. There was something oddly familiar about this woman. . . . Something oddly compelling. . . .

She turned.

Ashton stopped. So did his heart.

Sensing eyes upon her, Kelly whirled around.

And saw him. How could she not? He was unmistakable.

Ashton Hunter . . . Her breathing slowed and a dizzying sensation swept over her as her eyes took him in, his loose fitting black shirt, his body-hugging blue jeans, his powerful body. His *dreadlocks*. They were short, and incredibly attractive on him. In high school, Ashton had worn a low afro. He had looked fine then, but he looked even better now.

Kelly lifted her gaze to his compelling eyes, eyes that seemed to register shock at the sight of her.

She held Ashton's gaze as he sauntered toward her, his movements smooth and captivating and utterly sexy. He was just as gorgeous as he'd always been, except his boyish good looks had matured into the handsome face of a man. His skin was flawless and golden brown. And those dreadlocks. She couldn't get over them.

Along with that new look, he also sported a neatly trimmed goatee that framed his full, sensuous lips. The goatee added to his overall sex appeal.

As did his body. Kelly couldn't help but notice how good he made a pair of jeans look.

Still.

As he neared her, Kelly saw his eyes roam her body

leisurely from head to toe, and she swallowed. After all this time, he was still so damn appealing.

"Kelly?" He sounded cautious, although he must have known it was her.

Kelly found it easy to smile. "Hello, Ashton."

His eyes lit up as he smiled back, brightening his square shaped face, softening the hard, masculine edges. His eyes were still the most amazing combination of brown and green she had ever seen, sprinkled with flecks of gold. Kelly inhaled a deep, steadying breath, realizing that the spark in his eyes had more to do with the fact that he was relieved to have found her than any other reason.

Stupid fool that she was.

"Kelly . . . Wow. You look . . . different."

This was Kelly! Yes, her face looked the same, except older, naturally. But her body . . . Those curves were to die for. And he didn't know if she was wearing one of those push-up bras that were so popular now, but did she ever have a lot more cleavage than he remembered!

This was how she'd traveled on the plane? He didn't notice a jacket in her possession. Was she nuts? Didn't she realize there were a lot of crazy men out there who would pounce on a gorgeous woman like her?

"Different good, or different bad?" Kelly asked.

"Different fabulous," Ashton replied without hesitation.

Kelly folded her arms under her chest, and watched as Ashton suddenly averted his eyes. He was noticing her, all right. And just the way he was looking at her had her remembering. Remembering that one hot night.

Let him look all he wants. That's as close as he's gonna get.

"Thanks," she said in reply to his compliment. "You look great, too." And she meant it.

Kelly took the opportunity to check him out again.

At approximately six feet tall, he had an amazing physique. His shoulders were wide, his arms rippling with muscles. And his eyes—those hazel eyes. She could get lost in them.

Suddenly uncomfortable, Kelly turned her head to avoid getting caught up in past memories.

"I'm glad you could make it," Ashton said.

"Me, too."

Silence.

Their eyes met, held. God, it had been so long. So long since she felt the way Ashton had made her feel.

All right. So the sexual attraction was still there. That didn't mean she had to lose her head over him again.

Ashton cleared his throat, broke the silence. Folded his arms over his chest. Unfolded them. Then spoke. "How was the flight?"

The tension broke. "Fine. Where have you been, by the way?"

"I'm really sorry I kept you waiting." His deep voice was as smooth as silk, and washed over her like a warm and gentle breeze. "Traffic was a nightmare."

"I'll bet," was Kelly's mumbled reply. Traffic, or some woman who had been in his bed?

"Pardon me?" Ashton asked.

"Nothing." He was still looking at her precariously, as though he didn't believe she was who she was. "Uh, we'd better head to the car."

"Oh, yes. The car."

Ashton bent to pick up Kelly's luggage. So did she. Their heads collided with a *thunk*.

"Ouch!" Kelly wailed.

"Sorry," Ashton muttered. Holy, he was flustered. He hadn't been this nervous since high school. But then, it wasn't every day a man met up with the woman he'd abandoned.

Gently, he ran his fingers across her forehead. "Are you okay?"

His fingers were like a jolt of electricity as they caressed her skin. She remembered another time, another place. She pulled away. "I'm okay." At least she would be, if she could only get out of klutz mode around him. "You can have the luggage, if you really want it."

He chuckled, then retrieved the two small suitcases. Kelly's gaze fell to his lower body and she watched as his faded blue jeans strained against his muscular thighs. She'd always thought Glenn was good looking, but he was no match for Ashton. Everything about him was the definition of masculinity. Damn him for looking even better than he did in high school.

Swallowing a sigh, Kelly followed Ashton through the doors. When she stepped outside, the dim summer night enveloped her in a blanket of soothing warmth. It was a breath of fresh air, one that helped her put things in perspective. She had to stop lusting over Ashton.

Hadn't she learned her lesson the first time?

Kelly continued walking behind Ashton until he came to a stop. She whistled softly when she saw the black Mustang. "Nice car."

"Thanks."

While Ashton opened the trunk to put her luggage inside, Kelly walked the length of the car, observing it closely. It gleamed seductively under the streetlights, beckoning her touch. She obliged, running a finger along the smooth surface. She didn't know much about cars, but she certainly knew that the wide tires and five star rims were sporty enhancements. The windows were tinted an opaque black, and Kelly couldn't help remembering that night ten years ago when things had gotten so hot and heavy in Ashton's Buick, they almost hadn't made it to the hotel.

"Stop it," she chided herself.

"Stop what?"

Her eyes grew wide with horror. Good Lord, he'd heard her.

"Uh, nothing," she replied. "I was . . . talking to myself. You must think I'm crazy."

"Naw." He was the one who was crazy. He had walked away from her ten years ago, so why did he now find her so . . . intriguing? It was those curves. He was a sucker for a woman with curves like hers.

Yeah, he was crazy.

"I really appreciate you coming down," Ashton said, averting his thoughts. He opened the passenger door for Kelly. "Did you have trouble getting time off from work?"

So they were going to talk about everything *but* what had happened ten years ago. Fine with her. "Actually, I'm free for the summer. I'm a teacher, and school just ended a few days ago."

Ashton strolled to the driver's side and got in, and Kelly followed his example, slipping into the passenger's seat. "That's right," he said. "Karen mentioned that a while back. What do you teach?"

Kelly fastened her seat belt. "I teach fourth grade."

Ashton pursed his lips in a contemplative manner, as though trying to picture Kelly as a teacher. "How long have you been teaching?"

"Five years."

"I figured you were working at some high-powered job."

"Why would you say that?"

"I noticed your luggage. Designer, right?"

"Louis Vuitton." She shrugged. "What can I say? I like nice things. And it seems you do, too."

"The car, you mean?"

"Yeah, the car." Shifting her gaze to the car's interior,

Kelly ran her fingers along the edge of the cream-colored leather seat. Beautiful. The kind of car that attracted women. Definitely Ashton's style.

Ashton started the car's ignition, and the mustang came to life with a loud roar. A soft whirring sound drew Kelly's attention to the car's roof, and she realized it was opening. When the starless sky was in clear view, Kelly said, "I never understood why men were so obsessed with vehicles, but I have to say, this is a nice ride."

"Thanks." Stopping at a red light, Ashton faced her. "You'll never believe how I got it."

That piqued her curiosity. "How?"

"I won it."

Astonished at his admission, Kelly gawked at Ashton with wide eyes. "You *won* this car? How amazing."

Ashton nodded his agreement, a bright smile lighting his face. "It was a fluke actually. I stopped for a coffee and a doughnut one day and the cashier gave me a scratch card for some contest. Normally, I throw that kind of thing away, but this time I scratched it. And bingo. I won this car."

Kelly had never so much as won a jar of jelly beans at a school raffle, that's how bad her luck was. In fact, if she didn't have bad luck, she'd have no luck at all.

She continued to stare at Ashton, completely amazed at his good fortune. She liked his goatee. It suited him. Now that she thought about it, he kind of resembled that gorgeous actor, Shemar Moore.

He turned. Caught her staring. "What?"

She averted her eyes. "Uh . . . congratulations."

"Thanks."

Ashton focused his attention on the road, and Kelly took the opportunity to lay her head back and close her eyes. Her face was warm. In fact, her whole body was warm. Not even the cool breeze filtering through the open roof helped cool her skin. Being so close to

Ashton after all this time, she just couldn't forget the incredible night they had shared. Ashton, however, seemed to have long forgotten that night.

But she already knew that.

She willed away the memories and turned her attention to Ashton. Maybe casual conversation would help her feel less flustered. "What do you do for a living?"

"I'm a musician."

"Really?"

Casting a sidelong glance in Kelly's direction, Ashton nodded. "I write songs. I sing. I play keyboard."

Kelly digested the information, finding it a little shocking. She'd always assumed Ashton would be playing professional football somewhere in North America. She hadn't known he was interested in music. But then, what had she really known about him?

"Don't tell me," she said, "you're a rap artist?"

"A rap artist?" He laughed. "Actually, I sing soft, middle of the road melodies."

"As in—"

"As in slow jams. Love songs. Anything soft and mellow."

Kelly almost said "Puh-lease!" but bit her tongue. Ashton singing love songs? That was as hard to swallow as the Queen of England getting down and dirty to reggae. "Love songs?" Kelly asked, trying to hide her disbelief.

"That's what I do. My style is very much like Boyz II Men."

Kelly couldn't help throwing Ashton a doubtful glance. Boyz II Men was one of her favorite groups. The songs they sang put women on pedestals, something she couldn't see Ashton doing. Especially since the Ashton she knew hadn't cared one bit about her feelings. "Somehow that surprises me."

"Why?"

"Because . . ." The words died in her throat.

Ashton read her mind. "Because of what happened ten years ago. Between us."

She swallowed. "That wasn't what I was going to say."

"Wasn't it?"

"Look, Ashton, I've had a long day. I'm not really in the mood for a trip down memory lane."

"What about an apology?"

An apology? Like that would erase everything, make it all better. She turned and met his eyes. "Ten years after the fact? I'd say, save your breath."

"I am sorry, Kelly," Ashton went on anyway. "I was a jerk. You deserved better."

Kelly didn't respond. Maybe he shouldn't have mentioned anything. Clearly, she wasn't ready to deal with the past. He'd drop it for now, but they would have to deal with it if they were going to be working together.

They drove in silence for a long while.

Kelly sighed. Guilt gnawed at her. Ashton had apologized, and she should have accepted his apology. She was over him. But a part of her heart still ached from the pain he had caused, and she didn't want to make this easy for him.

Finally, she faced him. "Boyz II Men, huh?"

"Mmm hmm. I do a bit of funky stuff, too, but mostly slow jams."

In a short while, they were at the border. They both showed their identification and passed into Canada without any problems.

"You want to stop for food or something?" Ashton asked.

"No, I'm fine."

As Ashton continued to drive, Kelly laid her head back and closed her eyes. She didn't realize she had fallen asleep until Ashton touched her arm and said, "We're almost there."

Ashton turned right, bringing the city's Harbourfront into view. Kelly was overcome by the sweet scent of lilacs, and a flood of color dazzled her eyes as she looked at the various flowers in full bloom. Several boats of varying sizes floated gracefully on the water, underneath the gentle rays of the moon.

"So, when does Karen leave for the show?" Kelly asked.

"A week Sunday. I want to have the party for her on Saturday night."

Kelly nodded, then turned her gaze back to the breathtaking view of the lake. "This is a gorgeous area. I've always loved the water."

"We live in this building right here." Ashton pointed to a modern high-rise overlooking the lake. Kelly's eyes widened with delight as she viewed the beige-colored condominium with lots of windows. But delight soon turned to horror when she realized what Ashton had just said.

"We?" Kelly asked.

Ashton turned into the building's driveway, then used a security pass to gain access to the building's underground parking. "Yeah," he replied, as if it was the most natural thing in the world. "Didn't Karen tell you?"

Chapter 3

Kelly tried to swallow, but choked instead. Then coughed. Couldn't stop.

Ashton put the car in park and reached for her, placing a gentle hand on the back of her neck. "You okay?"

Kelly leaned forward, shrugging away from his touch. Trying to relieve the suffocating feeling, she slapped her chest. "Yes," she managed to say, then coughed again. She felt Ashton's hands on her back, rubbing in a circular motion.

"What happened?" he asked.

Strangely, she found comfort in his touch. She drew in deep, calming breaths before speaking. "I—I swallowed. My saliva went down the wrong . . . tube." Lord, she felt like a *total* moron! "I'm fine. Really."

"You're sure?"

She forced a smile. "Yes." *No!* "Oh, look," she said, pointing ahead, wanting Ashton to stop touching her. "The garage door closed."

Ashton eyed her a moment longer, apparently making sure she was okay, then backed up the driveway.

Once again, he placed his security pass against the electronic sensor. The garage door slowly began to open.

Karen and Ashton are living together? Kelly thought as the car began to move. She needed air. Her lungs wouldn't allow enough in.

Karen and Ashton . . . When did this happen? How long had they been lovers? How could she not have *known?* Kelly slipped a finger in her mouth and began gnawing on her manicured fingernail. None of this made sense. Karen and Ashton had been so different in high school. Yet now they were dating? Was this why Karen hadn't kept in better touch with her over the last few years?

Still, high school had been so long ago. Surely Karen couldn't believe that Kelly still had any kind of feelings for Ashton. But she must. Why else would she keep this news from her?

Considering what Karen must think, how would she react to this *surprise* Ashton had planned? Kelly suddenly wondered if coming to Toronto was a big mistake.

Kelly didn't even realize Ashton had parked the car until he opened the door and headed to the trunk. She waited until he closed the trunk before getting out of the car. Slowly, she followed him to the building's elevators, her mind churning. How was she going to handle staying with Karen and Ashton the next week, watching them as lovers? This was going to be a nightmare.

Didn't Ashton realize that Karen might be uncomfortable with this whole arrangement? Sure, she and Ashton had dated several years ago, but still . . . Men. They could be so obtuse sometimes.

"You seem a million miles away," Ashton said when they stepped into the elevator. "You okay?"

Kelly picked at an imaginary piece of lint on her dress. "I'm fine." *Just perfect.* If she had any guts, she would ask him how he could do this to Karen . . . and to her.

Ashton pressed the button for the third floor. "Are you sure that's all?"

"Yes. I'm just anxious about seeing Karen again."

"No need to be anxious. Karen's gonna be thrilled."

How can you be so sure, she wanted to ask, but didn't. "You must . . . know Karen . . . very well."

"I do."

"That's great. Just great."

Ashton's eyes narrowed as he eyed Kelly. Neither her tone nor her body language matched her words. Staring at the ground and twirling a braid between her fingers, she seemed more than anxious. Almost distraught. And he'd be willing to bet that he was the cause for her distress. She could hardly stand to be near him. He wished he could say something, *do* something, to ease the tension.

But maybe they could never be friends. And he wanted that. Right now, regaining Kelly's friendship was the most important thing to him.

The elevator doors opened with a soft "ping" sound. Immediately, Kelly started to move.

With one hand Ashton held the elevator door open, and with the other he grabbed Kelly's shoulder, stopping her. She flashed him a perplexed look. "Kelly," he began slowly, "I know you're upset with me—"

"Ashton, I got over you years ago."

Ouch. While he hadn't expected her to hurt for the rest of her life, her words cut through him like a knife. He wondered why he cared.

"You seem surprised," Kelly said.

Ashton gazed down at her. Her chin was tilted upward; her beautiful brown eyes challenged his. Eyes that had once regarded him with warmth and affection. Not

anymore. "No, I'm not surprised. We both had to get on
with our lives."

"The elevator."

"What?" Where did that come from?

"The elevator. You can't hold it all day."

"Oh. Yeah."

Ashton released her arm, and Kelly hurried out of
the confining space. *We both had to get on with our lives.*
He made it sound so simple. For him, of course, it had
been. But for her . . . Kelly wanted to yell at him, to get
the pain she thought had died years ago off her chest.
But she couldn't, because she didn't want him to think
she cared.

Because she didn't.

"Which way?" she asked.

Ashton cocked his head to the left. "This way."

Kelly's feet sank into the plush pink carpet as she followed Ashton down the hallway. The walls were decorated in peach-striped wallpaper, and the dim hallway
lights were encased in glass and brass. The building certainly was classy.

Moments later, Ashton stopped abruptly. Kelly's gaze—
for some reason—fell to his butt. His incredibly firm,
sexy butt. God, he certainly made a pair of jeans come
alive. Even after everything, she couldn't ignore his incredible sex appeal.

Turning to her, Ashton said, "Wait here." He looked
as excited as a young boy at his birthday party as he
walked a few steps to an apartment door. He knocked.

This is it. Kelly waited, a nervous tingling sensation
flooding her as she realized she was about to see her old
friend. She held her breath.

Nothing.

Ashton knocked again.

Again, nothing. Kelly released her breath.

Ashton glanced at her quickly, shrugging. Then knocked

once more. Once again, there was no response. Folding his arms over his brawny chest, he pursed his lips. Finally, he turned to her. "I don't think she's home."

"Not home? I thought you had this all planned."

"It was supposed to be a surprise." He glanced down at his wristwatch. "It's after ten. I thought she'd be home by now."

Kelly watched as Ashton stood, perplexed, fondling his goatee. "Well," she said after several moments, "aren't you going to open the door?"

"I wish I could."

"You w—" Kelly couldn't help rolling her eyes toward the ceiling. "Let me guess. You've lost your key?"

Ashton shook his head. "I don't have a key."

Kelly sighed, her patience wearing thin. "Wonderful. We can't stand in the hallway all night. Does the super have a key?"

"You'll have to see Karen in the morning."

"What? You are making *no* sense, Ashton. Just talk to the super. That way, we can get in *tonight.*" She spoke slowly, the way she did when explaining something to her students.

"I hope you don't mind, but you'll just have to stay at my place tonight."

"Y—" Kelly's mouth fell open. "Y-*your* place? What are you— Isn't this—"

"My place?"

"Yes!"

"You think I live with Karen?"

"Don't you?"

Ashton's sexy lips lifted in a crooked smile. "No. I don't."

"But you said— You told me that you live with Karen. That you both live . . . together."

"I said we both live in this *building*. But I don't live with Karen. I live down the hall."

"Oh. *Oh.*" He was grinning at her. Enjoying this, no doubt. He'd let her believe that he and Karen were living together. The louse! "Let me get this straight . . . you live down the hall?"

"Yes." He paused. "Anything else you want to ask me?"

"No," she answered quickly. "Well, yes. Are you and Karen . . ."

"Dating?"

"Yes."

Ashton's eyes roamed her body lazily, that wickedly sexy smile searing her skin. She squared her jaw, hoping he wouldn't see the unnerving effect he was having on her. "Would it bother you if we were?" he asked coolly.

"Oh, come on, Ashton! Just answer the question. You've led me on enough tonight."

"Led you on?" He chuckled.

"Is there an echo in here?" His smile, his gall, irritated her. "Yes, led me on. Let me believe something that wasn't true."

"Kelly, you made an assumption. An incorrect one."

"Are you dating Karen or not?"

"No, we're not dating. Karen and I are just friends."

Kelly threw her hands in the air, then let them drop, slapping her thighs. "Thank you."

"For what? Not dating Karen?" He was smiling.

"This is ridiculous. Which way to your place? No, forget it. Which way to the nearest hotel?"

"You are not staying at a hotel."

"Oh yeah? Try and stop me."

"I will, if that's what it takes."

Her eyes were wide with indignation, but Ashton held her gaze, letting her know he was not going to back down. He was crazy, but he wanted her. Wanted to take her in his arms and tear that sexy red dress off her body. Wanted to take her wildly, right here. Kelly had a lot of spunk and fire, and he wanted to turn that fire into a blazing passion.

"Fine," she huffed. "But first thing in the morning, I'm gone."

Not exactly what Ashton had hoped for, but it was the best he could expect. For now.

God help her, Ashton Hunter was infuriating! He had practically implied that he was living with Karen. Why? Just to get a reaction out of her? And fool she was, she had played right into his hands.

"Do I need to invite you in?"

She was standing in the doorway of his apartment, but had zoned out because of her thoughts. "Well, one never knows."

He flashed her a dubious look. "Kelly, after everything, you must know that's not true."

Not only was he looking at her with those incredibly sexy eyes, he was crowding her space. Suffocating her. "Yes, of course," she said, then marched into the spacious living room.

His leather sofa and love seat were a shade of teal green. Covering part of the shining hardwood floor was a colorful oriental rug. Across from the sofa, a large black entertainment unit was set up, beside which stood two large black speakers.

Except for the oriental rug, the apartment boasted dark colors. Definitely a man's place.

Kelly took a seat on the leather sofa.

Ashton moved to stand in front of her. "Can I get you anything to drink?"

Kelly couldn't help glancing at his thighs, which

were now at her eye level. His powerful thighs. His sexy thighs. Oh, how she'd love to reach out and touch him. . . .

"Kelly?"

Her eyes flew to his face, embarrassed that he'd caught her staring. "No, I'm fine."

"Not even a glass of wine?"

"Thanks for the offer, but I'm pretty tired. I'd just like to go to bed."

His eyes held hers a moment too long, but she wouldn't look away. Couldn't.

"No problem," Ashton said after a moment. "You've had a long day. The bedroom's down the hall on your right."

"You have a spare bedroom?"

"Only one. Mine."

Kelly gaped at Ashton. "Are you suggesting . . . ?"

"That you take the bed."

"I didn't mean to imply that you were suggesting . . ." Feeling flustered, Kelly stopped midsentence. If Ashton hadn't misconstrued her question, then she would only embarrass herself by blabbering on.

"I don't need the bed," she said simply. "I can sleep on the couch."

"Kelly." His deep voice made her skin tingle. "You're my guest."

"A guest who in no way wants to put you out. I'd be more than happy to go to a hotel. There must be some in the area."

"It scares you that much, does it? The idea of staying here with me?"

"No! Of course not. W-why would it?" And why was she suddenly tongue-tied?

"I don't know . . . maybe because of what happened between us."

Oh, dear God. He wasn't going *there*.

"Think about it. We've only spent the night under the same roof one other time. And that time—"

Kelly shot to her feet. "Okay. That's enough."

"We're never gonna discuss it?"

"Why, so you can get your kicks out of learning how you humiliated me?" As soon as the words left her mouth, Kelly regretted them. She hadn't wanted Ashton to know that he had hurt her in any way.

"I would never get my kicks out of that."

"Really?"

Ashton's eyes narrowed on her. "You think I deliberately set out to hurt you?"

"You did a damn good job, either way."

"I know this sounds lame—"

"So save it. Truly, Ashton. I got over you years ago. Besides," she went on, "I didn't come here so we could discuss our brief past. I came because of Karen. She's the only reason. And, quite frankly, I think we'd be better off keeping our conversations limited to Karen and the party you want me to help you plan."

"Is that so?"

"Yes, that's so." Before he could protest, she whirled around and scooped up the smaller of her two pieces of luggage. He'd said she could have the bedroom, and right now, she wanted to escape to it. "The bedroom's on the right?"

"Uh huh."

"Great."

She looked over her shoulder to flash him a quick smile. Then she disappeared down the hallway, wondering exactly what she'd gotten herself into by agreeing to come up to Toronto.

Chapter 4

Kelly was in his bed.

The very thought alone had Ashton shifting on the couch from one position to another. No new position helped him get comfortable. How could it, when Kelly was the reason he couldn't sleep?

Once. They'd made love one time, yet he hadn't been able to forget it. It was guilt, he was sure, for the cowardly way he had walked away without even a good-bye.

Yet how could he have told her that things wouldn't work out between them? She had looked at him with such hope. Such . . . love.

Until he had seen the vulnerability in her eyes, Ashton had actually wanted to believe that he could give a woman his heart. But the look was one he had seen on his father's face so many years before. A look of longing and hope and sadness and relief all mixed into one. It was the time his mother had returned to them after having packed her bags and left.

With that look, Ashton knew his father would have done anything to make his mother stick around. Yet only days later, she had taken off again. This time, she hadn't returned. And in the years that followed, she called rarely. Yet Ashton's father had never given up hope.

Neither had Ashton. At first. But once he had hit sixteen, he had known it was foolish to expect her to ever return. So he had hardened his heart and vowed not to let a woman hurt him the way his mother had hurt both him and his father.

Until Kelly.

Kelly had been different. Special. Her beautiful doe eyes said she was trustworthy, and Ashton had desperately wanted to trust her. Despite his promise to himself, he found himself falling for her. He had definitely been attracted to her, and the night of the graduation, one thing had led to another, and they'd ended up in a hotel making love.

The experience had been incredible. Too incredible. Far from just being the physical act, Ashton had connected with Kelly in a way that had scared him to death. He hadn't known how much he missed a woman in his life until that night. But once he and Kelly had parted ways, he had remembered his mother and how she had once made his father feel like he was the most special man in the world, and how, despite that, she had left him.

So, Ashton had taken off for his job in Alberta and hadn't looked back. Now, he felt the way he had in those first months after the end of their relationship—lonely, hot, bothered. He couldn't get the image of their lovemaking out of his mind. Then, her bright brown eyes had glistened with longing, her lips had grinned at him seductively. And when their bodies had finally come together, their coupling had been wild. Kelly had writhed beneath him, dug her nails into his back and buttocks, called out his name. Now, as he imagined her sleeping in his bed, he wanted her more than he had wanted her ten years ago. He wanted to press himself against her curves, sink his body into her softness.

He wanted to forget the reason he had left her. Forget the reason he had sworn off the idea of ever having a serious relationship. And make her his. Just once more.

Maybe then, he could finally forget her.

Hours later, Ashton was surprised when Kelly walked into the living room carrying her luggage. He sat up, swinging his legs over the side of the couch as he did. He dug his toes into the soft rug as he glanced at the wall clock. It was barely after nine.

"Good, you're awake," she said. "You weren't earlier."

"It's still early," Ashton said.

"I know."

Today she was wearing a form-fitting orange T-shirt with a fringed bottom. It made the plain blue jeans much more stylish.

Ashton couldn't help looking at her. Luscious golden skin, arresting brown eyes, and full, sensuous lips definitely made for kissing. He still couldn't believe she was the same girl he had known in high school.

He said, "You look like you're going somewhere."

"You said Karen would be around in the morning."

"Right." Ashton threw off the thin sheet that had been covering him and stood. He gave his body a good stretch. "Don't you want some breakfast first?"

"Not really."

At this rate, was she even going to want to spend any time with him to plan Karen's surprise party?

"All right. Let me put on some jeans."

Kelly gave a brief nod and looked away. She gave the

impression that she couldn't stand being in the room with him.

Which, he acknowledged sadly, she probably couldn't.

"Come on in, Ashton," Kelly heard Karen say, and a smile formed on her lips. After all this time, she was finally going to see Karen.

"I've got a surprise for you," Ashton told Karen. "But you've got to come into the hallway to get it."

"Ashton," Karen said in a wary voice. "I hope it's not some creepy crawly thing. You know I haven't forgiven you for that last incident."

"Trust me." He took Karen's hand and gently pulled her into the hallway.

"Ashton," she protested, clearly fearing the worst. But as she turned cautiously to her left and saw Kelly, Karen's mouth fell open and her eyes widened with excitement.

"Kelly!" Karen leaped toward Kelly and threw her arms around her. "I can't believe it. What on earth are you doing here?"

Kelly pulled back from her friend and looked at her, enjoying the wonderful sight of her after all these years. Her dark brown skin was smooth and perfect, and she was just as beautiful as Kelly remembered. In fact, Karen didn't look like she had aged at all.

Kelly took Karen's hands in hers and squeezed them gently. "Girl, you know I had to congratulate you in person on your enormous success."

"My success?"

"Maybe for a big star like you doing a musical tour across the country isn't a 'success,' but to a nobody like me, that's big news."

Karen's nose wrinkled and her lips pouted as she

made a silly face, one Kelly remembered well from high school. "This is definitely the biggest thing to happen for me in my career," Karen stated in an exaggerated tone. "I just had no idea that you knew."

"You have Ashton to thank for that."

Karen smiled up at Ashton, her bright brown eyes crinkling as she did. Then she let out a squeal of delight and pulled Kelly into the condo unit, leading her into the living room. Ashton followed with Kelly's luggage.

"I can't believe it. My girl is back in town."

"I know. It's been too long."

Kelly gave Karen's hand a squeeze, then released it. She sauntered to the window and peered outside.

"What do you think of my apartment?" Karen asked.

"It's beautiful." Kelly surveyed the small but quaint, modernly decorated condominium. Bright white walls contrasted with the black lacquer coffee table, the black and brass lamps, and the plush black and gold sofa. At the far end of the living room was a glass solarium overlooking the lake.

Kelly folded her arms across her chest as she walked into the solarium wide-eyed and peered through the glass out onto the lake, now able to get a closer look at the boats that were sailing. There was something about the view of the water that always lifted her spirits.

She turned around. The solarium boasted a beautiful glass dining table with black and brass trimmings. Two white candles rested on either end of the table in brass candleholders, complemented by a floral centerpiece.

"Check out the rest of the apartment," Karen told her.

Kelly did, discovering two bedrooms. The smaller one had a white day bed decorated with several cream-colored pillows. A large spider plant stood near the window, opposite an oak dresser. This was clearly a spare bedroom.

Great. She wouldn't have to stay on the sofa for the entire week.

"You really are doing well for yourself," Kelly announced as she strolled back into the living room.

"I wish I could say I'm paying for all this through my acting, but I'm not," Karen admitted. "This is a co-op, which means I pay a very affordable rate of rent, based on what I make."

Kelly's eyes lit up. "You can actually pay a fairly low rent for a gorgeous condo like this one?"

Karen nodded. "This is a great city. There are a lot of struggling artists living in this building, and with the rent structure, we're able to live affordably while concentrating on getting established at our craft. This was a godsend for me."

"But now you're gonna be a big star."

"I don't know about that."

"Well, I do," Kelly said. She hugged Karen again. "It's so good to see you again."

Chapter 5

"Hit me," Kelly said, the words sounding more like a question than a statement. Karen and Ashton had briefly explained the rules of Black Jack to her, and hours after Kelly had settled into Karen's spare bedroom, the three were playing for money: pennies.

In response to Kelly's request, Ashton placed another card before her. It was the ten of hearts. Kelly looked down at the card and shrugged, unsure what it meant.

"Brave move, but you just won," Karen explained. "I thought for sure you'd go over."

Kelly surveyed the cards before her. "But I have two tens and an ace. Doesn't that add up to thirty-one?"

"No," Karen answered, her short black bob bouncing as she shook her head. "Aces can either count for eleven or for one. So, in your case, it counts for one since you already had twenty. Therefore, you win."

Kelly narrowed her eyes, still confused. "But who decides what it counts for?"

Karen looked up at Ashton and shrugged. "Maybe you can do a better job at explaining it to her."

Kelly faced Ashton. His stunning hazel eyes captured hers, causing a highly charged current to surge through her.

"All right," he said, his voice deep and sexy. "You decide what the aces count for. But if you pick an ace and your cards are already close to totaling twenty-one, then obviously the ace will only count for one. But if you have an eight, and you pick an ace, that can count for eleven, for a total of nineteen. Understand?"

"I think I'm getting the picture," Kelly said, her gaze still locked with Ashton's. For the life of her, she couldn't turn away.

"Good," Karen said, patting Kelly on the shoulder.

Karen's physical contact released Kelly from Ashton's hypnotic effect. She averted her gaze instantly, embarrassed that she had let him get to her. Why, after all this time, did his striking hazel eyes still affect her this way? There had to be something wrong with her.

They continued passing the time with another few rounds of Black Jack, and when they were finished, Karen had accumulated the most pennies. Her winnings totaled eighteen cents. Kelly only had three pennies left, after having started with ten.

Smiling as though she'd won a million dollars, Karen swiped her hand across the coffee table, gathering all the pennies and letting them drop into her free hand.

"Next time we'll play for higher stakes," Ashton announced as Karen brought the pennies to a glass jar. But he was looking at Kelly. His eyes sparkled as he stared at her, and a mischievous smile played on his lips.

Kelly's stomach jumped. Was she mistaken, or was Ashton's statement ripe with sexual innuendo?

"Anyone want a drink?" Karen asked, walking into the kitchen.

Kelly was shocked to find that her nerves were too

tense and her throat was too dry to speak. Dammit. Why was Ashton having this effect on her?

"Cat got your tongue?" Ashton asked. His smile was smug, conceited.

"Huh, you two?" Karen asked. "I've got white wine and beer. Also some soda."

"I'll have a beer," Ashton replied.

"Me, too," Kelly finally replied, her voice deceptively calmer than her nerves. "As long as it's cold."

"I know," Ashton whispered. "It's pretty hot in here." He smiled at her as he sank into the nearby love seat.

Kelly gaped at Ashton. Clearly he was flirting with her.

Either that or making fun of her. What exactly was his game?

Surely he didn't think that after his apology yesterday, he could charm his way into her pants the way he had that night long ago.

But then, Kelly wouldn't put it past him. He was a charmer. Always had been. And he'd also been a joker. In high school, that had been part of his appeal. Now, it was annoying.

Karen returned with three beers, three glasses, and a bag of chips on a tray. Kelly lifted her beer off the tray and took a sip straight from the bottle, looking at Ashton with defiant eyes as she sat on the sofa across from him. Normally, she would have poured the beer into a glass, but today she knew she had to prove a point. Exactly what that point was, she really wasn't sure.

"Isn't it funny?" Karen said. "All three of us sitting here together? Who would have thought it after ten years? The last time you two saw each other was the night of our high school graduation."

Kelly's eyes flew to Karen's. As happy as she was to see her longtime friend, at this moment she wanted to shake some sense into the woman. Why on earth would she bring up the night of their graduation? Karen knew better than anyone how devastated Kelly had been after that night. Didn't she realize that she was opening an old wound?

"No need to remind me," Kelly mumbled.

"Gosh, didn't we have some crazy times back then?" Karen went on. "Ashton, you were such a charmer. Remember how you convinced Kelly to do your English papers?"

"Whatever."

"Like I'm lying. You remember, Kelly."

"How could I forget."

"Once," Ashton said, chuckling. "I have a vague memory of paying you to help me out on a paper once."

Kelly rolled her eyes. "It was at least three or four times."

"Two, max."

Throwing her head back, Kelly laughed. "Deny it all you want."

"A lot of good it did me," he said. "Mr. Duggan took me aside one day and said my recent paper didn't seem like my normal style. But when he suggested we discuss my theory that Shakespeare was a woman, I didn't know what to say. Stopped me cold from paying you to write another paper for me again. And it wasn't that I didn't *want* to write my own papers. But my football schedule kept me really busy."

"What ever happened with your football aspirations?" Kelly asked.

"Nothing." He shrugged. "Not every one can make it."

"Besides, Ashton was meant to be a musician," Karen said. "You'll have to listen to his CD."

"Yeah." With the attention off the night of their high

school graduation, Kelly felt much better. She glanced at Karen, then at Ashton. "I know you two didn't stay in touch after high school, so how did you meet up again? You saw each other in the lobby or something?"

"Not exactly, but it *was* a coincidental meeting," Ashton explained. "I met Karen at a voice class, one where you learn all about the jingle business, how to do a demo tape. Stuff like that. She noticed me first. We've been friends ever since."

"And what about this musical?" Kelly asked. "You haven't told me anything about it."

Karen's eyes lit up, dancing with excitement. She explained to a very curious Kelly that the musical was a romantic comedy, and that she was the understudy for the lead actress. She would be going on tour for at least four months, but possibly longer. It was her first major acting role, but she had done several commercials, and both small and large parts in television shows and films. Her true love was theater, however, and after years of doing community theater where she didn't get paid, and dinner theater where the pay was minimal, she was elated to be given the chance to understudy in a musical that was going national.

Kelly wrapped her arms around Karen and hugged her tightly. She was as excited for Karen as she would have been for herself. Kelly and Karen had met in the fourth grade, and the two had quickly become best friends. Even then, Karen had had an amazing singing voice and had been passionate about acting. She'd had fun practicing her acting with Kelly. Kelly had never considered a career on the stage, but certainly didn't mind role-playing with her friend. It provided a wonderful escape from their boredom.

"I can't wait to leave," Karen said. "Though I will miss Ashton's crazy sense of humor."

Kelly's eyes went from Karen to Ashton. Instantly, her stomach dropped.

Ashton had said the two weren't involved. But was she missing something here? Was there an underlying attraction between them?

"Is that all you'll miss?" Ashton asked, then winked.

"Oh, whatever!" Karen scooped up a small black pillow from the sofa and threw it at Ashton, hitting him on a leg. Ashton threw it back with lightning speed. It bonked Karen on the head. She shrieked, then grabbed the pillow and threw herself onto Ashton, smothering his face with it.

Easily, Ashton spun Karen over on the love seat, grasping her wrists with one hand and pinning her down. Karen kicked and wriggled wildly, struggling to be free of Ashton's grip. But her efforts were useless.

A sickening feeling spread through Kelly's body. There *was* an attraction between Karen and Ashton. When had this happened?

"All right!" Karen conceded. "You win."

With a victorious laugh, Ashton released her, and Karen scrambled to the opposite sofa for safety. She looked frazzled. Her short bob was more than a little out of place, and her breathing was labored. Ashton, on the other hand, looked as cool and confident as ever. Kelly's eyes lingered on Ashton's muscular thighs as they strained against the fabric of his jeans.

Not again, she thought. He was devastatingly sexy, she had to admit. But he was definitely lacking qualities she thought were essential in a man. Qualities like honesty and honor.

"How do you put up with him?" Kelly asked Karen, mock sympathy in her voice. But it was really a test to see if Karen would let something slip about her true feelings for Ashton.

"To tell the truth," Karen responded, rolling her eyes playfully, "I honestly don't know."

Ashton smiled sarcastically as the two women shared a laugh. "Fine. Pick on the oddball. Gang up on the only guy here."

"That's what I love about you, Ashton," Karen said. "You take it so well."

What she loved about him . . . Did Karen mean that in the literal sense?

"So," Karen began, turning to face Kelly, "how long are you staying?"

"I'm here for the week," Kelly replied. "Until you leave."

A soft sigh escaped Karen's throat. "I wish we could spend more than a week together. It's been so long."

"I know." Putting her arm around her friend's shoulder, Kelly rested her head against Karen's. "Too long."

Ashton gulped down the remainder of his beer, then replaced the empty bottle on the tray. "I sense one of those woman talks coming on," he said, placing a hand on each hip. "I think I'll go run some errands."

Slipping out of Kelly's embrace, Karen rose from the sofa and stood beside Ashton. At approximately five foot four inches, she looked quite petite compared to Ashton's height. "I'll see you out."

Were they going to have a private moment?

And why did that thought make her feel even a smidgen of jealousy?

Ashton cast a glance at Kelly and said, "See you later."

"Sure," Kelly responded dryly.

Ashton turned and walked leisurely to the door, with Karen at his heels. Kelly snuck one last glance at him, at his taut, sexy body, thinking once again that he certainly made a pair of jeans come to life.

Wrenching her gaze away, Kelly sighed. This was going to be the hardest week of her life. She couldn't keep pretending that she was immune to Ashton's charms, no matter how much that realization upset her. If only she could forget that passionate night they had shared . . .

But as bad as that was, it would be much worse if Karen started discussing Ashton with her—discussing her blossoming feelings for him. How would Kelly handle that?

"We could order some Chinese food if you're hungry," Karen suggested as she stepped back into the living room.

Looking up at Karen, Kelly shook her head resolutely. "These chips and beer have filled me up."

"Me, too." Karen sat beside her. "Tell me everything that's going on in your life. Only the important things, of course. Like are you dating someone? And if you're not," she smiled excitedly, "how was it seeing Ashton again?"

This was Kelly's chance to put an end to any idea Karen had that she was still hung up on Ashton. "Actually," Kelly began slowly, "I'm kind of seeing someone."

"Oh." She sounded disappointed. "You mean there's no chance for things to spark between you and Ashton again? Don't you think he looks great? I mean, those dreadlocks are *hot.*"

Kelly couldn't help saying, "Hmm. Sounds like you might be attracted to him."

"Me? Ha! Not hardly. Ashton's too . . ."

"Full of himself?" Kelly supplied.

"Free spirited is a better way to describe it. And so am I. He needs someone more level headed. Kind of like . . . you."

Kelly's lips curled into a slight smirk as she realized Karen hadn't changed much at all. She was still a hopeless romantic at heart, and a matchmaker. In high school, she had done all she could to make sure Kelly and Ashton spent time together. She had put them together the first time when she had been helping to produce a small school play. Karen had enlisted Kelly to coordinate the musical talent, and that had been Ashton. During that play, they had gotten to know each other fairly well, and the friendship had started.

It had taken nearly two more years for them to end up in bed.

And just like that, their relationship had ended.

"Ashton and I are so over," Kelly replied frankly. But she was secretly happy to know that Karen wasn't interested in him. That would have been awkward, at the very least.

"Okay, fine." But Karen sounded disappointed. "Tell me about this other guy. What's his name?"

"Glenn."

"Glenn." Karen shrugged, digesting the information. "And what does Glenn do?"

"He's a teacher. He teaches second grade at the same school where I work."

"Sounds boring already."

"Karen!"

"Sorry." She smiled sheepishly. "That was wrong of me. But a guy who teaches young children—"

"Is very sensitive."

"And predictable. Probably goes to church every Sunday—not that that's a bad thing, mind you, but you know he never misses a week. And his idea of excitement is probably a movie on a Friday night."

Just two weeks ago, Glenn had taken her to a movie on a Friday night. He had returned her home before the clock struck eleven P.M.

"I happen to like a guy who's sensitive," Kelly said in Glenn's defense.

"Okay, sensitive is great. But don't you want excitement? A guy who will surprise you."

"Glenn did surprise me. He proposed marriage just last week."

"What?"

"And . . . I'm considering it."

"Wow. I thought you said you were 'kind of' seeing him."

"Our relationship has been growing over the last year. And what is dating these days, anyway? Can anyone truly define it? Does it have to be hot and heavy as opposed to slow and steady?"

Karen shrugged.

"Maybe he's just what I need. I've had my share of excitement and unpredictability. Sure, there was a thrill factor—always followed up with a broken heart. Or the guys you couldn't get rid of. Glenn . . . he's safe."

"I guess I can see your point. I always thought I needed a more sedate kind of guy simply because I'm so out there." She wiggled her fingers beside her head. "Being an actress, my schedule is hardly normal. I've got a quirky sense of humor. One guy called me a live wire. But he was a banker," Karen added in her defense. "Anyway, two live wires in a relationship and one of us is bound to get electrocuted."

"Have you been seeing anyone?"

"Naw. The last one was a guy named Trevor. He's a director, and I met him when I auditioned for a dinner theater production. I got the part, then things quickly fell apart. It was brutal having to still work together. It made me realize that I couldn't date anyone I was working with."

"I hear you. And to tell the truth, that's what I worry about with Glenn. If things don't work out, I'll still see him at school. I dunno."

"Sounds like you're not convinced about Glenn, period."

"I'm . . . thinking about it," was all Kelly would commit to.

And she would. It was one of the ways she would use her time here.

One way or another, when she returned to Fort Lauderdale, she would know if she would become Mrs. Glenn Ritter.

Chapter 6

Kelly slept well that night, better than she thought she would have slept, considering she was in a strange bed. Sunlight spilled through the window, covering her like a warm caress and coaxing her to consciousness. She stirred, then finally opened her eyes. The bed was so warm and comfortable, she wanted to lie there forever.

Ashton, a quiet voice whispered in her head.

She had dreamt about him last night, and here she was thinking of him first thing in the morning? She sighed her frustration.

Kelly sat up and stretched. Why on earth couldn't she get the man out of her mind? Even though he and Karen weren't interested in each other, it had been clear to see through their interactions that Ashton was a huge flirt.

And a heartbreaker.

Determined to put Ashton out of her mind, Kelly went to the bathroom and turned on the faucets in the tub, preparing for a long, hot bubble bath. She knew from the previous night that Karen would be at work when she woke up. With the tour right around the corner, Karen was rehearsing long hours every day.

Being here alone would give Kelly the opportunity to stop and repose. Since school had finished a few days earlier and she'd wished all her students a happy summer, Kelly hadn't really taken a break. The marathon run had drained her. So had thoughts of whether or not she and Glenn could have a happy marriage.

Minutes later, Kelly slipped into the tub and reveled in the feel of the hot water against her skin, urging her into a relaxed state.

Nearly half an hour later, when she noticed that her fingers were starting to wrinkle like a prune, Kelly exited the bath and returned to her bedroom, feeling wonderfully refreshed. The small bedroom was growing hot beneath the sun's rays and Kelly went to the window and opened it. A much needed cool, gentle breeze filtered into the room.

It was a beautiful day and Kelly didn't want to stay inside for all of it. She slipped into a pink halter top and floral skirt, then placed her long braids into a ponytail. Her stomach rumbled, reminding her that she hadn't eaten.

She went to the kitchen and prepared a bowl of corn flakes. It was a quick and easy meal so that she could get outside as soon as possible.

Just as she sat down in the solarium to eat her cereal, Kelly heard a faint knock at the door. She pushed her chair back and rose, striding to the door in quick steps. She was about to swing the door open but thought better of it, and instead looked through the peephole.

"Ashton," she gasped, shocked to see him this early in the day, shocked by the intensity of his dazzling eyes. As she pulled her eye away, he rapped on the door once again.

"I know you're in there," he said, humor playing in his voice. "I just saw you look through the peephole."

Damn, Kelly thought. There was no avoiding him. Reluctantly, she opened the door, but not before looking in the hall mirror to make sure that she looked presentable.

"Good morning," Ashton said when the door opened. Without waiting for an invitation, he walked past Kelly and into the apartment.

"Karen's not here," Kelly informed him.

"That's good," Ashton replied. "Because I'm not here to see Karen. I'm here to see you."

Kelly's stomach tightened at Ashton's words, suddenly nervous. "What do you want with me?"

Something mysterious flashed in Ashton's eyes. "I could think of a number of things," he replied, a devilish grin prancing on his lips.

For a moment, Kelly was stunned, her throat too constricted for speech. Ashton's sexy smile and suggestive words suddenly had her tingling with longing.

"Excuse me?" Kelly asked. She barely got the question out.

Ashton lowered his face toward hers. "We have some unfinished business to attend to."

His head lingered for a moment, his eyes locked with hers. Kelly's breath caught in her throat as she tried to fight her unwanted attraction to Ashton, tried to fight her sexual expectation. And just as she thought he would surely kiss her, he said, "The party."

Kelly instantly felt foolish for jumping to conclusions, finding innuendo where there was none. "Oh, of course."

She closed the door and hustled back to the solarium. Ashton followed her. Kelly sat down.

"I hope you don't mind if I finish my cereal. I don't want it to get too soggy."

"No problem."

Kelly lifted a spoonful of corn flakes to her mouth.

She watched Ashton as she ate. She couldn't help but admire his wide shoulders, finely cut arms, and slim torso, which were easy to see in the flimsy white T-shirt he was wearing. A pair of gray knit shorts graced his muscular thighs, and were even more attractive on him than the jeans had been. Her eyes ventured past his shorts to his solid, golden brown calves. Every part of him was so well toned, so taut with muscles. Muscular, yet lean, the way Kelly liked it.

Ashton took a seat across from her. "If you didn't have any other plans, I figured I could show you around the city. It's changed in the years you've been away."

"What about planning the party?"

"That can wait for a while. Look, you go ahead and eat."

Kelly did, but with every spoonful she swallowed, she was acutely aware of Ashton watching her every move. It was unnerving.

"Maybe you ought to come back in half an hour," she said. "That'll give me a chance to get ready."

"You look great to me."

Was it Kelly's imagination, or did Ashton's smile mean that his words were suggestive? She would have been blind not to notice how he had looked at her when he picked her up from the airport. But then, it wasn't that Kelly thought Ashton didn't find her attractive. He just hadn't found it in his heart to commit to her.

"Okay, then," Kelly said.

She finished her cereal and stood. As she walked past Ashton, Kelly inhaled the spicy, masculine scent of his cologne. Good Lord, was it impossible not to notice his sexual appeal?

"Kelly."

Ashton's hand closed around her wrist, and a frisson of energy zapped through her body. "Yes."

"I was thinking maybe we could chat."

"We are chatting."

He paused, then said, "You know what I mean."

She did. He wanted to talk about that night ten years ago.

Kelly swallowed. "I think it's best we leave the past in the past."

"Do you?"

The unexpected softness in his tone caused Kelly's knees to wobble. She didn't want to be weak. She needed to be strong.

"You seem nervous around me," he went on. "Guarded. And there can only be one reason for that."

"Oh?"

"We need to resolve our situation."

Ashton sounded sincere, like he actually cared. And suddenly Kelly realized there was so much she wanted to ask him. So much she wanted to get off her chest.

He took the bowl from her hand, placed it on the table, then slowly stood. Kelly held her breath. Ashton said, "I don't want us to be enemies."

"You should have thought about that before—"

Before Kelly could finish her statement, Ashton's lips came crashing down on hers. Kelly couldn't have been more shocked if he'd slapped her.

But this was no slap. This was fire. The kind that turned into a blazing inferno before you could blink.

Despite her mind's warning, Kelly relaxed against Ashton's strong body, her lips opening beneath his. Goodness, it had been so long, yet she remembered this so well. Remembered with aching clarity all she had felt that day.

Ashton's tongue delved into her mouth. It tangled with hers in a mating dance as old as time.

"Damn, Kelly. You taste so sweet . . ."

His words instantly sobered her. Slipping her hand between their bodies, Kelly pushed him away from her.

"Kelly . . ."

"No, Ashton. You can't . . . you can't just kiss me like this. Not after everything."

"Not after how I left you."

Kelly frowned at him. "Does that make you feel good?"

"No. Of course not."

"I may be over you, Ashton, but what you did to me still hurts. You kissing me only makes things worse."

Ashton sighed wearily. "Sorry."

"That doesn't make anything better."

"I don't know what else to say."

"Nothing you say will make a difference."

Several seconds of silence passed. Despite her words, Kelly felt disappointed that Ashton didn't try to convince her with every ounce of his being that he hadn't meant to hurt her.

"My life was . . . messed up," he finally said. He looked down at her, his hazel eyes intense yet soft. After a momentary silence, he shrugged his strong shoulders. "In a lot of ways it still is. I don't know. I just wanted you to know that it wasn't your fault. It wasn't anything you did."

Kelly didn't want to go there. She didn't want to encourage any conversation on the topic.

"It doesn't matter," she forced out. And before Ashton could say anything else, she quickly said, "I'll get my purse. Then we can head out."

She hustled out of the solarium, not daring to look back.

The day was hot and hazy, and humidity hung in the air like a light mist, covering the city. It was the kind of day Kelly liked, but also the kind of day that required frequent stops to air conditioned facilities. After leaving a store where the air conditioning had been cranked up way too high for Kelly's liking, she and Ashton were now strolling leisurely along Yonge Street, the longest street in Toronto.

Kelly surveyed the street and its occupants. Hundreds of people of all ages swarmed the sidewalks, laughing, talking, and window shopping. Some walked slowly, as if totally carefree, while others walked briskly, dodging the slower ones, as if they were on some important mission. And every hundred feet or so, there were beggars. A young female in her late teens with green hair seemed able bodied to Kelly, yet she sat in the doorway of a closed business, a baseball cap before her, soliciting change. Kelly reached into her wallet for some loose coins and tossed them into the girl's hat. She smiled appreciatively.

Thus far, her time with Ashton had been pleasant. They had discussed the city and its changes. The weather. Safe topics.

A dark-haired woman strolled by them. She looked up at Ashton and smiled. Kelly quickly looked at Ashton. She saw him smile back at the woman.

That had to be at least the fifth woman to boldly ogle Ashton—not that she was counting. What was wrong with these women, anyway? To blatantly stare and smile at a guy despite the fact that he was with a woman—talk about gall!

But Ashton smiled back every time. Clearly, he loved the attention.

As they neared the Eaton Centre, Toronto's famous mall the size of a city block, Kelly watched as an attractive black woman winked at Ashton as she crossed his path. That was brazen enough as far as Kelly was concerned, but to make matters worse, Ashton turned to watch the woman walk away!

Kelly rolled her eyes. She was suddenly so irked that she couldn't help saying, "Do you mind?"

Ashton stopped in his path and turned to face Kelly. He gave her a questioning look as he asked, "Mind what?"

"Don't give me that. You know exactly what I'm talking about."

"If I did, I wouldn't ask."

"You are showing me no respect. Really Ashton, how do you expect me to feel?" Did he flirt with every woman he found attractive? Just this morning he had kissed her. Would he have locked lips with any of the women he'd exchanged smiles with if they were alone in a room?

"What on earth are you talking about?"

Kelly inhaled a deep breath, tasting heat and humidity. "You're walking around with me," she explained, "yet you're focusing all your attention on every attractive bimbo who walks by swaying her hips."

Pursing his lips, Ashton raised a suggestive eyebrow. "And that bothers you, does it?"

"Bother me? Why on earth would it bother me?"

His eyes didn't leave hers. "Then why even mention it?"

Trying desperately to concentrate on something other than Ashton's heated gaze, Kelly twirled one of her braids. She shouldn't have said anything. All she was doing was flattering Ashton's incredibly large ego.

"Huh?" he prompted.

"I'm simply pointing out that it's disrespectful to ogle other women when you've got a woman by your side. If you can't understand that—"

"Not that I was *ogling* anyone, but if I was, why would that matter to you . . . unless you'd rather I ogle you."

Kelly gaped at him. "I can't believe you."

"Am I wrong?"

Kelly was quickly losing control of this situation, but she laughed sarcastically to give Ashton the impression that he couldn't be more wrong. "You always have to twist everything to flatter yourself, don't you? I can't believe I ever let you seduce me ten years ago."

"Uh, I think it was the other way around."

"No it was—" But Kelly quickly shut her mouth. She had had a few drinks that night, and for a nondrinker, it had been enough to loosen her lips and boost her courage. She had always tried to block the memory of how flirtatious she had been with Ashton at the grad party, but now it came rushing back.

Her face erupted in heat.

She crossed her arms over her chest. "I'm not discussing that night with you."

Turning, Ashton surveyed the people around them. Then he looked at Kelly again, a smile tugging at the corners of his full mouth. "Kelly, everyone here thinks we're having a lovers' quarrel."

Horrified, Kelly glanced around surreptitiously, noting several curious faces. She grunted and turned on her heel, ready to walk anywhere—anywhere but this embarrassing situation. Ashton's strong fingers wrapped around her arm, forcing her to stop. "Honey, will you ever forgive me?" he asked, loud enough for the nosy spectators to hear. Then he pulled her into an embrace, squeezing her tightly.

For one fleeting moment, Kelly forgot that she was standing in the middle of one of Toronto's busiest streets, surrounded by curious onlookers. She could only think of the glorious feel of Ashton's hard body against hers.

But only for a moment.

"Let me go." Kelly's voice was soft but held a threatening quality.

"Promise me you'll be nice, and I'll let you go."

"Just let me go," Kelly demanded through clenched teeth.

"Not until you promise me that you'll be nice." Ashton's breath was warm against her ear as he chuckled softly.

Kelly closed her eyes, willing the unexpected tantalizing sensation to dissipate.

"I'm waiting . . ."

He was really enjoying this! Anger swirled within her chest. Kelly was so furious she wanted to belt Ashton, but she knew she couldn't. Not with an audience. And she couldn't continue to stand here in the middle of the street causing a scene. She had to put an end to this embarrassing situation as quickly as possible.

"All right," Kelly whispered into Ashton's ear.

"All right what?"

"All right. I'll be nice." She hoped he was happy. He had thoroughly humiliated her! The man was absolutely incorrigible!

Slowly, Ashton released his hold on Kelly, but still kept one hand firmly planted around her waist. He looked around proudly and smiled at the nosy passersby. "It's okay. She forgives me."

"She'd be a fool not to," a middle-aged woman muttered as she sauntered by, smiling at them.

Kelly could only stand there with a forced smile on her face. What else was she supposed to do?

"You are an absolute jerk," Kelly whispered, her tone as venomous as a rattlesnake's poison. "And you can let go of me now."

"Oh no, baby. I'm not through with you yet."

Chapter 7

Kelly had to be insane, because Ashton's words actually turned her on. She couldn't help thinking of Karen's comment that she needed a man who was unpredictable, rather than safe.

Ashton was definitely unpredictable.

And Glenn . . . she and Glenn would have had a pleasant day touring the city, then an equally pleasant dinner. Maybe they'd even go to a movie afterward, one he would let her choose.

It was a perfectly decent sounding scenario. So why did it have Kelly bored to tears?

She could hear her brother now. *Kelly, you're such a drama queen.* Was she?

She didn't have time to think of the answer to her question because Ashton suddenly whisked her across the street to the Hard Rock Café.

"What are you doing?" Kelly asked, certain that her interpretation of the situation had to be a mistake. He was *not* going to take her to dinner, not when he knew how angry she was.

"I'm taking you to dinner."

Enraged, Kelly shot Ashton an angry glance. "I'm not going to dinner with you."

Ashton chuckled, a self-confident, arrogant sound. "Yes you are."

"I want to go back to Karen's," Kelly protested, as Ashton led her inside the restaurant.

Ashton ignored her, and instead asked the red-haired hostess for a table for two in the nonsmoking section.

Kelly did her best to hide her disgust, but she was certain that she was failing. She was in no mood to sit down and dine with Ashton.

As though he expected her to dart for the door, Ashton continued to hold Kelly until they reached the table. "I think this table will suit you two well," the hostess announced. "It's pretty private." She smiled knowingly as she placed the two menus on the table, then walked away.

"For goodness sake, Ashton! Will you let me go?"

Ashton smiled down at Kelly, the same annoying smile that he always wore. "Temper temper," he said as he helped her into her seat. "You really need to calm down."

"What I need is to get away from you."

Ashton slid into his chair, then reached across the table and took Kelly's hand in his. "Kelly, I promise to be a perfect gentleman as long as you promise not to cause a scene."

"*Me* cause a scene?" she hissed. "*You're* the one—" Kelly stopped midsentence and inhaled a frustrated breath. She was about to tell Ashton exactly what she felt about him and his distorted memory, but she realized he was right. Getting more upset than she already was in the small confines of a restaurant certainly wouldn't do her any good. She needed to relax.

"Now, do you think you can be decent to me for the next forty minutes?"

"Oh, that's priceless." And it was the last straw. Kelly rose to her feet faster than Ashton could blink, grabbing her purse from her chair. But before she could get away, Ashton grabbed her by the waist and pulled her down onto his lap.

"Hey, none of that hanky panky until *after* dinner."

Horrified, Kelly looked up to see a pretty Asian woman with long black hair standing over the table with a pen and pad in her hand, a wide smile painted on her face. "We want to make sure you at least pay the bill," she added. "I'm Alice. What can I get you to drink?"

Kelly wanted to slink away and disappear.

"I'll take a beer," Ashton said. "Whatever you have on tap."

"And you, ma'am?" Alice asked.

"I'll have a water," Kelly said. *To throw all over you, Ashton,* she added silently.

"Bring her a strawberry margarita," Ashton instructed the waitress. "She'll like that."

The waitress made some notes on her pad, then slipped it in a pocket on her apron. Grinning, she walked away.

When the waitress was out of earshot, Kelly heaved herself off Ashton and stood beside him. "I hope you enjoy the strawberry margarita, because I certainly won't be here to drink it."

"Where are you going to go?" Ashton asked, his hazel eyes daring Kelly to answer him. "You know that if you walk out that door, I'll be right on your tail. So you may as well stay put, and enjoy your evening."

Knowing he meant every word he said, Kelly glared at Ashton for several moments, then slowly sank back into the seat across from him, resigning herself to a night of hell. The man really was impossible. But the more Kelly protested, the more Ashton would enjoy the situation. He obviously loved being in control.

The waitress returned with their drinks, and Ashton ordered a cheeseburger with fries. Kelly agreed to a plate of chicken fingers. After all the walking they had done, she had to admit that she was famished.

Kelly fiddled with her straw before finally putting it to her mouth and taking a sip of her strawberry margarita, feeling as though by drinking it, she was giving in to Ashton's control. To her delight, the drink was sweet and refreshing, with just a slight hint of alcohol. Kelly took another sip.

"You see," Ashton said, "this isn't so bad."

Kelly flashed Ashton a cynical grin. This situation was far from ideal. To have to look into his smug face and see those eyes, those brilliant hazel eyes. . . .

Stop it, Kelly told herself sternly. She may have been a fool once, but she'd be damned if she was going to be a fool again.

"Why don't we talk about something we can both agree on," Ashton suggested. "Karen's party."

Kelly expelled a sigh of relief. Karen's party was something that she could happily get into. With the focus off the tension between the two of them, her nerves could finally settle down. She could pretend, even if only for a few minutes, that she and Ashton were two normal people who enjoyed each other's company. That they didn't have a history.

"That sounds great. I assume you already have some ideas."

Ashton nodded. "Karen really enjoys a good party. So, I was thinking that instead of a small gathering at the condo, we should have the party at a restaurant."

Kelly rested her chin on a palm as she considered his suggestion. She had no objections. "Sounds good to me. Any ideas where?"

"I work part time at a restaurant that would be perfect. It has a dance floor, and one part of the restaurant is practically separated from the rest. That will be perfect for thirty to forty people. Those who want to eat dinner can do so first, then the others who want to dance can show up later."

"Sounds like you've got it all figured out."

"That's the easy part," Ashton said. "I've still got to hire a DJ, but as I work in the music field as my main career, I've already got someone in mind. The hard part is calling all Karen's friends and getting them to agree to come on such short notice."

When Kelly nodded, Ashton continued. "I need you to help me call all of Karen's friends. Believe me, she has a lot of them. I think Saturday will be the best day for the party, but I'll have to let my manager know the definite date very soon so we can reserve a section."

"I'm free to help you make the calls. And anything else you need. That's why I'm here."

Ashton smiled. "Great. Like I said, this is going to be pretty short notice. Do you think we can get started tonight?"

"Sure." Kelly actually felt a modicum of excitement, and thankfully, her earlier argument with Ashton was practically forgotten.

They discussed a few more details during dinner, and agreed that Kelly would take care of any decorations. Aside from calling Karen's friends and confirming their attendance, she wouldn't have much else to do. Which was fine with her. As long as she didn't have to spend every waking hour with Ashton.

Just after seven P.M., Kelly and Ashton arrived back at Karen's apartment. As Kelly inserted the key in the lock, she felt Ashton's presence directly behind her, and her knees wobbled. Good grief, what was wrong with her?

"Drama."

"What was that?" Ashton asked.

Kelly looked at him in alarm. She didn't realize she had spoken aloud.

"Nothing," she replied. She went back to the task at hand—trying to open the door. She fiddled with the key in the lock, but for some reason, the door would not open.

"Having trouble?" Ashton asked.

"No," she replied as calmly as she could.

"Looks like you're having trouble to me." Ashton put his hand on hers. "Let me help."

With his callused hand resting delicately on her soft one, Ashton turned the key in the lock, and it opened easily. "There. It just needed a soft touch."

A shiver of delight ran down Kelly's spine. His voice was warm and sexy and made her heart race.

Why oh why did she still react to him? Kelly didn't like that fact one bit. Sure, Ashton was attractive, even more so than before. But he had hurt her, and she shouldn't be feeling a surge of excitement at his touch. Yet she did. Her hand still tingled where his flesh had caressed hers.

Returning to the task at hand, Kelly quickly pulled the key from the lock and opened the door. She scurried into the apartment and Ashton followed her.

When she was in the living room, Kelly turned to face him. "Ashton, I know I said we could start making those calls tonight, but . . . but I'm a bit tired. At the very least I'd like to catch a power nap. I'll call you when I wake up, okay?"

"Oh. Well, let me go grab you the list of names."

"Can't this wait?" Kelly asked. She simply wanted to escape Ashton right now, and the unsettling effect he had on her.

Ashton's eyes narrowed with concern. "What's wrong, Kelly?"

"Nothing," Kelly said quickly. "I'm just . . . tired."

Ashton shook his head slowly. "One minute we seem to get along. The next you want to run and hide. Is this how you want things between us?"

"Of course it's not. It's never what *I* wanted."

Ashton folded his muscular arms over his firm chest. "Meaning it's what I wanted?"

Kelly merely shrugged and looked away.

"Don't do that. Don't turn away from me."

"Ashton, I'm tired . . ."

"I don't believe you."

"Don't you have women waiting on your call or something?" Goodness, where had that come from?

"Wow. Where's that coming from?" Ashton asked, echoing her thoughts.

She'd opened this can of worms. She may as well see it through. "You're a man, Ashton. One who . . . *appreciates* women from what I can tell."

"Are you saying I'm a player?"

"If the shoe fits."

Ashton took two steps closer to Kelly, and she lifted her chin defiantly, ready to do battle. "You don't even know me," he said, his voice softer than Kelly had anticipated. "How can you say that?"

Kelly held Ashton's gaze, unwilling to admit that he was right. She hadn't seen him since high school, so what right did she have to judge him? Just because he had given her one sizzling night then shattered her world the next day didn't mean he used women ruthlessly now.

But could a leopard change its spots? No. "I don't know. I get the impression you haven't changed much since high school."

"Meaning I haven't matured."

Kelly didn't answer. Suddenly she wasn't sure what to

think. She had based her assumptions of his character on her experience with him in high school. But maybe that wasn't fair.

Ashton took her by the wrist. "Or maybe," he said gently, "you want me to leave for another reason all together."

His voice was low, deep. Kelly's stomach fluttered. She shouldn't even indulge such crazy talk, yet she asked, "Like what?"

Ashton's eyes were steady on hers. "The chemistry between us. You have to admit, that's what all the arguing was about earlier. Pent up frustration, because you'd rather make love, not war."

"My God. You are—"

"Irresistible?"

Kelly's eyes flashed fire. "Impossible is more like it."

"And what if *I* find *you* irresistible?"

"I'd say poetic justice does exist."

"Are you saying you don't want me to kiss you right now?" Ashton gently stroked Kelly's face. She quivered at his touch, and knew that she was losing the battle to remain defiant. "Hmm, Kelly?"

Kelly's throat constricted, preventing any words from escaping. She was completely distracted by Ashton's touch, and she was desperately trying to fight the delicious sensation that was building inside her. As much as she wanted to scream "No!" she couldn't do a damn thing. She was paralyzed.

Before she knew what was happening, Ashton tilted her chin upward and lowered his lips to meet hers, surprising her with a delicate kiss. His mouth was as soft as velvet and lingered on hers, gently parting her lips with his tongue. Releasing her wrist, he reached for her face with both hands, cupping it tenderly. His tongue was warm as it danced with her own, teasing her.

Exciting her.

The kiss sent a tingling sensation all through Kelly's body, electrifying and awakening every cell. It grew in intensity until it seemed to have a life of its own, consuming them both.

When Ashton finally pulled away from her to catch his breath, Kelly felt as though someone had doused her with a glass of cold water. She hungered for more of what she had just experienced.

"You are the most beautiful woman I have ever laid my eyes on. I've been wanting to kiss you again for hours." Cupping Kelly's chin, Ashton smiled down at her. It was a genuine, dazzling smile. Kelly stared back at him in stunned silence.

But sanity suddenly crept back into Kelly's brain, and she abruptly turned her head. How dare Ashton kiss her? She had been a pawn in his game of seduction once, but never again. "I want you to leave."

Ever so lightly, Ashton brushed his fingers across Kelly's cheek. A flame of longing erupted in her belly. "Are you sure that's what you want?"

Kelly stepped backward, moving away from Ashton's distracting touch. "Of course that's what I want. And I don't appreciate you trying to take advantage of me."

Crinkling his brow, Ashton asked, "Advantage?"

"You told me I was beautiful . . . what were you hoping? That I'd allow you to have your way with me again?"

"My way with you?"

"You know what I'm talking about."

Ashton's eyes roamed lazily over her body. "If you're talking about sex, sure, I'm tempted." Kelly opened her mouth to protest, but Ashton continued. "But that's not what I was trying to do."

"You are . . . a jerk."

"Maybe this isn't about me at all. Maybe you've got issues with men."

"Excuse me?"

"I kiss you, and you jump to all sorts of conclusions. Do you have problems trusting men?"

Kelly guffawed. "I happen to be involved with a wonderful man whom I trust."

"You are, are you?" His tone was doubtful. "And when did that happen?"

"You don't believe me," Kelly stated in shock.

"You didn't mention anything."

"I wasn't aware that I had to report to you about whom I'm involved with."

"We've spent the better part of the day together. Hell, you've kissed me twice."

"*You* kissed *me.*"

"Semantics, babe. You were there as much as I was."

Kelly waved a dismissive hand. "It doesn't matter. It can't happen again."

"Because of this boyfriend of yours?"

"That's right."

Ashton stared at her in disbelief. "You really have a boyfriend?"

"Why is that so hard for you to believe?"

"There's obviously no reason you *couldn't* have one. You're beautiful. Sexy as hell. But you kissed me twice, and now you're telling me it can't happen again?"

"That's right, because I'm engaged," Kelly blurted out before she had a chance to think, before she had a chance to consider the consequences of her words.

Ashton tilted his head and looked at her as though she'd morphed into a Martian. "You're *what?*"

Chapter 8

She was lying. Surely she had to be. How could she have kissed him with such abandon if she was engaged?

"You're what?" Ashton asked again, when Kelly did not reply.

"*Involved,*" Kelly said this time. "Seriously involved."

Yeah, she was lying. "One minute you're engaged, the next you're 'seriously involved.' " He chuckled, feeling better. "Which one is it, Kelly? Or is it neither?"

Kelly just stared at him, seemingly at a loss for words.

"Well?" Ashton grilled. He didn't know what kind of game she was playing, but he wasn't going to let her use a fictitious man as a reason they should stay away from each other. Not that he thought they *shouldn't* stay away from each other. But he was thinking hypothetically, of course.

"I am . . . in a relationship," Kelly finally said. "You don't have to believe me. I've got nothing to prove to you."

The way Ashton saw it, she had a lot of proving to do. "So how long have you been *involved?*"

"About eighteen months. But I've known him for five years."

Ashton nodded, feigning belief. "Interesting. Eighteen months?"

"Yes." Again, Kelly paused. She was clearly making this story up as she went along. "And so you know, we *have* talked about marriage. We just haven't made it official."

"Is that so?"

"Yes, that's so. And . . . and the more I think about it, the more I realize that he's the perfect man for me."

"You sound so positive."

"Well, of course. Of course I'm sure. Totally."

Kelly strolled into the living room and sat on the love seat. Ashton followed her without hesitation. He didn't buy one bit of this story. This was her idea of payback because he had abandoned her ten years ago. If he kept the pressure on, he knew she would break down and admit that she was lying.

"Marriage is a serious commitment."

"Yeah, someone like you would point that out. Well, unlike you, I'm not afraid of commitment. Glenn and I *will* walk down the—"

His humorous outburst cut her off. Kelly glared at him, letting him know that she was less than impressed.

Ashton's laughter faded and died. She couldn't possibly be seriously involved . . . could she?

"I suppose someone like you would find that funny."

"Of course it's funny." Wasn't it? And why did it matter? "Not the idea of marriage, but this sudden story of yours. You've gotten yourself all tangled up in it."

Kelly looked at him calmly and said, "Sorry, Ashton. The joke's on you."

"You're not serious about this phantom boyfriend slash fiancé?"

"Do I look like I'm joking?" Her breathing slow and

deliberate, Kelly most certainly did not look like she was joking.

"You've really got a boyfriend?" Ashton asked, suddenly as serious as Kelly.

"Yes."

"Eighteen months?"

"Yes."

Eighteen months? How the hell was he supposed to compete with that?

And where on earth had *that* thought come from?

"You're really involved in a serious relationship with this . . . Glenn?"

"What part of this conversation don't you understand?" Kelly asked, a hint of a challenge in her voice.

"It's just that—" The words wouldn't come to him. All along, he'd thought Kelly had been making this story up—simply to get rid of him. But now she was telling him that she was seriously involved with this Glenn character and had talked about marriage! "I don't believe it."

Kelly guffawed. "Well, believe it. And please, in the future, don't forget it. That way, we can avoid any repeat episodes of the ones today."

Ashton eyed Kelly, hoping to see a hint of doubt. Something that would alert him to the fact that she was *indeed* lying. He saw nothing but determination, which left him thoroughly confused.

Especially since only a few minutes before, he had felt her wanton longing for him. He'd felt her body grow warm against his, had tasted the eagerness in her kiss. And now she was telling him that she was involved and that he couldn't kiss her again?

The problem was, he wanted to kiss her again.

Just because he loved a challenge? Or because something deep inside told him he wanted another chance with her?

Silence hung in the air between them, heavy and menacing. Ashton finally ventured to speak. "Kelly," he said, his voice calm. "Can I ask you a question?"

Kelly eyed him suspiciously, then slowly nodded. "Go ahead."

Ashton hesitated before speaking, carefully considering what he was going to say. "Do you actually love this guy?"

"Why on earth would you ask me that?"

"You don't think it's a fair question?"

"Well, I suppose." She paused. "Yes, of course I love him."

Ashton looked Kelly squarely in the eyes. "But are you *in* love with him?"

"What's the difference?"

"You have to ask?"

"You of all people shouldn't be lecturing me on love."

"I'm not lecturing you." Ashton paused. He didn't want this to turn into an argument. "I'm only trying to point out that there's a difference between loving someone and being in love."

"Like you would know anything about it." Kelly rolled her eyes. When was he going to stop hounding her? Why did he care whether or not she was in love anyway?

She almost wanted to ask, but stopped herself. Wouldn't she sound the complete idiot if she did? She couldn't believe herself. Even after all this time and the heartbreak he had caused her, there was a small part of her that still held onto some sort of hope.

Or maybe it was pride.

Yes, she thought, relieved. *It's my pride.* And now that she knew what her issue was, she could get over it.

"If you really plan to marry this guy, I hope you're truly in love with him."

Oh, wasn't that sweet of him?

"You don't need to worry about me."

Ashton strolled to the window. Kelly couldn't help watching him. His mood seemed to have suddenly changed. She could see it in the way he held his body.

And, crazy her, there was a part of her that wanted to reach out to him. A part of her that wanted to ask if he was upset because of what she'd told him.

She stood tentatively. "Ashton?"

"I mentioned that there were things I didn't tell you," he said without looking at her. His voice was quiet, but it held a note of . . . of resentment? Of pain? "My mother left me when I was young. I know it's no excuse for what I did to you, but . . ."

He didn't finish his statement.

Kelly held her breath as she stared at his back. "But what?"

"It wasn't only my mother."

"What does that mean? Someone else hurt you?"

"Forget it." He finally faced her. A mix of pain and anger flickered in his hazel eyes. "You said you wanted to rest."

He started toward the door. Kelly followed him. He was clearly hurt. Bitter, even. Though she had told him that she didn't care what he had to say about what had happened ten years ago, now she wanted to know.

Seeing Ashton was throwing her for a loop. He had always been so popular and attractive, she hadn't imagined he had any pain in his life. Was that why he had so often resorted to humor, to cover it up?

"Ashton."

He reached for the doorknob. "I'll talk to you later."

"Ashton," Kelly said, exasperated.

He paused. Faced her. "I thought I wanted to talk about this, but I realize now . . . I'm not ready."

Kelly could hardly believe her eyes. Ashton was genuinely hurt. It was a reality almost too bizarre to believe.

Which was an entirely unfair judgment. Everyone had a private life. Everyone had their issues.

Whatever the case, the pain she saw in his eyes was real. And to her surprise, part of her wanted to put her arms around him and whisper in his ear that everything would be all right. The part of her that was still a dreamer.

The sound of a key turning in the lock broke the moment between them. Ashton's disposition immediately changed. His saddened expression was replaced by a charming smile.

"Karen," he said happily when she opened the door. He immediately wrapped Karen in a hug.

When they pulled apart, Karen grinned at them both. "Hi, guys."

"Hey." Kelly hugged Karen, then walked with her to the living room. Ashton lagged behind.

Karen dropped herself onto the sofa with a sigh of exhaustion, then asked, "How was your day?"

"Better than yours, it looks like," Kelly uttered, smiling. "You look exhausted."

"I am. Some of the cast members are really stressed out." Karen sighed wearily. "Believe me, this job isn't as glamorous as it's cracked up to be."

Kelly sat down beside Karen, bringing a foot onto the sofa with her. Being a teacher, she had regular hours with weekends and all statutory holidays off. She couldn't imagine working at a job with irregular hours, no matter how much she loved it. One look at her friend told her that the stress and exhaustion must take a serious toll on one's body.

Looking as sexy as ever, Ashton appeared. "I'll see you gals tomorrow."

"You don't have to leave yet," Karen told him.

"You need your rest. We can hang out tomorrow."

Karen nodded her agreement.

Ashton then glanced down at Kelly. He held her gaze for a long moment. Too long.

"Oh, and thanks for taking Kelly around," Karen said, her eyelids closing as she laid her head back against the couch.

"No problem," Ashton replied. "Good night, ladies." He turned and headed for the door.

"Ashton," Kelly called after him, quickly rising to her feet. Suddenly, she wasn't quite ready to say good-bye to him.

When he faced her, she said, "I wanted to thank you as well. I appreciate you going out of your way to give me a tour of the city."

Ashton simply nodded. He seemed a little distant. "The pleasure was mine." And with that final statement, he disappeared.

Kelly stood silently for several moments. The weirdest feeling was coursing through her body.

Ashton's mother had really hurt him. And he didn't seem to be over it.

She cared. In a way that surprised her.

Kelly finally returned to the sofa. She sat, causing Karen to stir and awaken from her sleep.

Somewhat dazed, Karen looked at Kelly and asked, "Was I sleeping?"

"Why don't you go to bed?" Kelly suggested. "You've had a long day."

"Oh," Karen moaned. "But I wanted to spend some time with you. I've got to work the rest of the week."

Kelly stood. She took Karen's arm and gently helped her to her feet. "Don't worry about me. I'm pretty tired from all the walking I did around the city today. I'm heading to bed, too."

"Did you go up into the CN Tower?" Karen asked, her eyes temporarily widening with excitement.

"I most certainly did," Kelly informed her friend.

As she slowly made her way down the hallway to her bedroom, Karen asked, "Isn't it amazing? The world's tallest building. No, that's not right. I think they built a taller one in Japan. Or was it Hong Kong? I can't remember."

Kelly chuckled softly. Some things never changed. Karen always babbled when she was beginning to drift.

"Tell me in the morning," Kelly said.

"Okay."

Mechanically unbuttoning her shirt, Karen disappeared into her bedroom. She would probably drop it on the floor, along with the rest of her clothes.

Kelly sighed softly as she went to the spare bedroom to prepare for bed. She had packed a few novels in her suitcase, and this was the perfect time for her to pull one out.

A short while later, as she lay on the day bed with a suspense thriller in her hands, her mind suddenly drifted to Glenn.

Glenn.

She felt a measure of guilt for what she'd said to Ashton about him. As a general rule, she didn't believe in lying.

But when it came to Ashton, she had to keep her guard up. The last thing she could do was allow herself to become vulnerable to him again.

Glenn had asked her to call him. Kelly had told him that she would if she had the time. Now, she wondered if she should. Maybe it was a good thing for her to connect with him while away.

Especially since all the arguments she'd made about him to Ashton made perfect sense.

Glenn was stable. Glenn could commit. Glenn hadn't hurt her.

Are you in love with him? she heard Ashton ask.

She couldn't honestly say she was. But love was overrated . . . wasn't it?

Too bad it had electrified every cell in her very being.

"And what about electrifying kisses?" she asked herself. "Are those overrated too?"

Because the truth was, Ashton's kisses still electrified her. Glenn's didn't.

But Glenn was safe. Ashton was not. And Kelly needed safe. She needed someone who wouldn't break her heart.

Chapter 9

Kelly stood before the oval-shaped mirror in the bathroom, staring at her reflection. She had barely slept last night, and now she could see the slight dark circles that had formed beneath her eyes.

Damn Ashton Hunter, the cause of her unrest. Instead of being able to sleep peacefully, she had lain awake, wondering about the Ashton Hunter who had been hurt.

He had mentioned his mother, but he'd also said that someone else had hurt him. Did he mean a woman? Had he been in love and rejected? Was there a woman out there immune to Ashton's charms?

Kelly still remembered how his hazel eyes had darkened, pain evident in their depths. What had he refused to tell her?

She had let that question plague her until she'd had to accept that she wouldn't be able to guess the answer. But then she had been kept awake by the memory of their kisses.

And what a memory that had been! Would she ever forget the sweet taste of his lips, the spicy scent of his cologne as he'd held her close, the way her body had grown hotter than a Florida summer day. . . .

Kelly splashed cold water on her face, trying to douse the image. The last thing she needed to do was remember Ashton's kiss. She had succumbed to his charm, but it wouldn't happen again. Even if she was crazy enough to believe they might still have feelings for each other, things would never work out between them. Her life was now in Fort Lauderdale, and his was here.

Kelly suddenly lifted her head. Was that a knock on the door?

Yes, she realized, as she heard the unmistakable rapping on the door. Kelly grabbed her thick white towel and dried her face, then hustled out of the bathroom.

A quick glimpse through the peephole told her that her visitor was the man who had invaded her thoughts and her dreams all night. She scowled, knowing that she looked far from her best. Ashton could have at least called before showing up.

It doesn't matter what I look like, she told herself resolutely. *I'm not trying to impress Ashton.* With that thought, she swung open the door and smiled sweetly, determined to start today with a clean slate. "Good morning, Ashton."

Ashton's grin was warm as he stepped into the condo unit. He was clad only in black spandex shorts, and a black cotton tank top, allowing Kelly an unrestricted view of his gorgeous body. "Morning, Kelly. I hope I'm not too early."

Kelly was tempted to tell him what she really thought, that he should have called, but instead she shook her head. "No."

"Good. Because it's time to start making those calls." Ashton strolled into the living room and made himself comfortable on the love seat. "I've got the list of people to call. Most of the numbers will be in Karen's little black book. She keeps that on her dresser." Ashton extended a sheet of paper to Kelly.

Kelly took the paper from him and began to look at the list of names as she sank into the full-size sofa. There were probably about twenty names on the sheet.

"You can call those people, and I'll call the others." Ashton gestured to the paper in his hands. "I just need to look at Karen's phone book to get all the numbers I need."

Kelly watched as Ashton disappeared into Karen's bedroom. So far, it was strictly business. Ashton was being pleasant and didn't seem at all upset about last night. So why did she feel so . . . uncomfortable?

Kelly dismissed the nagging feeling and returned her attention to the list. She hoped that everyone would be able to make it to the party. This would be a truly great surprise for Karen. She still couldn't believe that her friend was going to be doing a cross-country tour! Several opportunities could develop out of this kind of exposure, and before long, Karen could be on Broadway. The thought made Kelly smile. She had to admire her friend for pursuing that kind of dream.

Ashton returned from the bedroom with a small black book. "This is it," he announced. "Will it bother you if I copy down the numbers here? I can do it at my place and then return the book to you, if it's a problem."

So he *was* upset about the previous evening. Well, Kelly couldn't blame him. Ever since she had arrived, the tension between them had been as intense as a Florida hurricane.

"Do what makes you feel comfortable," Kelly told him.

"All right. This shouldn't take long."

Sitting down once again, Ashton began to flip through Karen's address book. Kelly couldn't think of any small talk, and she sensed that Ashton wasn't in the mood for any. She got up and walked into the kitchen.

Looking through the cupboards, she found where Karen kept her tea. There was an assortment of teas, including peppermint, strawberry, and orange pekoe.

Deciding on peppermint, Kelly took the appropriate box from the cupboard and placed it on the counter. She then filled the electric kettle with water, and plugged it into the wall. As the water started to warm up, Kelly took a mug from the cupboard and placed a tea bag into it.

"Kelly."

Kelly froze, shocked not only that Ashton had called out to her, but at his tone. The sweet deepness of his voice, the softness it portrayed as he called her . . . Kelly's stomach suddenly felt like a home for frenzied butterflies.

"Kelly," he called again, bringing Kelly back to reality.

Cautiously, she walked back into the living room. "What is it, Ashton?"

"I've got the numbers I need." He stood and approached her slowly. Kelly made a determined effort to keep her eyes on Ashton's face, though it was oh so tempting to check out his magnificent body. "Here's Karen's book. You'll find all the numbers you need in it." His fingers curled around Kelly's hand, forcing it open. He placed Karen's little black book in the palm of her hand.

Kelly swallowed hard, trying to ignore the electrical current that surged through her body at Ashton's touch. "That's everything?"

Ashton's eyes roamed Kelly's face, questioningly, provocatively. . . . Heat rushed to her face as his gaze held her captive. What did he want from her?

The kettle whistled loudly, fizzling the sexual energy

that had permeated the air. Ashton blinked, stepped backward. Kelly took a much needed breath.

"Call me later, after you've had a chance to call those people." Ashton looked at Kelly for the briefest of moments, then turned and strolled to the door.

Tongue-tied, Kelly watched as he opened the door. She felt as though she should say something, as though Ashton expected her to. But what? A cold chill swept over her as Ashton left the apartment without even turning around to say good-bye.

Kelly sighed with frustration. For the life of her, she couldn't figure out why Ashton was acting so . . . so hurt. If anyone here had a right to feel hurt here, it was her.

"Ouch!" she wailed as she accidentally poured the scorching hot water from the kettle onto her hand. She mumbled a ladylike oath as she turned on the kitchen faucet and ran her burned hand under the cold water. Damn Ashton. He was the reason for this.

Kelly marched to the bathroom where she put some lotion on her injured hand to soothe it. The burn wasn't serious, but it did hurt something awful.

Maybe I shouldn't have come here, she thought. Her emotions were all out of whack after seeing Ashton again; there was no denying that. She didn't like the way she was feeling, the way Ashton's gaze alone made her feel. All she could think about was Mr. Heartbreaker, when she should be thinking about Glenn.

Glenn. Should she marry him?

The truth was, she hadn't seriously considered his proposal until she'd brought it up to Ashton. Last night, it had been easy to see all the reasons why she should marry him.

Rather, the reason. There truly was only one.

Because he wasn't Ashton.

Oh, goodness. What a horrible thought. Could she

marry someone, even a sweet man like Glenn who would probably be true to her forever, simply because he wasn't Ashton?

Glenn deserved better than that. He deserved her whole heart.

Kelly went back to the kitchen where she sweetened her tea and drank it. She had hoped the delicious liquid would help soothe her and take her mind off her dilemma. But it didn't.

Well, soon enough, she would be heading back to Florida and she could leave all thoughts of Ashton in the past.

If only she could survive the rest of the week.

The one way to do that was to stay busy. Making the calls for the party would take her mind off Ashton for the time being.

She strolled back into the living room and flipped through Karen's personal phone book, writing the phone numbers beside the corresponding names on her list.

She dialed the first one.

The phone was answered after two rings. "Hello?"

"Is this Bill McKnight?" Kelly inquired.

"Yes it is."

"Hello, Bill. I'm calling on behalf of Karen Stewart. You may already know that she's landed a part in a musical and is doing a cross country tour of the show."

"Yes, I do know."

"Great. Well, we're throwing a celebration for her on Saturday night as she's leaving next week. I hope you can make it."

There was silence for only a moment before Bill replied, "I did have other plans, but I'll cancel. Name the place."

Kelly informed him of the location for the party and the time. After she hung up, she smiled and wrote "yes" beside Bill's name. She hoped all the calls would go as smoothly.

Kelly spent the next thirty minutes calling the rest of the names on the list. There was no answer at some of the numbers she called, so she wrote "call back" by those names. Some of the numbers she called had answering machines so she left a message explaining why she had called, and gave Ashton's number to call with a response. Besides Bill McKnight, she reached six more of Karen's friends. Four confirmed that they would be able to attend the party. Two declined, but said to give Karen their best wishes.

Kelly stood and gave her body a good stretch. Thank goodness she had the party to concentrate on; that was the one thing that would help her make it through this week, help her keep her mind off the ever distracting Ashton Hunter. Already, she felt a sense of accomplishment at having confirmed five people. This party was going to be the best affair Toronto had ever seen; she was sure about that.

Strolling into the bedroom, Kelly looked out the window at the glorious view of the lake. The sun danced on the lake's waves, causing it to sparkle as though it were made of silver and gold. The weather was gorgeous, and there was no way she was going to spend the entire day inside.

She changed into blue spandex shorts and a matching blue top that exposed her firm, flat midriff. Back home, she jogged daily. Since her arrival in Toronto, she hadn't yet been jogging, and she felt a bit guilty for skipping her usual exercise routine. She wasn't obsessive about working out, but she knew how hard it was to keep up with an exercise routine once you started slacking off. She wasn't concerned about her weight; she'd never be a skinny minnie. But she did care about good health.

And a week was a long enough time to make it harder for her to get back into her routine once she returned home. *Well,* she thought, *there's no time like the present.*

Outside, Kelly walked the short distance to the water's edge. There was a path bordering the water that was divided into two lanes, one for walking and one for running. Other people were already jogging along the path and working up a sweat. Kelly stretched her leg and arm muscles in preparation for her exercise, then began to jog along the path.

This was exactly what she needed. The cool breeze off the lake was soothing against her skin, while the run was invigorating. Running was a great way to rid her body of stress.

As she trotted along the water's edge, Kelly tried to remember when she had first started jogging. She certainly hadn't been physically active in high school. In high school, some girls had been active with basketball, volleyball, cheerleading, and a number of other activities. Kelly had always taken her studies seriously, and when she wasn't studying, she was tutoring other students. Or dreaming of Ashton.

Ashton. Why on earth couldn't she get him out of her mind?

Kelly picked up her pace. This run was supposed to help her forget all the stressful things in her life. But for some reason, she couldn't forget the most stressful thing of all.

Her mind drifted back to high school. She and Ashton had met through Karen and the play she'd been helping to produce, but after that, they hadn't spoken much. Kelly had still been smitten, but too shy to pursue him.

The following year, they had ended up in the same English class. Ashton had sat with a few jocks in the back close to the window, while Kelly had sat near the front. So again, they hadn't had the opportunity to socialize.

But one Friday morning after leaving Mr. Duggan's class, Kelly had been walking down the hallway when she'd heard Ashton call, "Wait up." At first she hadn't realized that Ashton had been talking to her, but when he had called her by name, Kelly's pulse had quadrupled. She'd stopped in the hallway, her heart beating rapidly, turned her head to the side in a way she felt flattered her, and smiled shyly. She was certain that Ashton had come to his senses and realized that he just *had* to ask her out.

And he *had* asked her out. Just for a quick bite after school, but it had been the best day of her life. As they'd sat sipping their sodas and eating their sandwiches, Ashton had told Kelly how he'd been nervous that she wouldn't go out with him. Nearly choking on her drink—both from delight and shock—Kelly had assured Ashton that she was happy to spend time with him.

Then he had told her how much he respected her, how she wasn't like other girls, how he liked that about her. Beaming like a lovesick fool, Kelly had almost died with joy.

She'd hoped he would end the date with an invitation to a movie—or something. Something they could do to spend more private time together and get to know one another. He hadn't, but they had gone out a few more times for a bite after school.

A lot of time they discussed English class. Ashton just didn't get Shakespeare. So Kelly really shouldn't have been surprised the day he jokingly said, "I ought to pay you to write my paper for me."

"What?" Kelly had asked.

"You're so smart when it comes to all this. You could probably write your paper and mine in your sleep."

"Are you serious?"

"No." Ashton shook his head. "I'm not."

Kelly took a bite of her burger, still considering the suggestion. If she did write Ashton's paper, they could spend more time together.

And she would do anything to spend more time with him.

"How much?" Kelly asked.

Ashton swallowed his morsel of burger, then asked, "How much what?"

"How much would you pay me?"

"Honestly, I was joking."

"I wouldn't have to write the whole thing. Just *guide* you, so to speak."

"You really want to do this."

Kelly had smiled. "If the price is right . . ."

They had ended up deciding on twenty dollars. And every time they had met to discuss the ideas for the paper, Kelly's heart had pitter-pattered with joy.

That's why she had continued to work with him on more papers. All the while she'd believed they were growing closer. But the truth was, she and Ashton had never touched or kissed. Kelly had figured he was shy and taking things slowly.

Until graduation, when things had exploded between them.

Kelly blew out harried breaths as she continued to run, but she couldn't as easily blow away the memories of all that had happened after that night. Even as the days had grown into months, she had expected to hear from Ashton. Prayed for it, even. She had moved away, but their number had been forwarded. And just in case, she had called his father when they were settled in Florida to give him her new number.

But Ashton had never called. It had become painfully obvious that he had never really cared for her.

Kelly blew out an aggravated breath, willing the torturous memories to flee her mind. At this point in her life, no good would come of tormenting herself for having been dimwitted.

Bending forward and resting her hands against her knees, Kelly stopped to catch her breath.

"Don't stop now. I was getting some good exercise."
Kelly bolted upright and whipped her head around.
Ashton!

Chapter 10

Beads of sweat covered Ashton's beautiful brow. No wonder he had been dressed in black spandex earlier; he had been planning on jogging as well. Kelly silently prayed that he didn't think she had followed him out here.

"Aren't you full of surprises?" he chimed, his strong hands resting on his hips. "I had no idea you were heading out to jog."

"At home, I normally try to get a jog in every day."

A mischievous smile danced on Ashton's sexy lips. "You don't have to convince me of that. You're certainly in amazing shape." His eyes roamed her body lazily from head to toe, admiring the view.

Kelly shot him an outraged look. "Why are looking at me like that?"

"Like what?"

"Like you're checking me out?"

"What can I say? You are a beautiful woman."

"And one who has a boyfriend."

"I know, I know. You don't have to remind me."

"Good."

Kelly started to run again, this time sprinting off in the direction of the condo.

Ashton watched Kelly as she ran—ran for her life it seemed—back toward the condo.

Boyfriend schmoyfriend. That wasn't going to stop him from checking her out.

He didn't care if that was juvenile, but as far as he was concerned, if Kelly wasn't married, she was fair game. And not because he was the kind of guy who went after women who were involved, but because he sensed there was still an attraction between him and Kelly.

He had run from it ten years ago, but it was now apparent that he could only run so far.

Ashton looked out at the glittering water and inhaled deeply. The fresh scent of the lake filtered his nose. What he was thinking was crazy, but he couldn't will it away.

There was a part of him that still wanted her. A big part. And he felt in his soul that she wanted him, too.

He wanted another night with her. At least to see if the chemistry between them was still as strong as it had been ten years ago. Or maybe this was simply about closure. Another night together so they could get each other out of their systems and move on.

Kelly was only staying in town until after the party. Ashton didn't like that one bit. He didn't want her rushing back into the arms of Bozo the Boyfriend.

Turning, he started jogging toward the condo. He needed to figure out a way to make Kelly stick around after the party.

Somehow, he knew that wouldn't be an easy task.

* * *

Kelly had the strange sensation that someone was watching her, and she rolled over in the day bed, turning toward the door.

A figure engulfed in a dark shadow stood in the doorway of her bedroom. "I'm sorry, Kelly." It was Karen's soft voice. "I didn't mean to wake you."

"Hi," Kelly said, her voice husky. "I didn't even realize that I'd fallen asleep. Come on in."

Karen flicked on the light switch as she entered the small, cozy room. She took a seat on the pink quilted comforter beside Kelly. Rolling over onto her side, Kelly rested her head on the palm of her hand.

"I'm sorry I haven't been around much," Karen began, "but I've been so busy rehearsing."

Kelly smiled at her dear friend. "As long as you remember me when you make it big, I'll forgive you."

"Of course I'll remember you." Karen grinned, then frowned. "I just feel so bad because I haven't seen you in years, and I don't even have any real time to spend with you. I should be taking you all around the town."

"I'm surviving." As much as Kelly wished that she could be spending more time with Karen, she understood how busy her friend was right now. "But there's always the weekend. You don't have to rehearse then, do you?"

Karen shook her head. "Thank God I don't. I will definitely take you out."

Kelly threw the covers off her body and climbed out of bed. "I made some curried chicken; there's a lot left if you're hungry."

Karen's eyes lit up. "I'm starved."

Kelly and Karen walked into the kitchen, where Karen warmed the rice and peas and curried chicken in the microwave. Kelly poured herself a glass of orange juice.

Karen brought the warmed food into the solarium,

sitting down at the glass dining table. Kelly peered out the window, checking out the view of the darkened city. The Harbourfront was well lit and alive with action. "Is there ever a time when this place is dull?" Kelly asked.

Karen shook her head, waiting until she had finished chewing her food to speak. "Not a chance. There's always something going on, always something to do. I think this week it's the Jazz Festival."

Kelly slipped into the seat beside Karen. "Wow. I love jazz. I'll have to check that out. If I have time."

A weary sigh escaped Karen's lips. "I wish I could take you. But I can't. I'm just too busy."

"I know," Kelly said. "Don't worry about it."

Karen looked at Kelly as she said, "Well, I do worry. And since I can't spend much time with you, I hope you don't mind that I stopped by Ashton's apartment earlier and asked him to be your chaperon this week."

Oh no, Kelly thought, her smile fading. *That's the last thing I need.*

"And don't bother protesting," Karen told Kelly. "Ashton's already agreed."

"I don't need a baby-sitter."

Karen shook her head vehemently, obviously not wanting to hear any of Kelly's objections. "You need somebody to take you around. You don't know anybody else here. And there's no point sitting around bored when Ashton assures me he's more than happy to spend some time with you."

Kelly almost rolled her eyes to the ceiling, but fought the urge. Instead, she bit her bottom lip to avoid saying anything sarcastic.

"Besides," Karen said, her voice now playful and lighthearted, "Ashton's as hot as ever. You were crazy about him once. You might actually enjoy spending time with him now." Kelly opened her mouth to protest, but Karen continued. "I'm not talking sexually, or anything, because I know you're involved with Glenn. Your killer crush on Ashton was years ago."

"That's right. Ancient history." But her answer sounded weak even to her ears.

Karen shot Kelly a curious glance. "Are you sure about that, or does Ashton still set your heart fluttering?"

Kelly was too stunned to speak. All she could manage was an indignant stare.

Karen giggled like the schoolgirl Kelly remembered. "Don't mind me. I'm just being silly. I know you've got Glenn on the brain. Have you thought any more about his proposal?"

"Kind of. And . . . I'm still not sure what to do. I don't want to rush things."

"Of course not."

Kelly wanted to put down her guard and tell Karen how she was really feeling. How she was suddenly having doubts about her relationship with Glenn. How she knew that she wasn't ready to marry him—much less commit to a serious relationship with him. At least not until she had sorted out her feelings. Feelings that were out of whack after seeing Ashton again.

"You've got to admit, Ashton has certainly grown into one gorgeous hunk of a man."

Kelly shrugged and tried to appear nonchalant. "I guess he has."

"You guess?" Karen's eyes widened with surprise. "There's no guessing about it."

A disturbing thought entered Kelly's mind. Maybe Karen and Ashton weren't currently involved, but had they been? Kelly's stomach felt queasy just considering the thought.

She had to find out the truth. "Karen," Kelly began cautiously, "were you and Ashton ever—"

Instantly, Karen's big brown eyes bulged. "Intimate?"

She laughed. "No, Kelly. We were never lovers. Even if I wanted to, he was your guy. I'd never cross that line."

"He wasn't exactly my guy."

"Still, you were crazy about him. So, don't worry. Ashton and I have been nothing more than great friends. We would definitely not work out as a couple."

"I didn't say I was worried."

"Well, just in case you were."

Why would Karen say that? But the bad thing was, Kelly *was* relieved.

"Remember when we were younger?" Karen asked. "We used to spend so many summer evenings talking about our problems, and what was going on in our lives. Remember how obsessed I was with Malcolm Dixon?"

How could Kelly *not* remember Malcolm Dixon? He was Karen's first real crush. She had dated him, but she hadn't known at the time that he was dating almost every other girl in town. "I remember."

Kelly's eyes began to get misty. Karen always used to say that Kelly was the sister she'd never had, and Kelly used to say the same thing about her. Kelly had loved her brother, but she had driven him nuts trying to talk to him about her girl problems. Karen had never tired of Kelly's questions and concerns.

"I miss our talks," Karen said, then wiped at a tear that had escaped her eye.

Lord, how she missed their talks, too. Karen had been the one person Kelly had been able to tell everything. She wished desperately that she could confide her feelings with Karen now, but for some reason, she just wasn't ready. How could Kelly discuss her feelings when she was having a hard time accepting the fact that seeing Ashton again had thrown her for a loop?

Kelly squeezed Karen's hand and smiled at her. "I miss them, too. All the time."

Karen said, "Promise me that we'll always stay in touch."

Kelly leaned across the table and pressed her face against Karen's. "I promise."

Karen smiled at her. "And now, as much as I'd love to spend the evening reminiscing, I'm so exhausted I have to go to bed. Then get up tomorrow and do it all over again."

Kelly sighed, wishing she could spend the evening chatting with Karen. But her friend had another long day of rehearsal ahead of her.

She gave Karen a long hug, then, after a half hour of television, decided to go to bed herself. But in the darkness of her bedroom, she stared at the ceiling for what seemed like hours.

She couldn't sleep.

Kelly closed her eyes and tried to envision sheep, but after several seconds of picturing the white fluffy animals, a vision of Ashton invaded her mind.

Startled, Kelly opened her eyes and sat upright in the bed. Not Ashton again. Why wouldn't he give her any peace?

Kelly drew in a deep breath and let it out in an agitated rush, then plopped herself back down on the pillows.

Admit it, a voice told her. *You still want him.*

The thought shocked her. But when it settled, she knew it had a ring of truth.

Was this her problem, what had her so restless?

Maybe it was, but not because she wanted to be with him. Because she needed closure.

All this time, there hadn't been any closure, and his apology . . . well, it hadn't done much to make her feel better.

But another night with Ashton . . . surely that would

help put to rest the myth that they could have had a re-lationship.

Kelly had been a virgin when they'd slept together, which was no doubt why she still remembered that one hot night. Women foolishly held their first experience in higher regard than was normal. Perhaps even the memory was distorted in her mind.

So if she slept with him again, the truth would be clear.

"Are you even hearing yourself?" she asked aloud. "You have gone and lost your mind."

Yet the more she thought about it, the more she was convinced it might be the only way to put Ashton out of her system once and for all.

Chapter 11

Ashton stood quietly outside the door to Karen's apartment, anticipation and anxiety fighting for control of his emotions. He was looking forward to seeing Kelly again. He liked being around her. The light floral scent of the perfume she wore was etched in his senses, and he could easily picture her smile.

Yet would she want to see him? She had made it clear that he needed to stay away from her in any romantic sense.

And damn if he didn't like a challenge. He had spent the better part of the night thinking about kissing her sweet lips again.

His groin tightened as he felt the beginnings of an erection. Great. The last thing he needed was for her to open the door and see him like this.

He needed to regain control of his wayward emotions. He needed to stop fantasizing about the sexy but elusive Kelly Robbins.

Yet nothing he did to get her out of his mind so far was working. He had thought of other women from his past, even Camilla, but still Kelly had kept him awake.

He'd finally gotten out of bed and planted himself before his keyboard. Before he knew what was happening, he had written a song about a cute and feisty woman who wouldn't give him the time of day.

It had been a long time since Ashton had been inspired to write a song about a woman. Sure, he'd written lyrics about loving a woman, but those songs were a fantasy, something he didn't truly believe he'd experience, at least not in the sense one ought to. The last time he'd been inspired to write anything about a woman based on his feelings was after Camilla. And then, he had written about a woman who was self-absorbed, a woman who had used him while pretending to love him.

This time, he had written about . . .

Not love, Ashton told himself. He wouldn't allow himself life's greatest sorrow. He had watched his father live a life of despair after his mother ran out on them. And after his experience with Camilla, the one girl Ashton had grown to care for in college, he had sworn off love forever.

Camilla had been beautiful, stunningly so, and free spirited. *Too free spirited,* Ashton thought bitterly. In his first year of college, he had met the dark-haired, dark-skinned beauty and they'd begun dating. Ashton's college friends had all been immensely jealous every time they'd seen him with Camilla. She was a woman all men seemed willing to do almost anything for.

And she had been sold to the highest bidder. What might have been a sexual attraction to Ashton in the beginning soon turned to boredom when other men started showering her with gifts—all the things that really mattered to Camilla.

Ashton had never really loved her, but he had loved being with her. He still felt bitter about the callous way in which she had dumped him.

And what he knew of his father's relationship with his mother had confirmed for him that women were out to get what they could from men. Not all women, he had to admit. Karen was great. But most women. He was certain of that.

So why subject himself to love . . . to pain? He unquestionably didn't need the hassles. But he was a man with physical desires, and naturally, he noticed a beautiful woman. As long as the woman was willing, he wasn't opposed to a casual relationship. As long as she didn't care about love.

But since most women he met seemed hell bent on winning his heart, Ashton had been celibate for quite some time. His celibacy wasn't something he thought much about. He was too busy working and composing his music. But meeting Kelly again reminded Ashton just how celibate he was.

He knocked on the door to Karen's apartment, and several moments later, it opened. Kelly's eyes widened with surprise.

"I know, I should have called," he said. "But I figured it was easy enough to come by. What kind of progress have you made regarding the party?"

Kelly stepped backward. "Come in."

Ashton followed Kelly into the living room, his gaze lowering to her firm, round butt beneath her white shorts, then to her amazingly long and smooth legs.

Yeah, he wanted to her.

"Ashton?"

"Sorry," he said. Had she caught him staring? "What'd you say?"

"I said I've confirmed eight people."

"Oh."

Kelly picked up some papers from the coffee table. "I left messages for some, instructing them to call your number. Did anyone call you?" Tossing her head to the side, Kelly turned to face Ashton.

A simple tossing of the head, yet Ashton felt his blood growing hot. Kelly was a naturally beautiful woman, physically easy to look at. But it was more than that. She had an inner beauty that glowed through her personality—despite the fact that she liked to give him a tough time. She was so different from most of the women Ashton met, women who did everything to physically enhance their looks. Kelly's loveliness was simple, elegant, real. And the fact that she didn't seem the least bit obsessed about her appearance made her even more attractive to him.

"Ashton?"

Man, he was losing it. Ashton swallowed hard, attempting to gain control of his ravishing hormones. If Kelly sensed what he was thinking about, it would be trouble.

"I got four calls this morning," Ashton told her. "Three people confirmed that they can make it to the party. One can't. As for the people I called, eleven are definitely coming. A few more people said they'd have to let me know."

Kelly's full lips curved into a smile, revealing gleaming white teeth. "Great. That means there'll be at least twenty-five people at the party. I can't wait to see the look on Karen's face." She stood up, and Ashton resisted the urge to let his gaze roam over her body. "I was going to have a cup of tea before you came. Would you like one?"

Ashton nodded. "Sure."

"I'm having mint. Is that okay with you?"

"Mint tea sounds great," Ashton replied. "I haven't had it in years."

"It was a family ritual at our place growing up," Kelly said. A faint smile brightened her eyes. "Every morning before my parents went to work, and my brother and I went to school, we would have a cup of mint tea."

"That's right. I vaguely remember you having a brother. What's his name?"

"Michael."

"Right. He was a senior when we were freshmen?"

"Uh huh."

"What's he doing these days?"

"He's a cop. Though he was in the military for a while. Just got married a few months ago. One spoon of sugar, or two?"

"Two, thanks."

Ashton beamed inwardly as he watched Kelly disappear into the kitchen. She seemed different today, he noted. More relaxed. Since surprising her at the door, she had warmed up to him. At least that was a good sign. Getting down to business had proved to be the solution to the tension between them.

Several minutes later, Kelly returned with two cups of tea on saucers. She handed one to Ashton and placed hers on the coffee table before her as she sat down. Ashton thanked her, then took a sip. "This is great."

"Good. Now what else do we need to do?"

"Plan the rest of the party. Do you have any time today?"

"What did you have in mind?" Kelly asked. She fiddled with her teacup, mixing the hot liquid with a spoon while gently blowing it to cool it down.

"I figured you could come by my work place with me. Since we're having the party there, you should come by and check it out, get a feel for the place. I hope you're good with decorations and all that stuff because I'm definitely not."

Kelly chuckled. "Don't worry. I'll handle that. I was thinking of getting some kind of banner, and a few balloons."

"You'll get a better idea once you see the place." He paused. "So, you'll come by the restaurant with me today?"

Kelly was silent as she contemplated Ashton's offer. After several moments, she said, "Sure. When do you want to go?"

Ashton glanced at his watch. "I've got to work at four. I'll come get you around three-fifteen. Is that okay?"

"Mmm hmm. That's fine." She smiled.

Ashton returned Kelly's smile with one of his own, then finished the remainder of his tea. This was . . . pleasant. Sort of.

It was probably as good as things would get. Mint tea and friendly smiles.

For now.

Ashton stood. He didn't want to overstay his welcome. He had some things to do before he went to work. And considering the longer he stayed, the harder it would be to *not* kiss Kelly, he knew he'd better leave. He wanted to kiss her again, but this wasn't the time.

He headed to the door, and Kelly followed him.

"Three fifteen, then?" she asked.

A simple question, yet all the blood in his body rushed to his groin. He wanted to take Kelly in his arms and . . .

"Ashton."

Her soft, sensual voice brought him back to earth.

"Was there something else you wanted?"

"Uh," Ashton replied, suddenly at a loss for words. "I'll see you later." He opened the door and stepped into the hallway, daring only to turn his head when he heard the door click shut.

Man, he had almost lost it.

He inhaled a calming breath. Then he headed to his apartment to take a very cold shower.

Chapter 12

The tantalizing smell of sautéed onions, grilled chicken, and fried potatoes filled Kelly's nose as she followed Ashton into the spacious, upbeat, funky-style restaurant. Kelly looked around with interest, eyeing the large bar and medium-size dance floor on the left side. At the back of the restaurant, there were private booths on one side, and a kitchen area enclosed on the other. A young mother was holding her daughter up to the glass and pointing to different items on the grill.

"This is a very nice restaurant," Kelly commented, now examining the settings on a nearby table. "Does it get very busy?"

"At night. And especially in the summer," Ashton emphasized.

Suddenly realizing that she didn't know what Ashton's job was, Kelly asked, "Are you a waiter?" She tried to envision Ashton wearing a black bow tie, balancing plates on one arm while carrying a tray of drinks with his other.

"Actually, I'm a bartender."

That was more like Ashton, Kelly surmised. Pouring

drinks for a bar full of adoring females, raking in the tips and probably numerous phone numbers as well.

"If you're interested in bartending—" Ashton suggested, leaving the statement hanging in the air.

Kelly shot Ashton an "Are you out of your mind" look, and he chuckled. If there was one thing in life Kelly couldn't see herself doing, wearing a uniform and serving drinks a mile a minute was that one thing.

Ashton placed his hand on Kelly's back and led her to the bar. For some reason, the feel of Ashton's hand on her body caused her to involuntarily shudder. She was shocked that the mere touch of his hand on her skin could cause such a reaction. Especially since last night she'd finally put her feelings for Ashton where they belonged . . . in the past.

When he had been over earlier today, they had gotten along well, and for the first time, they hadn't ended up in some type of disagreement. Her resolve to put the past in the past had obviously worked, because she had been able to relax and even smile genuinely with Ashton. After all, she wouldn't be in town for much longer. After Karen left, she would go back to Fort Lauderdale and get on with her life.

He touched her once again, distracting her thoughts. This time, Ashton placed his hands on her waist and helped her onto a large bar stool. Excitement danced up her spine. "That really isn't necessary, Ashton," she said, turning to face him. "I'm quite capable of helping myself."

She looked up at Ashton, at his dazzling hazel eyes, and his gaze penetrated hers in such a sudden and tense way that Kelly had to turn her head to avoid being hypnotized. Damn, he was good looking. No one should look that good, she thought.

Even though Ashton seemed to rile her, and rattle her last nerve, Kelly was enjoying being near him now.

In fact, her body seemed to enjoy his touch while her mind tried to rationalize the reaction.

She wanted to run her hands through his dreadlocks and pull his face close for a kiss.

No, no. That wasn't what she wanted to do.

She asked, "Don't you have to get ready for work?" The sooner he moved away from her, the sooner she would regain her senses.

"That I do. Take a look around if you want. I won't be too long."

Kelly watched Ashton walk away, his sexy stroll making her think about what it would be like to feel his powerful thighs against hers, to have his tongue on her skin. Would it be as amazing as she remembered?

Disturbed by that sudden, inappropriate thought, Kelly turned her attention to the bar. The bartender, an attractive man with an olive complexion, smiled at her.

"You a friend of Ashton's?" he asked as he wiped the counter.

Kelly nodded. "Yes."

He paused in front of her. "What's your name?"

"Kelly," she responded quickly. She wasn't a very talkative person when it came to strangers, and nervousness had her shifting in her seat.

"I'm Tony." Tony extended his hand to her, and she shook it softly. "Ashton sure has kept you hidden from us. Hasn't even mentioned your name. Smart guy."

Kelly smirked. "What's that supposed to mean?"

"I haven't seen a woman as beautiful as you here in a long time," Tony replied, raising his eyebrows suggestively.

Kelly accepted Tony's compliment with a "Thanks." Unsure of what else to say, she was relieved when she saw Ashton appear from the back of the restaurant. He was following a short, stocky man with glasses, whom Kelly assumed was the manager. His light brown hair was receding, even though he couldn't have been older than thirty-five. He extended his hand to Kelly as he neared her, and he shook her hand firmly. "Hi, Kelly," he said. "I'm Marvin."

"Pleasure to meet you," Kelly responded.

Marvin asked, "Have you had a chance to check out the restaurant?"

Kelly shook her head. "Not really."

"Well then, follow me. I'll show you the area where you'll be seated Saturday night."

Kelly stepped down from the stool and followed Marvin as he took heavy, quick steps. He led them to the back section of the restaurant near the dance floor. "As you can see," Marvin began, "this area is relatively private from the rest of the restaurant, and can comfortably seat about forty people."

Kelly surveyed the area, noting approximately ten booths and tables. The walls were made of emerald marble, interspersed with gold strips that created a striking, classy atmosphere. The only direct light in this section came from artificial light fixtures on the wall, which at this point, were dimmed. Perfect for a party atmosphere, Kelly decided.

"I hope you like it," Marvin said.

Kelly nodded, then turned to face him. "Yes. It's gorgeous. Absolutely perfect."

"Have you decided what you want to do about dinner? Do you want a buffet?" Marvin looked at both Kelly and Ashton for an answer.

"I was thinking that it would be best to let everyone order individually," Ashton replied. "That way, those who don't want dinner can order only appetizers and drinks, and those who want a meal can order that, too. What do you think, Kelly?"

"Me?" Kelly swung her head to the left and faced Ashton, surprised. She hadn't even thought about meal arrangements. "It's gonna be late enough when we start the party. I guess it's best to forget a buffet because many people will have already eaten."

Marvin shrugged. "Whatever suits your needs."

"But you better get the kegs ready," Ashton added quickly. "I'm sure that all Karen's friends will consume a lot of alcohol. You know those actor types."

"That's what I like to hear," Marvin said. He glanced at the bar. "Business is picking up, Ashton."

"All right. I'll get to it." Ashton flashed Kelly a sexy smile, and a wave of heat washed over her. "Come by the bar when you're finished," he told her.

As Ashton sauntered to the bar, Kelly couldn't help thinking how adorable he looked in his white oxford shirt and bow tie, his corded muscles evident beneath his clothing. His loose dreadlocks provided an appealing contrast to his formal outfit. Another wave of heat enveloped her.

"Is there anything you'd like to ask me?"

Marvin's voice startled Kelly, and she turned to face him, crossing her arms over her chest. "Pardon me?"

"I was wondering if you had any questions for me."

Kelly shook her head. "No, you've been a great help. This place is perfect." She paused, then said, "You must get a lot of customers on the weekend, especially with a dance floor."

"We do get a lot of *guests,*" Marvin emphasized. "Not customers." When he saw Kelly's confused look, he explained, "We don't call people customers. We call them guests. That way, they feel more at home, more valued."

Kelly nodded and smiled faintly. She wasn't sure that the *guests* or *customers* cared what they were called, as long as they were treated well and were served good food. "Will there be a lot of people expecting to use the dance floor on Saturday night?"

"We'll make it clear there's a private party. And when you're ready to open up the floor, we'll open it."

"That's great. I'm definitely looking forward to this. Thanks so much for your help."

"No problem. I'll see you Saturday."

"Yeah. See you Saturday."

Kelly watched Marvin walk away, then turned on her heel and headed to the bar. Ashton smiled at her as she approached, and her heart nearly stopped. A week ago, she would never have imagined that she'd ever see Ashton again, yet here he was before her, smiling at her, making her feel things she hadn't felt since high school.

So much for putting her feelings for Ashton in the past.

As Kelly got comfortable on a barstool, Tony looked her way and winked.

Kelly did a double take. Surely she had to be imagining things.

Apparently not, because Ashton scowled at Tony. He kept his gaze on Tony as he made his way toward Kelly. His jaw was taut. He seemed tense.

Only when he faced her did he visibly relax. "You think you'll be able to make this place come alive for Karen's party?"

Kelly nodded. "I can't wait."

Tony strolled toward Ashton and Kelly, a curious expression on his face. He locked eyes with Kelly as he placed his arm on the bar, then slowly turned and faced Ashton. "So, Ashton," Tony said, "how long you been seeing Kelly?"

"Long enough," Ashton replied quickly, not bothering to turn and face Tony. "So don't get any ideas."

Kelly's mouth dropped to the counter of the bar in unmasked horror. Did Ashton say what she thought he just said? That she was his *girlfriend*?

"Lucky guy," Tony said. But his eyes were on Kelly's.

"I am *not* his girlfriend," Kelly stated emphatically. "As a matter of fact, I've only known him a few days."

"That's not true." Ashton squeezed Kelly's hand gently. "We go way back. High school."

"True, but we're hardly seeing each other."

Tony raised his eyebrows, clearly considering the possibilities. "In that case—"

"Not this case," Ashton responded, cutting Tony off. Then he exited the bar and marched toward Kelly. When he reached her, he scooped her off the barstool.

"Ashton!"

He ignored her protest as he took her hand and whisked her out of the restaurant. "Thanks for coming by," he said when they were on the sidewalk. "I'll see you later."

Kelly ran her fingers through her hair and flashed Ashton a dumbfounded look. His jaw had hardened, his eyes darkened. He wouldn't even look at her.

What was up with him and Tony? Some kind of macho competition?

"Ashton," Kelly began calmly, "why did you rush me away from Tony?"

He inhaled deeply, seemingly trying to calm his nerves. Kelly studied him, thinking that he was being completely ridiculous. She couldn't believe her eyes. He was acting jealous!

"You've got no right to—"

Ashton cut her off sharply. "Trust me. Stay away from Tony."

"But why?" Kelly demanded. If Ashton was going to tell her to stay away from a man when he had no claims on her, he'd better have a damn good reason.

"Don't ask me any questions," Ashton snapped, shocking Kelly. He must have sensed her hurt because he softened his tone as he said, "Just stay away from him. I know what I'm talking about."

"That's not good enough." Kelly looked up at him, noting the hard edges of his face. He continued to gaze beyond her, refusing to make eye contact with her. What on earth was wrong with him?

"I've got to go back in." Finally, he met her gaze. "I'll talk to you later, okay?"

Kelly rolled her eyes to the sky. "See ya," she said abruptly, then walked off in the direction she and Ashton had come from earlier.

Ashton's command that she not talk to Tony—no questions asked—was asinine. What on earth made him think he could tell her what to do? Because they'd had one night of passion a decade ago?

No, it had to be because of their stupid kisses. Though when Kelly thought back on it, she had a hard time thinking of them as stupid. Ashton's kisses had set off sparks in her body. Hell, when his lips had claimed hers, it had seemed like the Fourth of July.

Still, she had made it clear to him that the kisses meant nothing, and she had used Glenn to hopefully drive that point home. Clearly, she had failed.

Even her body wouldn't agree. It had a different agenda from her mind. No matter how much she tried to tell herself that she was over Ashton Hunter, her body practically ignited at the mere thought of him.

Thank God Saturday was right around the corner. The sooner she made her way back to Florida the better.

Chapter 13

The next day around noon, the phone rang. Kelly ran into the kitchen to answer it. "Hello?"

"I need to see you."

"Ashton?"

"Yeah. I'll be right over."

"Ashton, wait." But he had already hung up.

Kelly replaced the receiver, scooped up the fashion magazine she'd been reading and placed it on the coffee table, then headed to the bedroom. She didn't even make it before there was a knock on the door.

She stopped and turned, then did another one-eighty turn toward the bedroom door. She was still lounging in her nightgown and robe, hardly an appropriate way for her to answer the door.

Ashton knocked again.

Whimpering, Kelly realized she couldn't very well keep Ashton waiting. She rushed to the door and opened it.

Ashton immediately walked inside, but when he saw her, he stopped. His eyes roamed her body with interest, taking in her short silk nightie and robe immediately, before venturing down to her bare legs and bare feet.

Kelly recognized the raw sexual heat in Ashton's hazel eyes. His gaze seemed to burn right through her clothes, and as Kelly looked down at the flimsy robe covering her body, she suddenly felt very naked.

She folded her arms across her chest to distract Ashton's stare. "I've just been . . . well, you know. Lounging. Give me a minute to put some clothes on."

Ashton reached for her and softly ran his fingers down her arm, then encircled her wrist with his fingers. "Don't go."

His voice was deep and smooth and utterly sexy, causing Kelly's heart to flutter. She drew in a much needed breath and tried to remain focused. "I—I'm not decent."

"Oh, you are. You definitely are."

Kelly became all too aware of the nearness of his body, of the way his hand on her arm was igniting a burning passion deep within her.

Heat surged to her face. Silently, she cursed. Why was she blushing? Why was she so nervous? Why had her body temperature skyrocketed?

"Ashton please— I need to—" Why did she need his permission? "I'm going to get dressed."

"Please don't." He wrapped a muscular arm around her waist and pulled her soft body against his hard chest.

"Excuse me?" Kelly managed.

"I didn't mean that the way it sounded." Ashton looked down at her, his eyes glazed and dark. With gentle fingers, he cupped her chin. "Hell, I'm lying. Yeah, I meant that. I can't lie anymore. Not to myself, and definitely not to you."

"A-Ashton . . ."

"I know. This is crazy, Kelly. Maybe I just want to see if

it will be as good as it was ten years ago. I don't know. I only know that I want to be with you."

Kelly was paralyzed by Ashton's touch, by his smooth and captivating voice. Her brain knew she should say something, protest. But for the life of her, she couldn't say a word.

Ashton loosened the tie on her robe and slipped it off. It fell to the floor around her feet. Then, lowering his head, he brushed his velvet lips against her right shoulder. The touch was ever so light, but it set the skin beneath his lips ablaze.

"Oh, Kelly . . ."

Oh, Ashton! her mind cried.

Slowly, agonizingly, he trailed kisses along her sensitized flesh, from her shoulder to the base of her neck, then up to her mouth. The moan she'd held inside finally escaped. "Ashton . . ."

"Every time I see you, you drive me wild," he whispered into her ear.

Kelly was drifting out to sea. And she knew she would soon be lost in something beyond her control.

"Tell me this isn't one-sided," he rasped. "You've got to feel this, too."

"Oh, I do."

Ashton planted his lips on hers, hard. He kissed her like a man in the desert who'd just found water.

An electric bolt coursed through Kelly's veins, awakening her body to feelings she had never known existed. Feelings oh so tantalizing. This was more intense than that night ten years ago. It seemed impossible, yet it was. Maybe because her body had been taut with sexual desire from the moment she'd seen him again, a thirst that needed to be quenched.

Ashton slipped his hands beneath her nightie and trailed his fingers along her hips until they reached her waist. He slipped them beneath the waistband of her panties.

"Karen's gone for the day?" he asked.

Kelly clung to him. "Yes."

He moaned his happiness. Taking slow steps, he urged her body against the wall. He softly suckled her tongue.

"This isn't enough," he said. "God, Kelly. I want you."

She arched her neck as Ashton's tongue made its way down her skin.

"What's this fragrance you're wearing?"

"Enamored," Kelly replied.

"It should be illegal. It's driving me wild."

"You don't like it?"

"I love it."

He kissed her again, kissed her like he wanted to suck the very essence from her body. Then he said, "I know you have a boyfriend—"

"Not really," Kelly admitted on a sigh. "Glenn and I . . . we're close friends, but he wants more."

"So we can do this?" His voice shimmered with sultry promise.

Kelly looked up at Ashton, at the desire flickering in his eyes. She knew what he meant, but still she asked, "Do what?"

"Make love."

The scorching look in Ashton's eyes brought a hot flush to her cheeks. He was enticing her into a dizzying world of passion, but a very dangerous world as well. She wanted to say yes, but should she?

Dipping his head to her neck, Ashton brushed the tip of his nose against her skin. Then he raised his head and planted a soft kiss on her earlobe.

Reason lost out to lust.

"Yes, I want this," Kelly blurted.

He kissed her again, like a man starved. It was more passionate this time, all-consuming. His tongue sought hers with desperation, and to Kelly's surprise, her own tongue responded eagerly, exploring every part of his warm, enticing mouth.

She moaned as Ashton ran his fingers along her skin up to her breasts. She was drowning. Drowning in a sea of desire, and there wasn't a life preserver in sight. Being with Ashton Hunter felt so good, so right.

"Where?" he asked.

Kelly tore her lips from his to lead him the few steps to her bedroom door. She opened it, then looked at him. Was she really going to do this?

But before any second thoughts could take hold of her brain, Ashton walked into the bedroom and closed the door behind them. Then he whipped his T-shirt over his head and dropped it to the floor.

He closed the distance between them, reached for the hem of Kelly's nightie, and slipped it off her body.

"Oh, man." He bit down hard on his bottom lip as his eyes roamed her body, setting her skin ablaze.

Kelly felt powerful. And beautiful.

This was unlike the first time, when she had been in love with him. She wasn't desperate for a life with him. She simply wanted . . .

Sex.

Kelly slipped her arms around his neck and lifted her face to his. Ashton lifted her and whirled her around onto the daybed.

"I swear, Kelly. You have no clue how much I want this."

What did he mean by that?

Don't go there, she quickly told herself. *This isn't about love or even feelings of affection. This is about lust.*

She stopped thinking when Ashton tweaked her nipples into hard peaks. A sigh of satisfaction fell from her lips.

"That's right," Ashton said. Then he closed his mouth over one nipple.

A searing jolt of excitement raced right through her. Lord help her, she wanted this.

While Ashton suckled her breasts, he dipped a hand into her panties. He felt her wetness. "Oh, yeah, sweetheart."

Pulling back, Ashton undid his jeans.

The reality of what they were about to do made Kelly have a moment of sanity. She and Ashton had been with other people. Unprotected sex would be foolish.

"Do you have a condom?" she asked.

Ashton's shoulders visibly drooped. "No." He paused. "Damn."

Kelly slowly sat up. She covered her naked breasts with her hands. "We can't have sex without a condom."

"I can go to the store. It won't take long."

"No." Kelly shook her head. The mood was broken. "I don't think . . . I want to, but maybe we shouldn't. I've never really been into casual sex."

Ashton simply nodded, but he didn't say a word. Kelly's stomach sank. She knew what his silence meant. He *was* into casual sex.

It shouldn't matter to her, but it did. And it made her that much happier that they hadn't ended up making love. She couldn't get involved with Ashton. She couldn't let herself be seduced into a casual, meaningless fling. Because that's what it would be, meaningless.

Casual was one thing. Meaningless was another thing entirely.

"You should go," she said softly.

"Kelly—"

"No, Ashton. Just go."

Ashton raised his hands in submission. "All right." He retrieved his shirt and put it back on. Then he slowly walked out of the bedroom.

Kelly felt the cold draft hit her as he closed the door behind him.

Chapter 14

Ashton stood motionless under a spray of ice cold water, in a state of total shock and disbelief. What the hell had just happened?

One minute, he had been holding Kelly in his arms, inhaling her delicate floral scent, tasting the sweetness of her soft, luscious lips. The next minute, he'd been forced out of her apartment and into a very cold shower.

Was he really that way off base? It had been longer than he cared to admit since he had made love to a woman, but not that long that he couldn't tell when a woman wanted him.

And Kelly *had* wanted him. He'd felt her body's surrender in his arms, as well as the sweet heat that emanated from her skin. She had been as hot with desire as he had been.

And then she had turned stone cold.

It wouldn't have taken him long to pick up a package of condoms, so he knew that wasn't the issue.

Had he rushed things? It was seeing her in that white, silk nightgown that had made him lose all control. White—his favorite color on a woman. Though he had no doubt that she would look hot in any color.

She had looked so damned beautiful in that short nightgown, showing off her sexy curves and long legs, and those incredible naked feet.

There was a definite chemistry between them—he hadn't imagined it. Hell, he'd felt her wetness. He knew she wanted him. But for some reason, she had done a complete one-eighty.

Bozo the Boyfriend. That had to be the reason.

Yet in the heat of passion, she had admitted that her relationship with Glenn wasn't serious. And he'd been relieved about that, because everything he'd sensed about her said she was attracted to him.

So what had made her go cold? Had she had second thoughts because of Glenn?

Ashton glanced down at his erection and sighed wearily.

The shower wasn't doing him much good to forget about Kelly.

Six hours later, Kelly was still tense. Phoning every party supply place in town and jogging for an hour had not done a thing to help alleviate her stress.

She needed a drink. Something stiff.

She changed into a form-fitting white summer dress with spaghetti straps, and white sandals with a low heel. She needed to get out of the apartment before the walls closed in on her.

As Kelly walked along the Harbourfront, she hardly noticed the sounds of jazz music nor the hundreds of happy people on the street enjoying the Harbourfront's Jazz Festival. Her mind was in a state of turmoil.

She walked to Yonge Street, then headed north. Before she knew it, she was at *Delectables,* the restaurant where Ashton worked. One part of her brain asked her why she had come here—of all places—to have a drink. The other part told her that she knew why.

She felt bad about what had happened between them earlier.

While she made no apologies for not being into casual sex, she wanted him to know that she wasn't upset with him. She hoped they could put the incident behind them and move on. They still had to work together this week. There was no reason for added tension.

Tony was the first person Kelly saw when she sat at the bar. His brown eyes lit up when he glanced her way. Smiling, he strolled over to her immediately. "Hey. How you doing, gorgeous?"

"I need a drink. Something strong."

"One of those days?"

Kelly nodded. "One of those weeks. I think it will be until I get out of here."

Tony eyed her quizzically. "You just got here."

"Oh, you probably don't know, but I'm not from Toronto. I live in Fort Lauderdale, and I'm just here for my friend's going away party."

"The one Saturday night?"

"Yeah."

"That can't be what's stressing you out."

"No . . ." Her voice trailed off. "It's a private matter."

Tony nodded. "What can I get you to drink?"

"What do you suggest?"

Tony pursed his lips while he thought, then replied, "How about a Black Russian? It's got vodka and kahlua. It's strong."

"I'll have one." Turning, Kelly surveyed the crowded bar area, noticing a female bartender, but not Ashton. Maybe he wasn't working. Had she wasted a trip?

Tony mixed Kelly's drink, then passed it to her on a white cocktail napkin. She brought the glass to her lips immediately and took a swig, then winced when the liquid burned her throat. It was definitely strong.

Just what she needed.

A movement in Kelly's peripheral vision got her attention, and she turned in time to see Ashton enter the bar with a plate of chicken fingers and fries. Just one look at him, and her heartbeat accelerated.

But then her stomach dropped when she saw the expression on the female customer's face as she regarded Ashton. The look she was giving him could melt ice, that's how hot it was.

And Ashton was grinning at her like a lovesick fool!

Sure, the dark skinned woman was beautiful—stunningly so, as a matter of fact. But still. Just earlier today, Ashton had been ready to sleep with her. Yet here he was, flirting like there was no tomorrow.

Kelly took another sip of her drink. She watched as the woman leaned forward, her ample bosom practically popping out of her dress and onto the counter. A naughty smile playing on her lips, she covered Ashton's hand with hers.

Kelly's eyes nearly jumped out of her head when she saw the woman slip Ashton a piece of paper. Her phone number? Ashton put it into his pocket.

Throwing her head backward, Kelly swallowed a huge amount of the acrid alcohol. When she straightened her head, she felt a little woozy.

It was about time. The sooner she got drunk, the sooner she would be able to wash away the disturbing scene playing out before her.

Suddenly, Ashton looked her way. Kelly didn't have time to tell if he was surprised to see her, because she quickly averted her eyes and took another sip of her drink, pretending not to notice him.

Coming here to chat with him had seemed a good idea at the time. Now she realized it was foolish.

"What are you doing?" Ashton asked a moment later.

Kelly looked up in alarm. How had he gotten to her so fast? Glancing in the other woman's direction, she saw that she was happily eating her food. Did she have any idea how much of a player Ashton was, or did she even care?

Who was she kidding? This woman didn't seem to have a care in the world. Except, perhaps, how to keep her breasts inside her skimpy outfit.

"Obviously, I'm having a drink," Kelly said in reply to Ashton's question.

Her tone was sarcastic. And her words were a far cry from what she had planned to say when she saw him. She had been ready to tell him that he hadn't been the problem earlier, and why? Because she didn't want him to be hurt by what had happened. But it was clear she didn't need to be concerned about Ashton's feelings. He had long gotten over her rejection and had moved on to the next willing woman.

"A drink?" Ashton glanced at Tony, then back at her. "Here?"

Oooh. Kelly perked up. *He thinks I came here to see Tony.*

"She's hardly a minor," Tony chimed from over Ashton's shoulder. "What's your problem?"

Kelly didn't give Ashton a chance to answer Tony's question. "I'll have another one," she announced boldly, then downed the remainder of her drink in one large gulp. Ashton's curt tone with her hurt—more than it should. She wanted to burn that man from her memory and her life.

With a few more of these Black Russians, she was sure she could do it. Even if she had a killer headache in the morning.

"No problem," Tony agreed. He gave Ashton a wry smile as he added, "It's on me."

When Tony turned his back to prepare the drink for

Kelly, Ashton leaned across the bar to get closer to her. "Why are you doing this?"

Kelly looked him squarely in the eyes. "My God, Ashton. You're not trying to imply that you have the right to tell me what to do, are you? Because no one has told me what to do in aeons." Her parents had died tragically in a fire years ago, and since then, she had learned to fend for herself. With occasional help from her brother, of course.

Turning back to Kelly, Tony handed her another Black Russian. An impatient customer at the other end of the bar got Ashton's attention, and with obvious reluctance, he walked over to him. Taking an unnecessarily large sip of the new drink, Kelly watched Ashton march away.

"I've got a great idea," Tony said, drawing Kelly's attention. "Why don't we go for a drink tomorrow night? And please don't say no. You said yourself, you won't be in town much longer."

Kelly giggled loudly, attracting Ashton's attention from the other end of the bar. He needed to see this, to see her enjoying the company of another man. He wasn't the only one who could have members of the opposite sex worshiping at his feet. "Are you asking me out?"

"Just a friendly drink," Tony said. He leaned closer to her and smiled. "I won't take no for an answer."

"Is that so?"

Tony nodded. "That's so."

Continuing to smile fondly at Tony, Kelly considered his offer. What harm was there in going for a friendly drink with him? It was a much better option than sitting around Karen's apartment reading a book, or worse, thinking about Ashton. And given that she'd blurted out to Ashton that she and Glenn weren't really an item, going out with Tony would get the point across to

Ashton that she wasn't interested in him—once and for all. "Okay," she agreed. "I'd like that."

"Wonderful." Tony was all smiles. "There's a great piano bar across the street. I'm sure you'll love it."

Ashton couldn't make out what they were saying, but he could tell that although there was a black marble counter separating them, Kelly and Tony were getting pretty cozy. He watched as Kelly threw her head back and laughed, then Tony laughed. Then they both laughed together.

He didn't like it one bit.

Ashton continued to watch them, tapping his fingers impatiently on the sparkling marble. Why was she doing this? If Kelly wanted a drink, there were numerous places she could have gone much closer to the condo. Why did she come all the way here—dressed in a stunning *white* dress, no less—to have a drink and act as though he didn't even exist?

Ashton gritted his teeth. That louse Tony was enjoying every moment of this. No doubt, he was working up to asking her out, if he hadn't already. But would Kelly say yes? Or would she tell him about her *involvement* with Glenn?

Ashton would much rather she head back to Fort Lauderdale and into the arms of Bozo than get involved with Tony.

Kelly's loud laughter pierced the air. As Ashton's gaze swept over her, he suddenly got a wary feeling in his gut. She was fire and passion, friendly and beautiful, but he suspected she was also a little naive. He doubted she had much experience with men like Tony—men with loose tongues and loose morals.

Furtively, Ashton watched as Tony mixed another

drink and placed it before Kelly. He had tried to stay uninvolved, but Tony was going too far. In three quick strides, Ashton was over there, taking the drink from Kelly before she could put it to her mouth.

"Hey! That's my drink." She swayed ever so slightly as she reached forward to try and snatch the drink from Ashton's hands.

Damn. She was tipsy already, which confirmed what Ashton had suspected. Kelly wasn't a big drinker. Sure, she might be the type to have a glass of wine with dinner, but hard liquor? Considering it was barely five o'clock, she probably hadn't even eaten dinner. He could have pounded Tony for trying to take advantage of her like this.

"You've had enough," Ashton told her.

"Says who? Simon?" She giggled.

She was past tipsy. "Says me."

Tony reached for the drink in Ashton's hand, but Ashton pulled it away forcefully, spilling some of the contents of the glass onto the floor. "Get back to the other side of the bar," Tony ordered. "She's my customer."

Ashton glared down at Tony, who was a few inches shorter than he. "She's here on her own. Have some consideration for how she's going to get back home. She'll be a walking target after you finish with her."

"Ashton—" Kelly began, but didn't finish what she was going to say. Instead, she closed her eyes and moaned softly, then rested her head against the palm of her hand.

Yeah, she'd have a killer headache later, thanks to Tony. "You're going home." He dumped the contents of the glass into the sink, then exited the bar and walked swiftly over to her. "Let's go."

"No. I was talking to Tony."

"Not anymore."

Tony sneered at Ashton, but he didn't protest. To Kelly he said, "Meet me here tomorrow. Nine thirty."

Kelly nodded. Ashton wondered if she knew what was going on. Working at the bar, he had seen so many women like Kelly—inexperienced drinkers—have a couple drinks mixed with hard liquor, and before they knew it, it was game over. Some ended up over a toilet in the washroom, puking. Some passed out.

Kelly had been drinking straight alcohol. Ashton could only hope that she would be okay.

Placing his arm around Kelly's waist, Ashton helped her down from the stool. She instantly leaned against his chest. Warmth spread through him, surprising him. Surprising him because this was different than what he'd felt earlier. This warmth wasn't lust. It was something else.

It's a completely natural reaction, he told himself. *A purely male reaction to being able to provide a woman with comfort.*

His arm securely around her waist, Ashton walked Kelly to the door.

"Ooh. Not so fast. The world's spinning."

"I've got you," Ashton told her.

Outside he hailed a cab and helped Kelly into the backseat. He gave the driver her address, then passed him a twenty. "That should cover it. Don't worry about any change."

"Tank you," the driver said in an East Indian accent.

"Drink lots of water, and eat some crackers," Ashton advised Kelly. After a moment, he added, "We'll talk tomorrow."

He closed the cab's door. As it drove off, he curled his fist into a ball.

* * *

Lord have mercy, Kelly thought her head was going to explode.

Sliding across the backseat, she edged closer to the open window. A blast of cool breeze hit her in the face. The intensity was shocking, but it was also sobering.

She kept her head at the window for a good minute. Wow, she couldn't believe how dizzy she was. She'd only had three drinks.

Or was it four? She wasn't sure anymore.

But man had they had ever been strong. The kind of drink you were enjoying one minute, then wham! Before you knew what hit you, you were drunk.

And it didn't help that she hadn't even had anything to eat since this morning. She should have known better than to drink on an empty stomach.

She'd just been so tense, so frustrated, so unbelievably thrilled after nearly bedding Ashton. Kelly laid her head back in the cab, continuing to enjoy the feel of the wind whipping against her face. By the time she reached the condo, the effects of the alcohol were starting to wear off. Thank goodness.

"Thank you, sir," she said as she opened the door. "You did a great job getting me here in one piece. Thank you muchly. I mean, kindly." She giggled like an idiot. "You know what I mean."

"Yes." He chuckled. "Bye bye."

Kelly eyed him through the rearview mirror. Was he laughing with her or at her? She almost asked him, but realized it was the alcohol inspiring her to do so. "Bye bye," she mimicked instead, then got out of the cab.

Upstairs, she fell onto her bed and closed her eyes. Oh, yes. This was what she needed. This felt glorious.

But then she heard Ashton's voice. *"Drink lots of water, and eat some crackers."*

He was right, of course. She would feel so much worse if she didn't get anything into her stomach.

Grumbling, Kelly got up and made her way to the kitchen. There she made some dry toast to fill her stomach and drank two glasses of water. It hit the spot, but would it be enough?

Maybe a bath would help sober her up once and for all.

Ten minutes later, Kelly slipped into a bath filled with bubbles. The hot water felt glorious, and she leaned back in the tub, letting the steamy water work out all her tight muscles. There was nothing like a hot bath to make her feel like she had no problems in the world.

No problems except Ashton.

Why oh why couldn't she get him out of her mind?

And then there was Glenn. The longer she stayed here, the more she dreaded going back and facing him. When he had dropped her off at the airport, Kelly had told him that she would think about his proposal while she was away. Glenn had grinned from ear-to-ear.

"I'm not promising anything," she had pointed out. "I'm just saying . . . I'll think about it."

"That's all I can ask," he had replied. He'd sounded so reasonable, yet so hopeful. Then he had given her an awkward hug and kissed her on the cheek.

Kelly had the horrible feeling that Glenn expected her to return home and say yes to his proposal. Something she hadn't considered such a bad idea before. But now . . .

Now, she wished she felt even half the animal passion for Glenn that she felt for Ashton. If she felt that, she could marry Glenn and be assured that they would have a reasonably exciting life together.

Because Karen had been so right. Kelly couldn't settle for dull. No matter how safe it was.

Kelly dipped her sponge in the water, then held it above her body and squeezed, releasing a waterfall of bubbles and steam. Her mind drifted back to Ashton and the ferocity with which she had wanted him earlier. A quivering sensation ran throughout her body as she remembered the feel of Ashton's silken lips on hers, his fingers touching the most intimate part of her. She closed her eyes and let herself imagine. . . .

Ashton was resting against the doorjamb of the bathroom, his lips curved in the slightest of grins. His eyes were dark with desire as they probed every inch of Kelly's wet body. Slowly, he entered the bathroom, pulled his T-shirt over his head, and slipped out of his perfectly snug jeans. His body was magnificent, corded with muscles. Kelly gasped as Ashton pulled off his underwear, revealing his beautiful manhood and his obvious hunger for her.

How she wanted him! She needed him next to her, his warm skin pressing against her wet body. She looked up at him and softly called his name. Ashton came to her, and her lips parted in soft invitation. Stepping into the steaming bathtub, Ashton gradually lowered himself on top of Kelly's moistened body. She closed her eyes and unleashed a soft, passionate moan.

With exquisite tenderness, Ashton explored every part of her body with his hands. Caressing. Tweaking. Fondling. Teasing. Mercilessly, he ran his tongue along her wet, hot skin, tormenting her with passion as he glided his tongue in circles around one of her taut, throbbing nipples. And just when Kelly thought she was going to go crazy with desire, Ashton took her nipple in his mouth and sucked, sending ripples of pleasure coursing through her.

"Oh, Ashton."

Her own voice startled her, and the cold realization hit her.

Ashton was nowhere near the bathroom. She had been fantasizing.

Lord help her.

It was the alcohol.

How else could she explain fantasizing about him in such a vivid way?

Kelly got out of the tub and dried off, feeling more carnally frustrated than she had ever felt. Her body was thrumming with sexual longing, for which there was no cure.

Except Ashton.

"No, not Ashton," she told herself angrily.

Yes, Ashton, a voice countered.

She had the dreadful feeling that the voice was right.

Chapter 15

Kelly awoke to the mouthwatering smell of bacon, and despite her fatigue and slight headache, she could no longer stay in bed. Throwing off the covers, she glanced at the clock radio. It was 9:29 A.M.

After climbing out of bed and giving her body a good stretch, Kelly slipped into a gray robe that matched her nightgown, then made her way into the solarium where Karen was seated, eating. Sunlight spilled into the small room, filling it with warmth.

"I made scrambled eggs and bacon," Karen announced proudly. "I was getting tired of doughnuts."

Looking down at Karen, Kelly smiled fondly. "It smells delicious. It sure lured me out of bed."

"That's what I was hoping. There's enough for you in the kitchen. Help yourself."

Kelly didn't need to be told twice. She was starving. Pivoting on her heel, she scooted toward the kitchen, hoping that the bacon was crispy. As she neared the kitchen, she heard Karen say, "There's a fresh pot of coffee. I hear you might need it."

Kelly stopped dead in her tracks, her nape prickling. Ashton had spoken to Karen.

Anger washing over her like a bitter cold breeze, Kelly moved to the stove and helped herself to the remaining strips of bacon, as well as the scrambled eggs. She then filled a mug with coffee and rejoined Karen at the table.

"Thanks for breakfast," Kelly murmured. She picked up a crispy strip of bacon and brought it to her mouth, hoping that at least while her mouth was full Karen wouldn't ask her any questions.

Not a chance.

Curiosity danced in Karen's bright, brown eyes. "How're you feeling this morning?"

Damn Ashton, Kelly thought, rolling her eyes to the ceiling. "I'm fine." When Karen gave her a doubtful look, Kelly admitted, "I've just got a bit of a headache."

Karen's laughter permeated the air. "I should be glad you're not sitting around here twiddling your thumbs."

Kelly cast Karen a wry grin, then washed down some bacon with a swig of black coffee. "What did Ashton tell you?"

"Only that you were at *Delectables* last night and had a few drinks."

"A couple." Kelly took another sip of her coffee. Had Ashton also told Karen about what had almost happened between them? "Ashton totally overreacted. He sent me home in a cab."

"I think he was a bit worried about Tony."

That much was obvious. Kelly asked, "Why?"

"He doesn't want to see you taken advantage of." Karen threw Kelly a suspicious look. "So, were you . . . are you . . ."

"Attracted to Tony?" Kelly finished for her. "Tony is . . . charming."

"Oh, Kelly. Be careful."

"I just met him," Kelly responded. "And he's only a friend. Trust me."

"I wasn't trying to imply—"

"Good."

"It's just that Tony is a player. At least according to Ashton."

"I guess Ashton ought to know a thing or two about being a player," Kelly mumbled.

"Pardon me?"

"Nothing." Kelly blew out a frazzled breath. "Look, I've got enough stress thinking about Glenn. And Ashton—"

"Hold up," Karen quickly said. "What are you saying . . . you're thinking about Ashton?"

Oh, God. How had she let that slip?

Karen's eyes lit up. "Kelly!"

"I didn't mean that the way you think."

"Look, Kelly. I haven't spent much time with you this week, but I can certainly tell that something's bothering you. Is it Ashton?"

There was no point denying the truth. Karen knew her too well. Besides, she wanted to get this off her chest.

"Oh, Karen. I don't know what's happening to me. Before I came up here, I was considering marriage to a good friend I know will be decent to me. Sure, I don't love him, and I know love's important, but he's nice. He's safe. But I think what you said to me before is true. I don't want safe. I want excitement and drama. I want . . ."

"Ashton?"

"Yes," Kelly replied before she had a chance to think.

"Oh my."

"Oh, God. I just said that, didn't I?"

"Uh huh. And you can't take it back now."

"But I *need* to take it back. Ashton is all wrong for me."

"Why?"

"Why? You know why. Look what he did to me in high school."

"That was a long time ago. You need to let it go."

"What?"

"Ashton hurt you then, but he's a different person now."

"I don't think so. I saw him at the bar yesterday when he didn't know I was there. He was flirting with this woman, and then he took her number!"

"He's a bartender."

"So that means—"

"Hear me out. Ashton has told me that a lot of women hit on him. You can't blame them. He *is* hot. A lot give him their number. Sure, he'll take it—to be polite. That's all. He's got to appear friendly."

Karen's explanation made sense, but still, Kelly wasn't sure.

"He's wrong for me. My blood boils practically every time we're together."

"It's called passion."

Kelly gaped at her friend. "It's called insanity."

Karen shrugged. "I know you're confused. You hadn't seen Ashton in ten years, yet you still have feelings for him. For what it's worth, I think he still has feelings for you, too. You should have seen how concerned he was about you and Tony."

"Really?"

"Really."

Karen's warm smile faded when she looked beyond Kelly to the hall clock. "Goodness, I can't believe the time. As much as I'd love to stay and chat, stardom calls."

"Oh."

"We'll hang out tomorrow," Karen told her, clearing her plate and mug from the table. Then, with one last grin, Karen exited the room, leaving Kelly feeling a weird sense of joy and sadness.

Karen was such a dear friend, even after all this time. She wasn't judging her. Instead, she was simply there for her to support her.

When Kelly heard the door close, she got up from the table and strolled to the large solarium window. She closed her eyes and basked in the warm morning sunlight. The heat felt splendid on her skin.

Karen's condo was a corner unit, so one side of the condo overlooked the lake, while the other side overlooked part of the street. Opening her eyes, Kelly surveyed the street below. Already there was a lot of action. Businessmen with cell phones and briefcases were walking hastily along the sidewalk. Vendors were at the street corners selling hot dogs, peanuts, cotton candy, and other merchandise. Children and parents pranced along the paved path, enjoying another beautiful day. A gathering of people was heading west, no doubt to some cultural attraction. It was a wonder to see.

Across the street from her building, amid the strolling pedestrians, a male jogger caught Kelly's eye. Tall and well built, he reminded her of Ashton. As he darted out into the street, a fancy red sports car nearly hit him. Kelly winced. It still amazed her, the fearless mentality she'd noticed people possessed in this bustling city.

As the jogger got closer to her building, Kelly found he looked more and more like Ashton. He looked up, and Kelly did a double take.

It *was* Ashton!

He waved. Kelly abruptly stepped away from the window. She silently prayed that Ashton hadn't seen *her,* that he was waving to someone else. But knowing her luck, Ashton had probably spotted her just as quickly as a bull sees red.

When the sound of knuckles on wood penetrated the silence ten minutes later, Kelly knew it was Ashton. Walking briskly to the door, she knotted the tie around her gray cotton robe. At least today she was more decently dressed.

She was about to turn the door's handle when she paused. She didn't want a repeat of yesterday.

The knocking persisted. "Come on, Kelly," Ashton said playfully. "I know you're in there. I saw you spying on me through the window."

With that, Kelly swung the door open, and a gush of wind flew in from the hallway. Even with sweat glistening on his lovely brown brow, Ashton looked gorgeous. And in spite of the fact that he had been jogging, his scent was a combination of musk and spice—entirely masculine, and quite definitely captivating.

Boldly stepping inside the apartment, Ashton grinned and said, "I'm glad you're not in bed nursing a hangover." He held her gaze for only a moment, then let his eyes fall from Kelly's head to her bare toes.

Kelly pulled her soft cotton robe a little tighter around her body.

"What are you up to right now?" Ashton asked.

"I—uh—why?"

"Because I want your opinion of something. Will you come to my apartment with me?"

Was this a trick? Was he planning to seduce her? And why did that thought thrill her?

Not waiting for an answer, Ashton took her hand in his and pulled her into the hallway. He closed the apartment door, then led her down the beautifully decorated corridor.

"Ashton . . ." Kelly protested, well aware of how embarrassed she would be if someone appeared from a door. "Let me at least put some clothes on."

"No need. We're almost there."

A few seconds later, he was opening the door to unit 318. He stepped inside, leading Kelly in with him.

Kelly's heart instantly went berserk. The potential danger of this situation overwhelmed her. She was in Ashton's condo. He was holding her hand, causing her skin to prickle with anticipation. And she had a clear view of his bed through his open bedroom door.

She wrenched her hand from Ashton's grip, ready to turn on her heel and flee. "Ashton, this isn't a good idea."

"Relax." Gesturing to the open living room, Ashton added, "Have a seat."

Nervous, Kelly's eyes darted from Ashton to his living room. Warily, she took a few steps into the room. Sunlight came through the large living room window, spilling onto a variety of vibrant green plants.

"Sit," Ashton repeated.

Swallowing a spate of nervousness, Kelly moved to the love seat and did just that. Ashton disappeared into his solarium.

Kelly folded her arms, then unfolded them. Leaned forward, then backward. Sucked in a sharp breath, then blew it out in an irritated rush. Finally she announced, "I don't know why you dragged me over here, but I was in the middle of—"

Ashton appeared from the solarium. "I want you to listen to something." He disappeared again.

"Oh?" Curious, Kelly stood. She sauntered to the solarium.

Ashton's sexy back was to her. Kelly let her gaze travel over his wide shoulders, broad back, slim waist, cute butt, and muscular legs. She swallowed the surge of anticipation that crawled up her throat. The man certainly had a body to die for.

He was huddled over a rather sophisticated synthesizer, which was hooked up to two speakers. A guitar lay on the floor, a computer stood in the corner, and other gadgets Kelly couldn't identify filled the room. This was clearly Ashton's home studio.

Kelly took a step inside. "Wow."

"This is where I create," Ashton told her.

"You said you were a musician, but it didn't really seem real until right now."

Turning to face her, Ashton smiled. "It's real all right. And I want your opinion of something I've written."

"*My* opinion?"

"Sure." Ashton fiddled with something on the synthesizer. "Why not?"

Kelly shrugged. She didn't know if she should feel flattered. "What do you want me to do?"

Ashton slipped onto the stool before his keyboard, adjusted something, then said, "I want you to listen."

His fingers hit the keys, creating a wonderful, romantic melody. Pleasantly surprised, Kelly found herself warming to the rhythm, and she swayed her body. Then Ashton's voice filled the small room.

Despite having seen Ashton's elaborate home studio, she still wasn't prepared for the reality that he was a genuine musician. She wasn't prepared for the soft, silky-smooth voice that warmed the air and warmed her heart. The man could sing. His voice was as well honed as any professional vocalist.

A few minutes later, Ashton ended the delightful melody and slowly turned to Kelly. He had a sparkle in his eyes that sent a searing jolt of sensation right through her body. Lord, he was sexy. *And* he could sing.

He was dangerous, indeed.

"Well," Ashton drawled slowly, "what do you think?"

"I . . . it's wonderful Ashton. Absolutely wonderful."

Ashton's eyes crinkled as his sexy mouth lifted in a wide grin. "You really think so?"

Kelly nodded. "Most definitely. I'm still in shock. I didn't think you would be this good. I don't mean any offense by that. I'm just . . . surprised. Did you write the lyrics?"

"Everything. The words, the music. Sometimes it's a struggle to make it work. Other times, it flows."

"That surely flows." The words were beautiful. He sang of a woman he loved and longed to be with, yet she didn't return his feelings. Kelly wondered if the song had been inspired by something he had experienced. "Is it . . . based on a true experience?"

"Everybody asks me that about what I write," Ashton replied. "Sometimes, I write from experience. Other times I write what I'd like to experience. It just depends."

Kelly felt a weird tingling sensation in her stomach. Crooning a love song the way he just did had Kelly seeing a whole new side to Ashton Hunter. While he sang, he seemed like a warm, sensitive man looking for the right woman to love him. He seemed like a man who was vulnerable and not immune to pain. And despite all her resolutions, she found herself more attracted to him than ever.

Rising from the stool, Ashton approached her slowly, deliberately. "What are you thinking?"

Kelly swallowed. "I'm wondering if you'll tell me about your mother."

Ashton took a step backward. Pain flashed in his eyes. "I told you."

"No, not really."

"She walked out on my father and me. It devastated my father."

"And what about you?"

"We've all been hurt at some point, haven't we? You get over it."

"But you didn't, did you?"

"Kelly."

Surprising both of them, she reached for his face. "Tell me."

"How does one get over something like that?" Ashton asked, his voice intense with emotion. "She left and you know how often I heard from her? Once in a blue moon. People get separated and divorced all the time. They don't leave their kids."

"I'm sorry, Ashton."

"It's not your fault."

Kelly eyed him cautiously. "She wasn't the only one," she ventured slowly. "You mentioned that a couple days ago. Who else hurt you, Ashton?"

"Let's just say, the women I've known have said one thing and meant another. Like that they care about you, but they really care about what you can give them."

"And you think all women are like that?"

Ashton didn't answer.

Kelly didn't know why, but she desperately wanted Ashton to know that all women were not callous gold diggers. Maybe because she knew how much pain he was in.

And because she couldn't help feeling that this was what had kept him from her all those years ago.

She put her arms around his neck and tipped up on her toes.

Ashton's eyes widened in surprise. "Kelly?"

She held her mouth seductively close to Ashton's.

"What are you doing?" His voice held a hopeful note.

Kelly parted her lips in soft invitation. "This," she replied, then planted her mouth on Ashton's.

Chapter 16

Their mouths came together in a soft, yet dazzling kiss. Ashton didn't resist. Instead, his lips courted hers in a sensual dance, nipping gently, sucking softly. Framing her face with his hands, Ashton slipped his wet, hot tongue into her mouth, sending a jolt of white-hot desire straight to the center of her womanhood.

Kelly groaned against Ashton's lips, surrendering completely to him. Her fingers played with his dreadlocks the way she had wanted to do from the moment she'd seen him again. Lord, she was crazy, but she wanted him.

Delicious sensations swirled through her as Ashton nibbled on her bottom lip, then nibbled on her chin, and then her neck. Kelly dipped her head backward, giving Ashton access to more of her. His tongue ignited a trail of fire along every inch of skin it touched.

Urgency building, Ashton opened Kelly's robe and nudged it off her shoulders. Kelly shivered when he brought his velvet-soft mouth to her shoulder, teasing the sensitive flesh with soft flicks of his tongue.

Kelly drew in a sharp breath when Ashton's hands

found her breasts. He stroked their fullness through the fabric of her nightgown with aching tenderness before ever so lightly grazing his thumbs along the tips. Her nipples responded instantly, hardening beneath his touch.

Ashton groaned. "Yeah, sweetheart. That's what I like to feel."

Kelly mewled.

Lowering his head, Ashton brought his lips to one of her breasts, brushing his lips across the pebbled nipple through her nightgown. He groaned again, a deep rumbling sound from his chest, then slipped her nightgown off her shoulders and down her arms, exposing her full, round breasts and dark, taut peaks. His tongue was moist as it flicked out to taste a dark tip, his lips cool on her heated skin. Kelly clamped her teeth together to strangle the moan that was welling up in her throat.

But the moan wouldn't be suppressed. Nothing had ever felt as glorious as Ashton's tongue on her body. Kelly bit her bottom lip as Ashton suckled, as hot moisture pooled between her legs. She was getting swept away in a sea of desire. "Ashton . . ."

"Yesterday you didn't want to do this," he whispered against her ear. "Are you sure?"

"You have a condom?"

"A whole pack," he replied, a smile in his voice.

"Oh. Pretty ambitious, aren't you?"

"I've got to make up for lost time."

"Mmm."

Ashton dipped his hand beneath Kelly's nightgown and trickled his fingers up her inner thigh. A shudder rocked her body as he pulled her lacy panties down, then found and delicately stroked the sensitive flesh between her legs. Kelly leaned into Ashton's touch.

Grasping his back with both hands, Kelly moaned passionately as Ashton plunged a finger deep within her. It felt so, so good. He withdrew and plunged again, and Kelly bit her bottom lip so hard she thought she would draw blood.

Ashton spun her around and led her to the stool, leaning her against it for support. As he continued to fondle her, he found a burning nipple and drew it into his mouth, suckling firmly. The combination of both actions set her body ablaze.

And then she was digging her nails into Ashton's shoulders and moaning loudly, shamelessly, as wave after wave of contractions rocked her body. She clung to Ashton's brawny shoulders, clung to him as if her life depended on it, until the wonderful spasms subsided.

Ashton kissed her fiercely, then scooped her into his arms. He carried her to the bedroom.

In a frenzy of activity, they stripped out of their clothes. They touched, they kissed. There was no going back now.

And Kelly didn't want to turn back.

Ashton broke the kiss and asked, "You're sure?"

Kelly stroked his erection. "Where are the condoms?"

Kelly's gaze fell to Ashton's firm butt as he walked to his dresser. She heard him open a package and as the moments passed, she knew he was putting the condom on.

The fact that he'd gone out to buy them made her feel happy. It was good to know that Ashton didn't keep a supply of condoms in his apartment.

He turned and faced her. Kelly bit down on her bottom lip and stepped backward to the bed. It was hard to believe she was about to make love to Ashton—again. But she was helpless to stop it.

She didn't want to stop it. No matter what came tomorrow, she wanted right now.

Ashton's gentle kiss melted her fears. Cradling her

in his arms, he gently lay her on the bed. He ran his hands down her body until his fingers found her center.

"Please, Ashton." Kelly's breathing was ragged. "Don't tease me. I need to feel you inside me."

Ashton didn't need any further invitation. Spreading her legs, he settled himself between her legs and guided his erection inside her.

Kelly instantly cried out as Ashton filled her. Oh, how she'd needed this. Needed him.

She stroked his face. He opened his eyes and met her gaze. His eyes didn't waver as he thrust deep inside her. Kelly felt the connection between them, real and intense. She could see into his soul, and what she saw said he cared.

That this wasn't casual.

Kelly closed her eyes and clung to him, refusing to believe anything else.

Later, Ashton and Kelly lay in bed together, Kelly's back against the front of Ashton's body. He brushed her braids aside and planted a wet kiss on the back of her neck.

They'd made love twice already, yet desire gripped Kelly once again.

"Ashton," she said in mocking disapproval.

"I know. It's just that I can't get enough of you."

Kelly giggled. No other man had ever made her feel so sexually powerful. "Is that right?"

"Yeah, that's right."

Kelly rolled over and faced him. As she looked at him, her expression grew serious. "Ashton?"

"Hmm?"

"What's next for us?" Maybe she was rushing the issue, but she wanted to know where Ashton's head was at. She had a life in Fort Lauderdale, and if they wanted to be together, they were going to have to make some kind of plans toward that.

He didn't answer right away. "I don't know," he finally said.

Kelly didn't like that answer. Didn't like it one bit. "Well, what do you want? In an ideal world, that is."

"Kelly, what are you getting at?"

"I just . . . just want to figure out what you're thinking."

"Like what? Am I ready to propose marriage?"

Kelly stiffened at Ashton's words. Was it a mocking statement of what he actually felt for her? "Why would you say that?"

Groaning, Ashton sat up. "Why is it that women always expect a proclamation of undying commitment after sex?"

"Excuse me?"

"Can't two people go to bed together and that just be it?"

Kelly certainly hadn't expected a proclamation of love, but she had expected more than this. At least some respect.

"No one was talking about love or commitment here, Ashton." He wasn't even looking at her. "But damn it, I at least expect some respect."

He blew out an agitated breath. "Sorry. That . . . that came out wrong."

Kelly rose, taking the blanket with her to cover her nakedness. "No, I don't think it did."

"It's just that . . ."

"One minute, you say that no woman has really cared about you for you. And you know what—I believed you. But now I realize that the problem isn't the other women. It's you. You don't know how to accept love. You never did."

Kelly snatched up her nightgown, then fled from the bedroom and into the bathroom.

"Kelly."

"Do me a favor, Ashton," Kelly said from behind the bathroom door. "Shut up."

When she stepped out of the bathroom, Ashton was standing there. His eyes held contrition when he looked at her, but he didn't say a word.

Kelly all but ran to the living room and retrieved her robe. But as she reached for the apartment door, Ashton called out to her.

"Kelly, I just want to say—"

"I understand, Ashton. This was your way of telling me that what happened between us wasn't only sex, it was meaningless." God, why did her voice have to tremble.

"No, that's not what I said."

Kelly summoned all her courage. "Don't say anything else. Please."

Then she ran out of the apartment. She didn't stop until she'd reached Karen's. In her bedroom, she finally allowed herself to cry.

Well, he'd messed up but good!

Ashton's stomach was a ball of mangled nerves as he got ready for work. Things between him and Kelly hadn't ended nearly the way he'd wanted them to.

He'd enjoyed their time together. Enjoyed it immensely. That's what he had wanted to convey to her. Until she'd asked him what was on his mind.

It was the same question he'd heard from other women—women he hadn't cared about. And it was the question he dreaded, so whenever he heard it, it instantly set him on guard. His response to Kelly had been the result of frustrated feelings he'd felt over other women. Women who had initially told him they wanted a no-strings-attached relationship, only to change their minds. It wasn't that they weren't necessarily decent women. It's just that he didn't see them as long-term partners.

The problem isn't the other women. It's you. You don't know how to accept love.

Ashton heard Kelly's words. And he had to wonder . . . were they true?

For the longest time, he had been wary of relationships. No doubt because of his mother. Somehow, he had ended up with women who were either emotionally void or too needy. Women who weren't relationship material. Was that an accident, or was it his way of making sure he didn't have to commit?

The only time he had truly connected with a woman, he had pushed her away.

That woman was Kelly, and what he had felt for her had scared him to death.

Because he didn't want to be hurt the way his father had been hurt, and he knew in his gut that Kelly had the power to hurt him.

It didn't matter that she hadn't given him a reason to think that she would.

Groaning, Ashton placed his hands on the edges of the bathroom sink and leaned forward. He stared at his reflection and had a stunning revelation.

He didn't know who he was anymore.

Chapter 17

Kelly took a cab to the east side of the city where she planned to get all the supplies she needed for the party. Having called every store in the yellow pages, she found one in particular that she wanted to check out. The woman on the phone had seemed genuinely interested in her story about the surprise party, and the prices she quoted had been reasonable.

It was the least she could do to get her mind off Ashton. Today's situation had been nothing short of disastrous. She had fallen into his bed and had her heart broken all over again.

No, not her heart. He didn't have it anymore. But still, he had hurt her.

How could she have been so stupid? How could she have let Ashton lure her to his apartment, a place she knew would be dangerous? How could she have melted in his arms like warm butter? Between wanting him and being angry with him over the past, her emotions were measuring pretty high on the Richter scale.

She couldn't take the roller coaster ride any more. She wanted off. One minute they were arguing, the next they were . . . Kelly closed her eyes at the mental image of Ashton fondling her body. She had totally lost perspective by letting him get past the barrier she had erected specifically for him. Yet she hadn't been able to stop what had been set in motion from the moment she had seen him again.

Today, her ego had paid the price, but at least she knew better. It wouldn't happen again.

"That's eighteen twenty-five," the cab driver said, alerting Kelly to the fact that she had arrived at her destination. She sighed wearily as she reached into her purse. She certainly hadn't expected the cab ride to cost her this much. But then, the driver could have driven around the city ten times for all she knew. She hadn't seen a single sight since she'd stepped into the cab. Her thoughts had been completely focused on Ashton.

Kelly handed the driver a twenty dollar bill, then waved her hand at him to indicate that he could keep the change. She slipped out of the cab and planted her feet firmly on the sidewalk. She stood, quietly observing the party supply store for several moments before she went inside.

If there was one store in the world that had every conceivable notion, decoration, and gadget for any occasion, this was it. The entire length of the walls and shelves in this large, rectangular shaped store were covered with colorful streamers, banners, ribbons, and numerous other ornaments. Gold and silver glittered under the fluorescent lights, and for a moment, Kelly was awe stricken.

"Let me guess—wedding invitations?" asked a short, cute, petite blonde. Her eyes sparkled as she stared at Kelly expectantly.

"Actually"—Kelly began slowly, lowering her gaze to the woman—"a party. For a friend of mine, who's landed a part in a musical."

"Oh yes," the woman chimed, then flashed her best customer service smile. "You called earlier."

Kelly's lips curled into a genuine grin, pleased that in a city of this size, this young woman actually remembered a specific phone call. "Yes, I did."

"Follow me. I've got just what you're looking for."

Kelly followed the woman to a section at the back of the store where an array of party banners and balloons was displayed brilliantly. Everything from "Congratulations" to "It's a Boy" to "Happy Silver Anniversary" was displayed in vivid colors, even with matching stationery on tables below.

"There's a book of banners to choose from, in case you don't see something that you like. And if you need something specially made, we can do that too."

Kelly found it extremely hard to believe that this store didn't stock every conceivable banner available. She wouldn't be surprised if she found one that read, "Congratulations on Landing a Part in a Musical!" Kelly chuckled softly. To be honest, she would be *very* surprised if this store had a banner that said that.

"I'm sure I'll find something," she said cheerfully.

Soft chimes suddenly played in the background, and the sales clerk immediately looked to her right. An attractive couple had just entered the store, arms linked. "My name is Misty. Give a holler if you need any help," she told Kelly, then scurried off to greet her new customers, her short blond bob bouncing with each giddy step.

Kelly took a deep breath and looked around at the available selection of party decorations. There were so many to choose from. All the more reason to pick something reasonable and then leave. If she started looking through the catalog, she might just be here all day.

Ten minutes later, Kelly decided that twenty balloons in varying colors with the word "Congratulations" written on them would be fine, as well as some streamers and a banner. After closely scrutinizing the banners on display, she decided to get a broad white one with the words "Way to Go!" printed on it in glittering gold. That would stand out well in the dim lights of the restaurant.

Kelly turned around to get Misty's attention, but Misty was right there, her white teeth glistening as she smiled. "Did you find anything that you like?"

Kelly nodded, then pointed out her selections to Misty.

"Great," Misty said. "It'll take only a few minutes to retrieve the items from the back of the store."

While Misty headed to the back, Kelly strolled leisurely through the store. Furtively, she eyed the young man and woman who were happily looking through a large book. Curious, Kelly edged closer to them but a large, shimmering white book caught her eye. Wedding invitations. She paused to flip through it.

A nasty lump formed in her throat as she viewed the variety of invitations a would-be bride had to choose from. Some were simple and to the point, while some were much more exquisite, with imprints of champagne flutes, pearls, and flowers. She glanced at the happy couple, their eyes wide with excitement as they viewed the various invitations.

And she thought of Glenn. She suddenly wondered if she was giving him enough credit. Didn't every woman want a man who would be true to her? A man like Glenn?

She had promised Glenn that she would think about his proposal, but that shouldn't have included bedding Ashton to get a better perspective on things.

"Thinking he might pop the question soon?"

Kelly whirled around on her heel, closing the wedding book in one quick motion. Misty stared at her curiously.

"Uh—well—no," Kelly stammered. Misty didn't need to know about her mixed-up love life. That someone had proposed marriage, but she wasn't truly in love with him. And the guy she felt passionately about saw her only as a bed partner.

"A beautiful woman like you—he's bound to ask soon. Probably your high school sweetheart, right?"

Kelly's eyebrows shot up at Misty's remark. Was this woman psychic? While Kelly wasn't engaged to Ashton, he certainly had been occupying her thoughts all day. And he certainly had been the light of her life back in high school, although that didn't really qualify him as her high school sweetheart. "Well, kinda sorta. It's a long story."

"I knew it. I get a sixth sense around certain people sometimes. And when I look at you, I hear wedding bells. Trust me, he's going to ask you to marry him— soon. And when he does, come on back here. We've got everything you need."

Kelly shifted uncomfortably. "I'll keep that in mind. Do you have my decorations?" She'd had enough of Fortunes By Misty.

"In a bag at the front counter. We can take care of the bill if you're ready."

"I'm ready."

As Kelly followed her through the store, Misty's words played in her mind. It was a nice fantasy to believe that the man of her dreams would ask her to marry him, but Kelly knew it would never come true. How could it, when Ashton didn't care about her?

The moment Kelly walked into *Delectables,* she was overcome by the sounds of clanking cutlery, loud laughter, a buzz of chatter, and funky music. Waiters scurried along the tiled floor, some carrying trays of drinks and food, others rushing toward the kitchen as if their lives depended on it. Every table in the restaurant was occupied, and a crowd of people waited in the restaurant's foyer.

"It's going to be a half hour wait," a male host informed Kelly, his tone weary. He ran a hand through his sandy brown hair as his eyes darted from Kelly to the occupied tables. The poor guy couldn't have been older than nineteen, yet he seemed stressed beyond his years. Keeping a crowd of impatient people happy was no doubt a demanding job.

Kelly smiled warmly at him. "Actually, I'm meeting somebody. The bartender, Tony."

"Oh," the host said, clearly relieved. "Well, you can wait at the bar . . . Oh, here he is."

Whirling around, Kelly saw Tony, his hands on his hips and a wide grin on his face. She smiled back.

"That smile," Tony said, throwing a hand to his eyes and squinting. "You're killing me."

Kelly playfully punched Tony's arm. "Stop it."

"I can't," Tony said. "That smile is the most beautiful smile I've ever seen."

"I don't have a beautiful smile," Kelly protested.

"Then what do you call that?" Tony asked, softly touching her cheek.

"Okay," Kelly conceded, beaming. "People always tell me that I have a beautiful smile, but I don't seem to accept compliments very well."

"In that case, I will make it my personal duty to see to it that you realize just how beautiful you are."

"And just how do you propose to do that?"

"While we're at the piano bar across the street, I'll conduct a survey. I'll ask all the waiters, managers, and even the customers whether or not they think you have the most beautiful smile they've ever seen. I'm sure they'll all agree with me."

Kelly chuckled softly. "Gimme a break, Tony."

Tony shook his head. "Nope. I'm serious. After my survey, you'll have no justifiable reason to refuse any compliments whatsoever."

Kelly threw her hands into the air, acknowledging defeat. "Okay, Tony. You win."

"I win?" He raised an eyebrow suggestively. "Tell me, my fair lady, what do I win?"

"I will accept any compliment that you might give me."

Tony pursed his lips, silently contemplating Kelly's offer. "Fair enough," he finally said. "I'm not quite finished my shift yet. Why don't you go to the bar and wait for me? I've got to go to the kitchen to pick up some food."

Kelly nodded, then watched as Tony sauntered off in the direction of the kitchen. The moment she turned to her left in an effort to go to the bar, she felt an overpowering presence and realized that someone was blocking her path. She recognized the spicy scent of his cologne without even having to look up. But as soon as she lifted her head and saw Ashton, excitement and anger fought for control of her emotions.

"Kelly. What are you doing here?"

"Ashton." Kelly inhaled a deep breath before continuing. "I'm . . . I'm here to see Tony."

"Tony?" Ashton's hazel eyes darkened. "Why on earth would you be here to see Tony?"

Kelly narrowed her eyes and glared at him. "Please, do not even *attempt* to tell me what to do. And I don't want to hear a word about how Tony might take advantage of me, because, quite frankly, you're the one who's guilty of that, not Tony."

"Is that why you're here to see him? Because of what happened between us earlier?"

"I'm not going to dignify that with an answer."

Kelly started off, and Ashton followed her. "You have every right to be angry with me—"

"Really?" Kelly said sarcastically, not breaking stride.

Ashton placed his hands on her shoulders and stopped her dead in her tracks. "Why don't we talk? I'll see if I can take a break."

Kelly looked squarely into his eyes. What on earth had she ever found attractive about him? Ashton was the lowest of the low, a man who could sleep with you, then throw you aside. "I'm here to see Tony. Not you."

Ashton met her fury with soft eyes. "I didn't mean what I said earlier."

"Oh, for God's sake. Stop pitying me. I'm a big girl, Ashton. I know the deal. So save your smooth talking for someone you haven't fooled before. 'Cause I've been there, done that."

She turned quickly, determined to get away from Ashton, to forget that she had ever wasted any precious time hoping that he might care for her.

Ashton grabbed Kelly's arm. "So you're just gonna run to Tony?"

Kelly looked down at her arm where Ashton held her, then up at him with the iciest of stares. "Let go of my arm."

"I'm trying to tell you that I'm ready to talk—"

"You heard the lady."

Ashton and Kelly both turned to see Tony standing behind them with his hands planted firmly on his hips. Ashton immediately released Kelly's arm and turned to fully face Tony. "Why don't you get lost?"

Tony looked at Kelly. "Do you want me to get lost? It looked to me as though you needed some help, so I came over."

Kelly ran her hand through her hair. "No, I don't want you to leave. Thank you, Tony."

Ashton's hard stare turned to one of complete confusion. "Don't pretend that you're actually afraid of me, Kelly. You and I both know that's not true."

"Things have changed," Kelly said.

"What's that supposed to mean?"

Kelly ignored him and turned to Tony. The last thing she needed was for Ashton to let slip what had happened between them today. "Tony, I am *so* ready to leave. Are you?"

"Almost. I've just got to finish up at the bar."

"Okay. I'll go to the washroom and freshen up, then I'll meet you at the bar."

"Perfect." Tony's eyes were on Ashton as he spoke.

Kelly flashed Ashton a devilish grin as she brushed passed him and walked toward the ladies' room. That would show him. Normally, Kelly wasn't the type of person to rub something in another person's face, but Ashton had been asking for it. After all, didn't he deserve to be hurt, the way he had hurt her?

Hopefully he had gotten the picture. Hopefully, he would leave her alone.

Chapter 18

Ashton saw Kelly the moment she exited the washroom, her floral sundress bouncing against her curves with every move. She was fire. She was ice.

He couldn't get his mind off her.

Ashton watched her take a seat on a vacant bar stool. Her braids gently caressed her shoulders. He swallowed, trying to ignore the sudden desire he had to run his fingers along her smooth skin, to sweep her hair aside and kiss her sweet neck, to take her in his arms and make wild, passionate love to her.

Again.

But after today, he doubted he'd have the chance.

Granted, he'd messed up, but was that enough reason for her to get all dolled up and come here to meet Tony?

And why did he care so much, anyway?

"Hello . . .?"

The female voice got Ashton's attention, and he turned. Two young women smiled at him.

"Hey, ladies."

"We thought you were ignoring us," the blonde said.

"Naw," Ashton replied. He resisted the urge to glance Kelly's way. These women were easy on the eyes. It shouldn't be hard to give them his undivided attention. And unlike Kelly, they looked like the type who would appreciate it. "So, did you leave the men at home for a ladies' night out?"

The other woman giggled, shaking her long red mane in the process. "No, we didn't leave the men at home," she replied. "I'm single and so is Amber."

"Ah," Ashton said. "So you're here on the prowl. I guess all the single men should be on the lookout, hmm?"

The two women smiled coyly at Ashton, almost as if they had rehearsed their seduction act. "Not exactly," replied Amber, taking a strand of curly blonde hair between her fingers. "Unless of course, *you're* single."

Ashton couldn't help it. He glanced to his right. Kelly was watching his interaction with these two women.

If this were another time, when Kelly hadn't been in his life, Ashton would have been tempted to pursue one of these ladies. Ever since his bitter experience with Camilla, when he had been prepared to put his heart on the line, he had vowed never to get involved in a serious relationship with a woman ever again.

But he remembered Kelly's words earlier, and a lump formed in his throat. He had run from relationships in an effort to make sure he'd never get hurt, but had that brought him happiness?

"Sorry, ladies. You're gonna have to keep looking. I'm engaged."

The blonde shook her head and clucked her tongue, dismayed. "Too bad."

"Hey, it happens to the best of us."

Ashton looked Kelly's way. Again, he caught her watching.

She quickly turned her head.

* * *

Kelly couldn't help glancing in Ashton's direction once again, and when she did, she didn't like what she saw. Ashton was still talking with the two bimbos at his end of the bar. He leaned against the marble counter and said something to them. Then they all burst into laughter.

Kelly squeezed her hands into tight balls. Well, there went the last nail in the coffin enclosing her infatuation for Ashton. Sleeping with her one minute, flirting like he'd invented the word the next.

At least this proved that Ashton had never really been interested in her. He was a playboy, a womanizer, a man who didn't give a damn about a real relationship.

Unable to stomach another moment of his flirtation, Kelly looked away. She was determined to forget Ashton once and for all. At least she had regained her sound mind before she'd made the mistake of giving him her heart again.

"Don't let that guy eat away at your sanity," Tony advised Kelly, drawing her gaze to him.

Giving Tony a puzzled look, Kelly asked, "What guy?" As if it wasn't obvious to probably everyone at the bar. Hell, probably everyone in the restaurant.

"Ashton," Tony replied. "He probably let you think he liked you, right? Yet he's hitting on those two women over there."

Kelly shrugged, trying to appear as nonchalant as possible. "Ashton can do what he wants. It doesn't matter to me."

Tony smiled. "I'm glad to hear that. Because Ashton's not the type of guy who takes women seriously. He goes through so many women a year, I've lost count."

Kelly swallowed hard to get rid of the lump that was now forming in her throat. She already knew that Ashton was a womanizer. But hearing the truth from somebody else really made her realize how much of an idiot she had been. One of the world's biggest fools, was a more accurate description. She couldn't even head back to Fort Lauderdale with her dignity.

"I'm just gonna change, then we can leave," Tony told her. "I won't be too long."

Kelly nodded, then took a sip of her water as Tony disappeared. She couldn't wait to get out of the restaurant and away from Ashton.

Thank God, she only had one more day to put up with him.

But right now, the sooner she got away from him, the better.

Kelly was glad that she had agreed to go on this friendly date with Tony. The piano bar was very quaint, classy, and the moment she had entered the place, she'd felt her tattered nerves start to relax. A man dressed in a black tuxedo was playing a jazzy tune at the piano. This was exactly the kind of atmosphere she needed right now.

Tony smiled fondly at her from across the table where they were seated, then took her hands in his. "You've got beautiful hands. Has anyone ever told you that?"

"As a matter of fact, I think *you* told me that a couple of times already, Tony."

"Those hands should be in a commercial. You know, advertising dish soap or something." Tony raised Kelly's left hand to his lips, then kissed it very softly.

A shiver of apprehension slid down Kelly's spine. She smiled politely, then pulled her hand away.

"I know what you need," Tony announced. "Another drink."

Before Kelly could protest, he slid out of the booth

and disappeared in the direction of the bar. She'd already finished one glass of wine, and wasn't planning on having another drink.

Glancing around the bar, she surveyed the people—singles and couples—who were laughing, drinking, smoking, and having a good time. Tony was being friendly, and most importantly, his company was helping to keep her mind off of Ashton.

What would another drink hurt?

Tony appeared carrying a bottle of beer and a large, creamy, chocolate-looking drink. He placed the creamy drink in front of her, then took his seat across from her.

"What is this?" Kelly asked, looking down at the drink garnished with a banana slice and a mini umbrella.

"That, my dear, is a chocolate monkey. Try it. I guarantee it's delicious. If you don't like it, I'll get you something else."

This was stronger than a glass of wine . . . but it was only her second drink. And she'd eaten dinner.

"Don't be silly," Kelly said, her tone light. "I'm sure I'll like it." She leaned forward and took a sip of the drink through the straw. A burst of chocolate and banana flooded her mouth, and she savored the flavors on her tongue before swallowing. "Mmm. This *is* delicious."

"Nothing but the best for a very beautiful lady," Tony said. Then suddenly he stood up and took Kelly's hand. "Let's dance."

Kelly didn't protest, but that feeling of apprehension swept over her again. Tony was being so nice to her. *A little too nice*, a voice in her mind said. But she pushed that thought aside, certain that Tony didn't have any ill intentions. After all, he knew she was only in town for another couple days. What could he possibly want from her other than friendly companionship?

The pianist was playing a modern love ballad, and Tony pulled Kelly's body close to his as he led them in a dance. He smelled as though he had bathed in a bottle of cologne. Not like Ashton, whose cologne was always subtle, unobtrusive. Kelly stiffened, uncomfortable with how close Tony was holding her.

"You can relax," Tony whispered into her ear. "I'm not gonna bite."

Heat immediately warmed Kelly's face. She hadn't wanted to portray her unease to Tony. Clearly, she was still tense. About Ashton, about everything. "I'm sorry. I'm just not very comfortable on a dance floor."

"That's okay. I'll lead." Tony held Kelly close, moving their bodies to the soulful rhythm. Unexpectedly, he slid his hands to the small of her back. Kelly drew in a startled breath. "Tony . . ."

"Shh," he whispered. "I love this song."

Kelly's mouth was open, ready to protest again, when she noticed a familiar face out of the corner of her eye. *Ashton!* He was standing at the bar, casually leaning one elbow against it, staring at her. "Oh my goodness," she muttered.

Easing his head back, Tony looked at Kelly. "What's the matter?"

"I don't believe it," she added, now a little more annoyed.

"Hon, what's wrong? Is it me?"

Kelly shook her head, her eyes still on Ashton. "No. It's . . . Ashton." He must have followed them. Why wouldn't he leave her alone? She wanted to walk right over to him and give him a piece of her mind. "I can't believe he followed me here!"

Tony pulled Kelly close once again. "Ignore him. You're here with me."

But Kelly couldn't ignore him. The gold in his eyes glittered beneath the dim lights as he stared at her, but his eyes held no warmth. Was it pain she saw? Yes, she was certain of it. Pain and perhaps anger. *Why?* Kelly wondered. He'd made it clear earlier that he didn't care about her.

Tony swiftly swung Kelly around, forcing Ashton out of her view. "I want your undivided attention." He smiled, but it didn't reach his eyes.

"You have it," Kelly said.

Tony pulled his head back and looked into her eyes. "Since Ashton followed us here, why don't we give him a little show?"

"A show?"

"Yeah," Tony said. "Kiss me."

Chapter 19

Kelly blinked at least five times as she looked up at Tony, certain she had not heard him correctly. *"What?"*

"You want Ashton to get the picture that you're not interested, right?"

"Well, yes, but—"

"Then kiss me. That'll get your point across."

Kelly glanced over at Ashton as she contemplated Tony's offer. He was still staring at her, his striking hazel eyes boring into her like daggers. Why he was doing this to her, standing there trying to make her feel uncomfortable, she didn't know.

Maybe Tony was right when he said that the only way to get Ashton to leave her alone was to give him proof that she wasn't interested. As long as Tony knew what the real deal was, what harm could come of a simple kiss?

No, Kelly quickly decided. Kissing Tony was not an option. She had already made it clear to Ashton that there wouldn't be a repeat incident of what had happened today.

"Actually Tony, I just want to go."

"You want to go somewhere else?"

Shaking her head, Kelly pulled away from Tony. "No. I'm tired. I'd like to get some fresh air."

"Let's go then." Tony wrapped his arm around Kelly's shoulders and led her toward the exit. They walked across the dance floor, through couples who were moving their bodies to the soft melody, then past the bar—and Ashton—on their way to the exit. Kelly glanced at Ashton surreptitiously, then quickly averted her gaze. She didn't owe him any explanations.

Then why did she feel so uncomfortable with Ashton watching them? Why did she feel a pang of guilt? Why did she have a nagging feeling that Ashton's kisses and touches had meant something, despite what he'd said to her?

Wishful thinking.

Kelly was glad when she stepped outside and onto the sidewalk. The air outside was cool and gentle, and much more refreshing than the stale, smoke-filled air in the bar. She sighed, her mind a mix of so many conflicting emotions, then cradled her body with her arms.

"You cold?" Tony asked.

"No, I'm okay."

"I can rub your arms for you," he offered.

"Really, I'm fine."

They strolled leisurely along the street, which at this hour, was still fairly populated. Kelly was awkwardly silent, and so was Tony. They walked together for a few more minutes before Kelly said, "Thanks for the evening."

"No problem."

"You don't have to walk me all the way home. I'd, um, actually like to be alone for a while."

Tony chuckled lightly. "I don't know what it's like where you live, but here, it's not safe for a woman to walk home alone at night. Especially a beautiful one like you."

"Okay. If you insist."

"Are you in a rush to get home?" Tony asked.

Kelly shook her head. "Not really."

"Then why don't you let me show you a great park? It's just around the corner."

"Oh, I don't know. I think I'd prefer to walk."

Tony stopped walking and faced Kelly. He tilted her chin up so that he could look into her eyes. "You aren't staying here much longer. Other than the main attractions, have you seen much else of the city?"

Kelly shook her head slowly. "No."

"Then why don't you take the time to go to this park with me. It's especially beautiful at night. It will give us a chance to talk."

Talk. So her sudden apprehension regarding Tony had been justified.

After fearing that he might be interested in her, she had been dreading this moment, secretly hoping that Tony would go his way and she would go hers, and then they would never have to see each other again. But since he seemed persistent on sticking around, they may as well talk. Kelly sensed that despite the fact Tony knew she wasn't going to be in town much longer, he was infatuated with her. She may as well take this opportunity to tell him that although she really liked him as a person, there was no chance for a relationship with them. "Okay," Kelly agreed. "We do need to talk."

Taking Kelly's hand, Tony led her to the park. She felt a bit uneasy, but told herself that Tony was only holding her hand to make it easier for her to follow him.

The park was like an oasis in a desert. Hyacinths, petunias, impatiens, and lilacs were in full bloom everywhere, their delicate sweet scent hanging in the air. Stylish streetlights were scattered around the beautiful landscape, and coupled with the moonlight, they gave this park a very romantic aura. Kelly looked all around, surveying the grass, the flowers, the cobblestone path. In various areas of the park, there were several young couples. Some were locked in an embrace. Some were sitting quietly talking. Some were kissing.

A warning bell went off in Kelly's head, telling her that this was not the place that she and Tony should be talking. This seemed more like a lovers' lane. . . . What was Tony expecting?

"Let's sit," Tony instructed Kelly, interrupting her thoughts. He lowered himself onto a park bench and pulled her down beside him. "Isn't this place beautiful?"

Kelly nodded stiffly. "Yes, Tony. It is. But this looks like some type of lovers' hangout," she said, speaking her mind. "Why would you bring me here?"

"A lot of lovers come to this park, but it's open to everyone," Tony responded. He was still holding Kelly's hand. "And like I said, I wanted to show you some parts of the city that you've never seen—before you go back home."

Kelly inhaled a deep breath of the cool summer air, trying to relax. At least Tony didn't have romance on the brain.

"Thank you. This is . . . nice. And private, so it's a great place to talk."

Tony brought Kelly's hand to his mouth and kissed it. "I can think of much better things to do than talking."

Kelly cleared her throat, hoping to make Tony realize how uncomfortable she was with what he seemed to be suggesting. It was obvious to her now that he wanted some kind of an intimate relationship with her. But what? A one night stand? All the more reason to come right out and tell him that she was not interested in him.

"Tony, I want to talk about us. To clear the air."

"I hope I'm not gonna hear Ashton's name."

Kelly shook her head vehemently. "Absolutely not. I already told you that I have no feelings for Ashton. In fact, he repulses me."

Tony edged a little bit closer to her, putting his arm around her shoulders. "That's exactly what I wanted to hear."

"But that's not all," Kelly protested.

"I know, baby. You don't have to say it. I can feel the vibes you're sending me. You're as attracted to me as I am to you. So let's stop talking and start doing what we both want."

What we both want? Kelly thought, horrified. What did he mean by *that?*

Before Kelly could set Tony straight, his mouth was on hers fiercely. His tongue invaded her mouth harshly and probed it in the most disgusting way. He tasted of beer and smoke, and Kelly instantly felt sick. Tony's rough hands held her firmly in place, preventing her from moving even an inch. And then slowly, with the weight of his body, Tony forced her down onto the hard park bench.

"Tony . . ." Kelly managed to say, but her voice was lost under Tony's own moaning when his hand touched her inner thigh.

"You feel so good, so soft."

Squirming with all her strength, Kelly managed to squeeze her legs tightly together so that Tony's hand couldn't venture any farther upward. "Please," Kelly managed to say.

"Don't worry, baby." Tony's eyes glossed over with lust as he looked down at her. "I'll take care of you." Like a savage beast, he flicked his tongue out and ran it along her neck.

Kelly tried her best to inhale and exhale slowly, but

she felt as though she were suffocating. She could hardly breathe with Tony's large body pinning her to the bench. Panic swept over her as she wondered exactly what Tony was planning to do, how far he was planning to go.

"Tony, stop. I don't want to do this."

Tony's laugh was almost maniacal. He looked at Kelly with hard, dark eyes. "What the hell are you saying?"

A cold tremor of fear rocked Kelly's body. She didn't like the look in Tony's eyes, nor his irrational behavior. Would he try to hurt her if she voiced her opposition? "I only wanted to talk."

"You've been leading me on. Teasing me all night."

"No, Tony."

Tony ignored her and pulled the fabric of her dress off her shoulder, then kissed the skin beneath it. "You can't turn me on like this and expect to walk away."

Kelly's worst fears were confirmed. He was going to violate her.

Horror shot through her body. With all her strength, she tried to push Tony off her, but he was just too strong. The more she squirmed, the more he seemed to enjoy his power over her.

"Tony, stop," she begged, as her eyes filled with tears. "Please don't do this."

"Get off of her."

That wasn't Tony's voice. A sob, part startled, part relieved, escaped Kelly's lips, and she tilted her head backward to see who was there. In a blur of tears, she saw a face that looked like Ashton's.

"Get out of here, Ashton," Tony said angrily, still pinning Kelly's body possessively. "She doesn't want you. Get over it."

"You slimy S.O.B.!" Ashton grabbed Tony by the shirt and dragged him off Kelly, freeing her from his violating grip. He hauled him across the pebbled walkway and slammed him against a lamppost. As Ashton held him by the collar of his shirt, his eyes filled with rage. "Can't you get it through your head when a woman isn't interested in you? Or doesn't it matter what they want?"

Kelly's tears fell freely now, realizing how close she had come to being violated. She looked down at her once cute summer dress. It was torn at the shoulder, and it was all wrinkled and disheveled. God, she had been so stupid. She should have never gone out with Tony. She should have listened to Ashton.

"She was enjoying it!" Tony barked. "Until you came along."

Ashton pulled Tony's collar fiercely, dragging him away from the lamppost. "You're a pathetic moron," he said, then gave Tony a powerful right hook that knocked him flat on his back.

A startled gasp fell from Kelly's lips, and she placed a hand over her mouth. Tony wiped his hand across his lips and looked at the blood on his fingers. "I swear to God, Ashton . . ."

"You want a piece of me?" Ashton roared. He marched toward Tony, his hands balled into fists.

"No!" Kelly cried. She darted over to Ashton and grabbed his arm. "Please, Ashton, let's just go."

Still nursing his mouth, Tony got to his feet. "Come on. Let's do it."

"No, Ashton," Kelly protested. She didn't want them to get into an all-out brawl. "Take me home."

Ashton eyed Tony, anger distorting his attractive features.

"Come on," Tony egged him on.

"Ashton . . ."

"If you ever so much as look at Kelly again, I'll rip your head off."

"Whatever, buddy."

"Get out of here, Tony. Before I make sure Kelly calls the cops."

Tony took a few tentative steps backward, his bravado fading. Then he turned and started to run.

Only when he was out of view did Kelly allow herself to breathe a sigh of relief.

Ashton turned to her. "Are you okay?" he asked. His voice was laced with concern.

Too upset to say anything, Kelly nodded.

"Let's go." Ashton wrapped a protective arm around her and pulled her close. "I'll take you home."

Kelly wiped her tears. "Ashton, if you hadn't shown up . . ."

"Shh. Don't talk. We'll be home soon enough, and we can talk then."

The night air no longer seemed warm and inviting to Kelly; it was cold and harsh. She slipped her arm around Ashton's waist, needing to feel his warmth.

Her head was spinning. So much had happened in such a short time. One minute she had been at the bar with Tony, enjoying the music and the atmosphere. The next . . .

A tremor shook Kelly's body. She didn't want to think about tonight. She wanted to forget all about Tony, about the restaurant, about this city. Now more than ever she wanted to be back at home in Fort Lauderdale, in the comfort of her own bed.

Yes, she wanted to go home. Because as good as she felt in Ashton's arms right now, it was only a temporary anchor. And worse, it was a tease. A taste of what she wanted but could never have.

Oh, she could lie to herself all she wanted, but it was obvious every time she was near Ashton that something between them hadn't died. The spark that had made her come alive years ago was still there. Even if it was one-sided.

And with each passing day, it was getting harder and harder to be near him and not be with him.

Ashton released Kelly, and she looked up, surprised that they were at the condo already. Deep in thought, she'd been like a zombie while walking with him. Ashton opened the glass lobby door with his key, then held it open for her. Hugging her body, she walked past him, still feeling a chill.

Minutes later, they were at Karen's door. Ashton said, "I want to talk to you, Kelly. Are you up to it?"

She nodded. "Okay."

"You'd better change first. Wash up if you want, even. When you're ready, come over to my apartment."

There was an urgency to Ashton's words, even though he had spoken calmly.

"Maybe an hour?" Kelly said tentatively.

"Whenever. I'll be there."

Chapter 20

Kelly bit down on her bottom lip to suppress a sob as she entered Karen's apartment. Emotion threatened to overwhelm her as the reality of the day's events came crashing down on her full force. Her emotions had run the gamut from desire to despair to devastation.

She immediately went to the bathroom and turned on the shower. She stripped out of her dress and threw it into the garbage. It would forever be a reminder of what had happened with Tony, and she never wanted to see it again.

Pulling back the shower curtain, Kelly stepped into the tub. Moving forward, she let the spray of hot water beat against her face until she stood back and gasped for air.

She scrubbed the makeup off her face, perhaps harsher than was necessary. She lathered herself up several times, washing away the memory of Tony's hands and mouth on her body. But it wasn't enough. The pungent smell of smoke was still in her hair. She carefully washed her braids, hoping once would be enough to do the trick.

The shower left her feeling refreshed. She wrapped a towel around her hair, but knew it wouldn't dry fully until the morning.

In her bedroom, she changed into loose-fitting jeans and a white T-shirt. She didn't bother to put on any more makeup. Tonight had been a disaster, and she wanted to change her look completely from what it had been earlier. Besides, she wasn't out to impress Ashton. Only talk to him.

As Kelly headed to Ashton's condo unit, her stomach clenched. She knew what he wanted to talk to her about. He was going to tell her how foolish she had been. He was going to tell her that he had warned her about Tony, but that she had been too stubborn to listen.

Which was true. He *had* warned her, but she had assumed that Ashton had only wanted to control her; that in some way she had hurt his ego by going out with Tony.

Which, truthfully, was exactly what she had wanted to do. She'd wanted Ashton to feel what it was like to be rejected and pushed away, the way he had rejected and pushed her away both times they had made love. But all she had succeeded in doing was hurting herself.

As Kelly stood outside Ashton's door, she braced herself for the "I told you so" lecture, then slowly raised her hand to the door and knocked.

Ashton opened the door almost immediately. His jaw was set in a firm line.

"Come in," was all he said.

Kelly swallowed hard as she followed Ashton into his living room. He was mad at her, she knew. For her stubbornness, for her stupidity.

When he turned to face her, his eyes were expressionless. Kelly hugged her torso, bracing for the words he was going to say.

"I'm not going to waste your time or mine," Ashton announced matter-of-factly. "I think we need to talk about what happened tonight. What it means . . . for us."

Kelly nodded, unable to find a voice to express any words.

"I'd have to be a fool not to know why you went out with Tony."

"I know, I was—"

"It's my fault. And I'm really sorry about that."

His fault? Kelly thought.

"Believe me, if I needed further reason to realize how much I hurt you, I don't anymore. When I saw you with Tony . . . If he had raped you, I don't know what I would have done."

Despite the circumstances, Kelly felt a smidgen of hope. It sounded to her that Ashton was telling her he cared about her.

"I'm going to give you what you want, Kelly. I'm going to leave you alone. And in a couple of days, I'll be out of your life forever."

His words stunned her. Yes, she had been telling herself that she and Ashton had to put an end to what they'd started, but hearing him say the words made her heart sink.

"We've been playing some weird game since you came to Toronto. I don't know. Maybe we needed to go where we went today to put some closure on the past. But you kept telling me we shouldn't, and I pursued you anyway. Sure, there was an attraction between us, but we're both adults. I should have been able to keep my hands off you. And now . . . You put yourself in danger to prove a point to me." Ashton let out a ragged breath, and Kelly sensed this was difficult for him. "I'll never forgive myself for that. Look, I'm going to leave you alone. That's what you want, isn't it?"

Now that Ashton was truly offering Kelly what she had begged him for, she couldn't help but wonder why she wasn't happy. She couldn't understand why she was feeling a deep sense of loss—for the second time. She swallowed, reminding herself that it was for the best.

"Yes," Kelly said softly.

Ashton gritted his teeth. "I'm such a hypocrite. There I was, telling Tony that 'no means no,' when you'd been telling me no all along."

Kelly's heart ached. Ashton was nothing like Tony. She closed her eyes briefly, then reopened them. "Don't compare yourself to Tony. You . . . were right. Things escalated between us because I do feel something for you. It's just that it wouldn't work between us. Maybe if things were different . . ."

Ashton's jaw flinched. Why did he seem to be in pain? "I know. I've got more problems than you can shake a stick at, right?"

Whoa. Where had *that* come from? "It's not—"

"It's okay, Kelly. I know. I guess the one good thing that has come from today is that I realize I've got to find a way to work on my issues. I don't want to hurt anyone else." He shook his head. "And I'm just angry with myself that it took Tony nearly raping you for me to get the hint."

Kelly reached out and gently placed her hand on Ashton's arm. "Please, Ashton. Don't blame yourself for that. I'm a big girl. I made the decision to go out with him. And you . . . you saved me from that creep. Thank you for that."

"No, Kelly. Don't thank me. It was the least I could do."

Kelly's eyes filled with tears as pent-up emotions overwhelmed her. "I'm sorry, Ashton. I'm so sorry I didn't listen to you. You were right and I—"

"Shh," he whispered softly. He took Kelly in his arms

and held her close. "It's okay now. Everything is all right."

Kelly's tears fell freely. Ashton's touch provided her more comfort than she would have expected, and she was angry at herself for ever having doubted his advice about Tony. "No. It's not all right. I was stupid, and I was stubborn. All you were trying to do was look out for me. But I was too stupid to listen to you."

Ashton gently framed Kelly's face with his hands, using his thumbs to wipe away her tears. He looked down at her with concerned, sympathetic eyes. Maybe more. Was she imagining it?

"You are not stupid," Ashton told her emphatically. "You are a beautiful, caring, and trusting person . . . as sweet and delicate as a rose." He pushed a stray braid off her face, then merely gazed at her, gazed at her mouth with dark, passionate eyes. Kelly's lips parted, waiting, inviting. Despite all they'd said, she wished she and Ashton could stay this way forever.

Ashton groaned softly, then stepped away from her, breaking the intimacy of the moment. Once again, his eyes became distant. "The only stupid person in this situation is Tony. No means no. He doesn't have the brains to figure that out."

"I know," Kelly agreed, "but if I had just listened to you."

Ashton wrapped Kelly in his arms again, hugging her tightly. She felt so safe in his arms, so . . . loved. But how could that be?

He said, "I just thank God that I trusted my instincts and followed you two."

Pulling out of Ashton's embrace, Kelly looked up at him with a puzzled expression. "You followed us?"

Ashton nodded. "That's how . . . I was able to help you."

"You saw everything that was happening?"

"Yes."

"Then why didn't you come over sooner?"

Ashton shook his head. "I feel like a fool for thinking you were actually interested in Tony, but that's what I was thinking. At the bar, you two seemed so cozy. Then you went to that park."

"It was just to talk," Kelly interjected.

"I believe you. But at the time, it looked to me like you two were getting closer."

Kelly was still confused. "Then why did you follow us?"

"I always told you that Tony was bad news. A voice in my head kept telling me that something wasn't right. So I followed you."

Kelly slipped her arms around Ashton's waist, resting her head against his strong chest. "I'm so glad you did."

Ashton stiffened as she held him, and Kelly's throat constricted. He abruptly cut the hug short and moved away from her. His face was contorted with unreadable emotions, and Kelly wondered if he was fighting his attraction for her. But was that all it was—a physical attraction?

Yet if it was only physical, then why could she see agony written on his face? Guilt?

She wished he could accept the comfort she was offering him.

"Yeah. Well, it's over and you're safe," Ashton said. "I'm just sorry you had to go through that at all, especially because of me."

Kelly swallowed, but the lump in her throat didn't go away. Had someone opened a window? She really felt quite a chill now. "I guess I'd better go. It's been a long day."

"See you around."

"You mean tomorrow," Kelly corrected him. "At the party."

Ashton nodded. "Yeah. I'll try to stay out of your way."

Kelly didn't like the finality of his words, nor his tone. She stepped into the hallway, then turned to face Ashton one last time. "I don't think that's necessary. I'd really like it if we could try to be friends."

"I'm not sure that's a good idea."

"You don't?"

"I think the less we see of each other, the better. That way, we'll be sure to keep things in perspective."

The words stung Kelly like a slap in the face. The thought of cutting off all ties with Ashton saddened her deeply. But he was right. The less they saw of each other, the less temptation there would be.

"Okay," Kelly replied, her voice almost a whisper. "See you."

Ashton closed his apartment door, disappearing from Kelly's view, from her life.

And with that, Kelly felt the world around her start to crumble.

She didn't think she could feel such sadness over Ashton again, such raw pain. After all, she wasn't in high school anymore. She wasn't the love-struck teenager he'd abandoned.

She was an adult now, a confident one with a successful career as a teacher.

So why couldn't she get him out of her system—out of her heart?

Because she'd seen something in his eyes, sensed something in his touch that told her he cared? Was Ashton hurting now, just like she was?

Later, as Kelly prepared for bed, she couldn't help remembering the look she'd seen in his eyes. The look of pain when he told her that he would stay out of her life.

She had initially thought that Ashton had no feelings

for her, except perhaps lust. Their talk after they'd made love had convinced her of that.

Is it possible? she wondered, as she pulled the covers up under her chin. *Is it possible that I'm wrong?*

Chapter 21

Ashton sat at his keyboard, his fingers poised and ready to play, his mind ready to compose lyrics. He'd hardly slept last night. His mind had been in turmoil because of Kelly.

When she'd left last night, he had felt a wrenching physical pain that to him was inexplicable. He'd never felt deep pain like that before, not even after Camilla had dumped him.

Except when his mother had taken off.

All his life, everything Ashton had done had been an attempt to save himself the agony he had suffered when his mother abandoned him and his father. To a large extent, he had succeeded.

That's why his feelings yesterday were so foreign to him. He wasn't used to feeling this way. He wasn't *supposed* to feel this way. He had hardened his heart.

Hadn't he?

He needed to write. Get his feelings out.

He pressed a few keys, getting a flavor for what he would create. And then the words started flowing.

It happened by surprise,
When I looked into her eyes,
Something happened, something happened to my heart.
Suddenly I can hardly wait,
At night I anticipate,
Just seeing, seeing her lovely smile.
She's as sweet and delicate as a rose,
She's stolen my heart but I don't think she knows,
So I'm sitting here, sitting at home alone.
I just want her in my life,
I want her to be my wife . . .

Ashton's fingers immediately froze. *Wife?* Why did he sing *that?*

Because it rhymed?

Because it was the truth?

Ashton pounded the keys, creating a mishmash of contrasting sounds. He had lost it. He was certifiable.

"It doesn't matter what I want," he said aloud. "Kelly doesn't want me. So, Ashton Hunter, you'd better accept that."

Kelly lay awake in her bed, unable to bring herself to get up. It was the day of the party, but she didn't feel in a festive mood. She couldn't get her mind off Ashton and what had happened the night before.

All night, she had considered the possibility that Ashton may genuinely care for her. There was something about the way he had looked at her yesterday, something in his eyes. . . .

Could Ashton's attitude toward Tony have been based on jealousy, not just a hurt ego as she'd originally thought? And if he *had* been jealous, didn't that mean he cared?

Unleashing an agitated breath, Kelly rolled over. It wasn't true. It couldn't be. Her teenage fantasies were getting the better of her.

Maybe she was just feeling closer to Ashton because he had saved her from Tony.

If Ashton *hadn't* been so stubborn, if he *had* left her alone . . . Kelly shuddered at the thought of how disastrous last night with Tony could have been.

"Girl, you are drama with a capital D," one of her friends had told her once.

Maybe she was. She'd come up here considering one man's proposal, only to fall into bed with the guy who'd first stolen her heart, and then get attacked by another guy on the same day because she'd been foolish enough to go out with him to make a point. If that wasn't drama, then Kelly didn't know what was.

But Ashton had been there for her.

Why *had* he looked out for her? Was it a sense of honor, an inherent sense of goodness? Maybe he would have done the same thing for any other woman. But something in Kelly's heart told her that Ashton had been looking out for her for other reasons.

"Is it possible he really does have feelings for me?" Kelly asked out loud, then sat up. In her heart, she secretly wanted the answer to be yes. Hell, she had cared so much for him once before.

But then she remembered Glenn, and she felt so confused.

With Ashton, Kelly could only speculate as to his real feelings. He was so different from Glenn. He was so much more . . . passionate. His kisses set her heart racing, his touch set her skin on fire. Ashton stirred a raging passion within her that Glenn never would.

But what she needed was stability. A man who she could count on to be there for her, to take care of her, to support her. A man who would help curb the drama in her life, not enhance it. A man like Glenn.

Kelly sighed once again. Was that the kind of life she really wanted? A boring, stable one? Or did she want excitement and passion?

Why didn't she feel about Glenn the way she did about Ashton? Why did she know in her heart that Glenn's touch would never excite her the way Ashton's did?

Love. The thought caught Kelly off guard, disturbing her. Oh, God. Was it possible? Was it possible that she was falling in love with Ashton?

"Oh, Ashton," Kelly sighed. "How can fate be so cruel? Why, if we're attracted to each other, can't we make it work? Why have you come back into my life at all? Why now?"

Were they meant to love each other yesterday, for one last time?

Kelly ran her fingers through her braids. Thinking about Ashton and whether or not he loved her was making her crazy.

Maybe she *was* feeling this way because Ashton had saved her from Tony. Or maybe, for the first time in her life, she was really, truly in love.

Or maybe, she had always been in love with Ashton.

After he'd dumped her so callously, she had convinced herself that she had been infatuated with him. In serious lust, but not love. After all, she'd been so young. She didn't know what love was.

Groaning, Kelly got out of bed. She had to stop thinking about Ashton. Her nerves were frazzled, and her heart ached. This wasn't good for her at all. She slipped on a robe, then strolled into the living room. Wondering what she should do, she paced the room several times, looking at the phone. She finally picked up the telephone receiver and pressed "0." Anxious as hell, Kelly brought her Peter Pointer to her mouth, nibbling at the nail until the operator answered. "I'd like to make a collect call," she announced, then continued gnawing on her nail. She gave the operator Glenn's telephone number, then waited nervously for him to answer the phone.

After two rings, Glenn answered the phone. "Hello?"

Kelly paused for a moment, her stomach suddenly tightening with tension. "Hi, Glenn," she said softly. "It's Kelly."

"Kelly . . . Oh, hi."

Kelly pulled her nail from her mouth and placed her hand on her hip. "How have you been?"

"I'm fine," Glenn responded. "Taking it easy. Doing some gardening. Reading."

Kelly tucked a stray braid behind her ear. "Sounds like a great way to unwind."

"It is. How's your friend?"

"Oh, she's fine." So far, no "I miss you." But of course, it wasn't like Glenn to pressure her. "The party's tonight." Then she lied, "But I thought I might stay around another week or so."

"Why?" Glenn asked.

"I'm still . . . thinking. About your proposal."

"That's good to hear."

"Yeah. I figured that when I head back, I'd like to be able to give you an answer, one way or another."

"Take the time you need. You know I'll be here."

He was the epitome of patience. So why did that bother her?

Because right now, Kelly didn't want patience. She wanted, needed, something else. She needed . . . emotion. If Glenn felt passionately for her, she wanted him to tell her to come home. Demand that she give him an answer.

Good Lord, she wanted drama. It was in her blood.

"Kelly?"

Glenn's voice brought Kelly back to reality. "Yes."

"You okay?"

"Yes, of course. I . . . I'm just hungry. I'd better get something to eat."

"All right."

Brother, but Glenn was passive. Would he ever challenge her in any way? Get her blood boiling with a good argument so that they could make up in the heat of passion afterward?

"Will you call me later?"

"Sure. I'll let you know when I make my travel arrangements."

There was a short pause, then Glenn asked, "You sure you're okay?"

The question took Kelly by surprise. Did he sense her apprehension about him? "Yes. I'm fine."

"All right. Well, have fun tonight."

"Thanks. I will."

Before Kelly could say anything else, she heard a loud dial tone. Slowly, she let the receiver fall from her ear, holding it against her chest for several moments.

She hadn't had the conversation she'd expected. In fact, Glenn didn't seem necessarily happy to hear from her.

He'd treated her like . . . like a friend. Not like a woman he was in love with.

It wasn't that he'd told her he loved her. Instead, when he had proposed to her, he had told her that they could be good together because he believed friendship was the best foundation for a marriage.

Yet today, when she told him she was still thinking about his proposal, he'd barely responded.

Was it only she who had doubts about his proposal? Or was Glenn having second thoughts? After all, he hadn't even told her that he missed her.

But maybe that was just Glenn. Not the type to get emotional.

Kelly sighed. She felt more confused. She had called Glenn hoping to get some perspective. If he'd given her any true indication that he cared about her, she could return to Fort Lauderdale with an easy decision.

But he hadn't.

All this thinking was making Kelly more and more confused. She placed a collect call to her brother's place. It was early and he would probably be at work, but Diamond should be home as she didn't do her radio show until the afternoon.

"Kelly, what's up, girl?" Diamond asked when she accepted the call.

A smile pulled at Kelly's lips when she heard her sister-in-law's voice. "Diamond, it is so good to hear your voice."

"You enjoying your time up in Siberia?"

"Toronto."

"Whatever." Diamond laughed. "If it's a place that gets snow, it may as well be Siberia. Girl, I hate snow."

"It was eighty-nine degrees here yesterday," Kelly pointed out.

"Get out."

"It's not cold here every day." Kelly loved Florida, but so many Floridians thought of winter when she mentioned Canada. It was crazy. "You ought to come up here one day and check it out."

"True dat. I do need to travel more."

"Besides, if you and Michael come up here, he can show you some great spots. Like Niagara Falls, honeymoon capital of the world."

"Oooh, now you know I'm down with that. 'Cause me and your brother, we're never gonna stop honeymooning."

"Don't I know it," Kelly said, feigning annoyance.

"But I'm sure you didn't call to talk about me and Michael."

"No." Kelly paused. "I called for advice."

"Hit me."

"Remember my old high school crush? The guy I'd slept with but—"

"Ashton! Of course I remember! Uh oh, girl. Don't tell me you went up there and fell for him again?"

There was no point in lying. Diamond had a knack for figuring out what was really on people's minds. It was an occupational hazard, considering she gave advice on relationships for a living.

"Actually . . ."

"Girl, tell me all about it."

"I just wish I had exciting news to share. Things have been up and down, to say the least."

"What happened?"

Kelly spent the next several minutes filling Diamond in on all that had transpired—including how she and Ashton had ended up in bed. "The problem is, now I'm more confused than ever. One minute I think he likes me, then I'm sure he doesn't, now I'm not so sure again."

"Can you say d-r-a-m-a?"

"Diamond . . ."

"I know, but it's the truth. And if you want my opinion—which I think you do, or you wouldn't have called me—I'd forget about Glenn as husband material. He's not for you. If he was, you would have jumped at his proposal."

"What about growing to love someone?"

"Maybe for someone else, but not for you. Girl, you'd die of boredom."

"Fair enough. But what should I do about Ashton? Try and talk to him again? Gosh, I don't know why I can't leave that alone."

"You can't leave it alone because you're in love with

him. I saw that the first time you told me about him that day you showed up at Michael's place in Naples. Come on. You hadn't seen the guy in nearly ten years, yet you were telling me about him, a virtual stranger at the time?"

"You were Lady D, host of *The Love Chronicles*. I knew I could talk to you."

"People don't bring up someone from their past if they don't care about them. The thing is, you figured you didn't have another chance with him so you had to put him behind you. Then he calls out of the blue. Now, you see him again and the sparks are still flying."

"But how can things work out? He's been hurt and it's messed him up. He doesn't know how to love."

"If your brother can turn himself around, *anybody* can turn around."

Diamond made it sound so simple. Of course, Kelly knew it hadn't been simple for them. Her brother's depression had cut him off from the world. The fact that Diamond had been able to get through to him and help him to love again was nothing short of a miracle.

"You make it sound so easy."

"If it's meant to be, Ashton will be the man you need him to be. If not, then you're better off without him."

Such succinct advice. It didn't make Kelly feel better.

She was only going to be in Toronto a short while longer. She and Ashton didn't have much time to get their act together.

If they even had an act.

"All right, Diamond. I appreciate your advice."

"The love game, it's not easy. But I'm not convinced it's supposed to be easy. I think we appreciate it more when we have to work for it."

"I guess that's true."

"I hope it all works out, Kelly."

"Thanks."

Chapter 22

"So after I came back from the moon, I was really depressed. After all, none of my friends on earth wanted to talk to me anymore. I think it was because I had turned green, don't you?"

"Mmm hmm."

Leaning across the table in the booth, Karen took both of Kelly's hands in hers and squeezed hard. "You haven't heard a word I've said."

Kelly directed her gaze at Karen and blinked innocently. "Yes I have. I've been listening." But when she saw the skeptical look in Karen's eyes, she frowned and said, "I'm sorry. What did you say?"

"Other than my moon story?"

Narrowing her eyes, Kelly flashed Karen a confused look. "What?"

Karen chuckled softly. "Never mind. Sweetie, I've got the time, and I think you should tell me what's bothering you."

Kelly groaned. "I'm really sorry. You've taken me out for brunch, but I'm not very good company, am I?"

"Truthfully? I *have* had more interesting conversations with a brick wall." Karen squeezed Kelly's hands affectionately. "We're not going anywhere until you tell me what's going on."

Kelly did her best to give Karen an "everything's perfectly fine" smile. "I'm just tired. That's all." Then, out of habit, Kelly slipped her a fingernail into her mouth and started chewing.

"Oh no. It's worse than I thought. It always is when you chew your nail like that."

Quite clearly, Karen knew Kelly better than she thought. What point was there in continuing to pretend to her friend that nothing was wrong? Especially when she needed to relieve her mind of her very heavy burden. She'd talked to Diamond about it, but clearly she wouldn't feel better until she'd talked to the whole world!

Kelly blew out a hurried breath and looked at Karen with a weary expression. "It's about Glenn."

"Uh-oh." Karen's eyes instantly grew wide with concern.

Moaning loudly, Kelly ran a hand through her hair. "I realized I can't marry him."

"Kelly . . . what are you saying?"

"I know . . . I don't know. That's my problem."

Karen raised her eyebrows in confusion. "That might make sense to a brick wall—"

"I know." Kelly sighed again, trying to think of the right words to say. "The thing is, I feel like a heel. How am I going to make Glenn understand that?"

Karen chuckled softly at Kelly's cryptic words. Then she said, "Didn't you say that you and Glenn weren't really involved? That you were good friends and he proposed to you?"

"Yes."

"Then he's got to be prepared for you to say no to his proposal."

"I can't help thinking that I'm going to hurt him."

"You never promised him anything."

"No, but . . ."

"But nothing." Karen paused. "Is that what's really bothering you?"

Kelly was practically relieved when Karen asked the question. "No."

"This is about Ashton."

"I slept with him."

"You *what*?"

Several people in the restaurant quickly looked their way at Karen's outburst.

Kelly groaned.

"I'm sorry," Karen said in a lowered voice. "I didn't mean to attract attention, but I was just so shocked. Did I hear you correctly?"

"Yes."

"When?"

"Yesterday."

"Oh. My. Goodness. And?"

"And . . . it was horrible. Well, not the act. That was amazing. Even better than the first time."

"But what?"

Kelly told Karen all that Ashton had said afterward, and how she had felt like a fool.

"I don't believe it," Karen said.

"That's what he said."

"That's not what I mean. I don't think he was telling the truth. I've known Ashton a while. And I've never seen the spark in his eyes that I saw since you came around. Something's going on between you two, whether or not he's ready to admit it."

Kelly's eyes grew wide with interest. "You think so?"

"You'll just have to ask him, won't you?"

Groaning, Kelly's brow furrowed in a scowl. "I can't ask him that. We talked about it last night—after what happened with Tony."

"Tony?" Karen's eyebrows shot up. "What happened with Tony?"

"Please don't say I told you so, but you and Ashton were right. It was awful. I agreed to go out with him for a friendly drink the night before, and the only reason I kept the date was because Ashton had pushed me away. I know, it was silly. But I thought the guy was just a friend."

The waiter appeared. "More coffee?" he asked.

Karen shooed him away.

When he was gone, Kelly continued. "He tried to rape me."

"Oh, my God!"

"Thank the good Lord, it didn't happen. Ashton had followed us to the bar we went to, then followed us again as Tony took me to a park. He saved me from that creep."

"Kelly, I'm so sorry you had to go through that."

"So am I. And believe me, I'm so grateful for Ashton." She inhaled deeply, blew the air out slowly. "After he brought me home, we talked. And . . . I don't know. There was something about him that seemed . . . seemed like he cared."

"Because he does."

"Even though he told me he'd stay away from me?"

"I'm sure he thinks that's what you want."

"He did say something about that."

"See."

"I don't know, Karen. This is all so hard."

Karen's shoulders rose and fell in a shrug. "It seems quite simple to me. You follow your heart. Life is short. You know the routine."

Kelly *did* know the routine. But that didn't make things any easier. How could she follow her heart, when her heart always seemed to get stuck in her throat?

Whether or not she should ask Ashton about his feelings was the thought that plagued Kelly on the short walk back to the condo, and for another forty-five minutes after that until Karen knocked on her bedroom door and announced, "Ashton's at the door. He wants to speak to *you.*"

Kelly's heart started racing, considering the possibilities. "Did he say why?"

"Oh, will you just go to the door!"

Kelly had no choice but to obey Karen's command. Avoiding Ashton forever wasn't going to solve any of her problems . . . would it?

No, it wouldn't.

Cautiously, Kelly approached the door, a guarded expression on her face. The sight of Ashton in the doorway, looking so damn sexy with those dreadlocks of his, caused butterflies to do a frantic aerobic exercise in her stomach.

Inhaling a steadying breath, Kelly managed a "Hi."

"Hi," Ashton answered, then rubbed the back of his neck with his right hand. "Uh, we've got to talk. Some unfinished business."

"Uh . . . sure."

Ashton peered into the living room where Karen was sitting and said to Kelly, "We need privacy." Sauntering into the living room, he looked down at Karen, who was pretending to be absorbed in a book. "Karen, if you don't mind, I'd really like to speak to Kelly alone—"

"Don't say another word," Karen said, slamming the book shut. "I've got to go pick up some . . . milk." She jumped up from the sofa and pranced to the doorway.

"I really appreciate this," Ashton told her.

Karen slipped into a pair of sandals. "Don't mention it." Moving to Kelly, she flashed a smile at her and winked. "Go for it," she whispered in Kelly's ear.

Kelly smiled tightly as Karen stepped into the hallway. And then, with the click of the door, Karen was gone. Kelly was alone with Ashton. Despite the many deep breaths she drew in, her heart wouldn't slow its frantic pace. Turning from the door, she faced Ashton, who was standing a few feet away from her. "So . . ."

"I won't keep you long," Ashton stated impersonally, his eyes unreadable. "I just came to pick up the decorations you bought for the party. Seeing that the party is tonight."

So that was why he had wanted privacy. "Oh."

"I can bring everything to the restaurant. All you have to do after this is show up."

Kelly turned away from Ashton's gaze and hugged her elbows. "So . . . that's all you wanted?"

"I know this is awkward, Kelly. I promised I'd stay out of your way. If I could have avoided this, I would have. But I still want the party to be a surprise. Then after tonight . . . well, you won't have to worry about seeing me."

Karen was wrong. There was nothing simple about this.

She cleared her throat and mustered her most pleasant expression. "Just give me a minute to get the decorations." She scurried to the bedroom, and once there, dropped herself onto the bed, where she stifled a cry with her pillow.

Sure, Ashton had feelings for her!

And last night, the cow jumped over the moon!

A lone tear escaped Kelly's eye and slowly trickled down her cheek. How could she have been so incredibly stupid—*again*?

Kelly swiped at the tear. Now wasn't the time to think about that. She had to pull herself together and go out and face Ashton as though nothing was wrong. She couldn't let him see just how much his rejection of her was tearing her apart.

If she had only left the past in the past.

There was a knock on her bedroom door.

Quickly jumping from the bed, Kelly wiped her eyes again to make sure she erased all evidence that she had been crying. "Just a second."

She went to the closet and retrieved the bag of decorations. Then, crossing from the closet to the bedroom door, she filled her lungs with air. There was no way she was going to let Ashton see her upset. Blowing out the breath and forcing a smile, Kelly opened the bedroom door and stepped out to meet Ashton.

"Here you go," she said in her most cheerful voice, sounding like one of those salespeople with the plastic smiles. "I'm sure you can manage from here."

"Yes . . . well, I would ask for your help putting them up, but since this is Karen's day off . . ."

"Yes, I know."

Moving to the door, Ashton placed his hand on the knob. "Thanks for all your help. I'll see you later."

Kelly's face hurt from grinning so hard. "Of course. See ya."

Opening the door, Ashton stepped into the hallway. Kelly promptly shut it.

Trying desperately to fight the tears that threatened to fall again, Kelly said, "I will not cry over you anymore, Ashton. I *won't.*"

But despite her words, the tears fell anyway.

Ashton stood beneath the warm water pulsating from the shower nozzle with his eyes closed. He was going insane. Kelly was driving him insane. Why the hell couldn't he get her out of his system?

Somewhere along the way his sexual attraction for her had started to feel like just a bit more than a mere sexual attraction.

A whole lot more than a sexual attraction was more like it.

Despite what Kelly thought of him, he wasn't just out for a carefree romp in the sac. Sure, his brain wanted a no-strings-attached love affair, but his heart wanted something more. Something he didn't want to want.

He wasn't sure when the truth had snuck up and bit him in the butt. Was it the moment when he saw Tony lying on top of Kelly, and he heard her desperate cries? When he had realized what Tony was trying to do to her, his emotions had overwhelmed him, like someone had been trying to violate *him*. He knew at that moment that he would have given his life to protect her, if he'd had to.

That alone was proof that he cared about her in more than a casual way.

An image of Bozo the Boyfriend flashed in his mind. He was no doubt established, cultured, clean cut, and attractive. Why did he have the urge to strangle this guy if he ever laid eyes on him?

Because, God help him, he wanted Kelly.

But she didn't want him. He had to remember that. She'd put herself in danger with Tony just to get that point through his thick skull.

But their lovemaking . . . the feel of her soft skin against his . . . it had all felt so right . . . so perfect.

And then he'd gone and told her that he didn't want a serious commitment.

Which he didn't.

At least he hadn't.

Love was complicated. Love hurt.

It had hurt his father. Devastated him. He had never remarried. The one woman he'd loved to death had left him with a broken heart that he'd never recover from.

Kelly's not your mother.

That she wasn't. In fact, she was nothing like his mother. Thankfully.

But was that enough for him? Enough to make him feel secure enough to put his heart on the line?

Chapter 23

Karen was not an easy person to surprise. Kelly had had to pull Karen's teeth to convince her that *she* should be the one to take *her* out, that that was the least she could do as her way of saying congratulations.

"But I wanted to take you to this wonderful Greek restaurant," Karen had told Kelly. "You'll love it."

"I hate Greek food," Kelly had responded.

"Since when?" Karen had asked suspiciously.

"Since I graduated from high school."

"Well," Karen had protested, "they serve a variety of food. Hell, if you want a burger, you can have one."

"No."

"Oh, come on."

"I've already made reservations," Kelly had finally said. "It was *supposed* to be a surprise."

"Oh," Karen had responded, smiling. "Where are we going?"

"That *will* be a surprise. So just get ready. Upscale casual, or sexy . . . whatever you want."

After trying on a dozen or so outfits each and carefully scrutinizing their choices, Kelly and Karen had finally decided on ensembles that they thought were appropriate. Kelly had to admit that she looked fine in her knee-length black pleated skirt and form-fitting red cotton shirt that zipped up at the front. She would never have spent so much time deciding what to wear if she had been on her own—but with her and Karen together, it had been a throwback to high school days.

Hadn't everything been a throwback to high school days since Kelly had arrived in Toronto?

Karen gave herself the once over in the hallway mirror, smoothing down her short black wrap-around skirt and adjusting her white satin blouse.

"You look great," Kelly assured her.

"You think so?" Karen asked, turning sideways to examine her outfit.

Kelly nodded. "Yes. Besides, you're not going there to impress anyone."

Tilting her head to the side, Karen gave Kelly a sly look. "You never know."

The apartment buzzer went off, alerting them that their taxi was waiting. Grabbing their respective purses, Kelly and Karen made their way downstairs.

When the taxi pulled up in front of *Delectables,* Karen said, "This is where Ashton works." She eyed Kelly curiously. "You never did tell me how your *meeting* with him earlier went, and I didn't want to press the issue. But if we're here, I assume that means things went well."

"Let's just go inside," Kelly said, then paid the taxi driver.

The hostess greeted them with a wide grin. Kelly told her that they had a reservation for Karen Stewart. Her eyes sparkling, the hostess smiled and said, "Follow me."

Karen surveyed the bar area as they walked by it. "I don't see Ashton."

"Hmm," Kelly said coolly. "Maybe he's not working."

They walked a few more feet, then swung to the left

around the bar. Immediately, Kelly saw the banner pro-
claiming, "Way to Go!" amidst pink and white streamers
and colorful balloons. Grinning widely, she turned to
face her friend, noting the sudden gleam in Karen's eyes
and the startled but pleased expression on her face.

"Surprise!" everyone at the tables yelled in unison.

Karen brought a shaky hand to her mouth and stifled her cry of delight.

Kelly threw her arm around Karen's shoulder and
drew her close. "Congratulations, sweetie!"

"You bugger," Karen said, then wrapped her arms
tightly around Kelly.

Instantly, Ashton was at Karen's side, followed by several more of her friends. After all the hugs and well
wishes, Karen and Kelly made their way to the center
table. The chair that was lavishly decorated with balloons and streamers was clearly for Karen. Kelly took
the seat beside her.

Before they could pull their chairs close to the table,
Ashton approached them with a bottle of wine. Kelly
averted her gaze, avoiding eye contact with him as he
filled their wineglasses. It hurt too much to look at him.

When their glasses were filled, Ashton announced,
"I'd like to propose a toast." Everyone at the tables
lifted their glasses. Ashton looked down at Karen
warmly. "To Karen, a dear friend, and a wonderful person. I wish you many years of success doing what you
love most."

"Here here," someone said, then everyone raised
their glasses and began clinking them with the people's
around them. Ashton touched his glass lightly against
Kelly's, and she forced a smile.

After several more toasts, the DJ began playing an
upbeat dance tune that instantly had several members
of the party jumping up from their chairs. Kelly watched
them scurry to the small dance floor, wondering at the

power of a simple song to get people moving. She was glad that Karen was still seated beside her, because she didn't want to be alone right now.

But just as she turned to face Karen, a handsome man in his midthirties approached their table with a wide grin on his face, and Kelly knew he wasn't smiling at her. "Dance with me," he said, taking Karen by the arm and easing her out of her seat. As the man led her to the dance floor, Karen looked over her shoulder at Kelly, a "What can I do?" expression written on her face.

So now she was alone. After observing the happy crowd of dancers for a moment, Kelly turned her gaze to the bar. Relief washed over her when she didn't see Tony anywhere. She hoped that if he *were* here he would have the sense to leave her alone.

"He's not here."

At the sound of Ashton's sexy voice, Kelly spun around and saw him standing behind her chair with his hands clasped together. "I spoke with the manager about what happened," he continued, "so he told Tony not to come in tonight."

Despite Ashton's humble demeanor, tension filled the air between them. Nervous, Kelly twirled a braid between her fingers. "Thanks," she said softly.

Even in the dim light, Ashton's hazel eyes were as intense as ever as he gazed down at her. "Do you mind if I join you?"

Kelly looked up at him warily, and in defiance of the inner voice that told her she should say no, she found herself vocalizing the words, "Go ahead."

Ashton pulled out the chair beside her and eased himself onto it. He was wearing beige dress pants with a white cotton shirt. As he sat, Kelly couldn't help noticing the way the muscles in his thighs strained against the soft fabric. He looked good.

Too damned good.

"I've got to ask you something," Ashton said, his voice gently washing over Kelly.

Kelly's body immediately grew taut, dreading any type of personal conversation. "What?"

"What did you hope for when you came up here, when you saw me again?"

"Excuse me?"

"I need to know, Kelly."

"What, so I can stroke your ego again? My God, Ashton. Isn't it enough that you abandoned me in high school, slept with me yesterday, then pushed me away? Do you really need to feel as if I'll always be broken-hearted over you?"

"I didn't mean it that way."

"Didn't you?"

"I just . . . I needed to know . . ."

"It doesn't matter, Ashton."

Not wanting to talk about this anymore, Kelly stood. Ashton quickly jumped up, grabbing her by the arm. His touch sent a jolt of electricity right through her, and she looked away, determined not to let Ashton see the effect he was having on her.

"Let me go," Kelly said, her eyes steadfast on the foot of a chair.

"I wish I could."

"Of course you can."

"No." Ashton sighed. "I don't know why, but I feel there's so much unresolved between us. And yeah, I know what I said earlier, but I don't want you heading back to Florida angry with me."

"Fine." Kelly forced a smile. "I'm not angry with you."

In one smooth motion, Ashton's hand was against Kelly's face. "I . . . I want more than that."

This was a game. *She* was a game to him. The man couldn't get his act together.

"I'm marrying Glenn," she said before he could say anything else.

"Really?"

"Yes, really."

"And when did you make that decision?"

"Today. After I talked to him and realized . . . and realized . . ." Ashton was gently stroking her face, making it impossible for her to think.

"If you really care about him, then why does it feel so good when I do this?" Ashton slowly ran his fingers along Kelly's face, down her jawbone, then down to the base of her neck. His eyes glistened with desire, a desire that Kelly was fighting with all her might to ignore.

"Ashton—" The man was a modern day Dr. Jekyll and Mr. Hyde. *Come to me, leave me.* Kelly could hardly stand it.

"And this?" Ashton leaned forward and gave Kelly a feathery kiss on the lips. Just enough to make her shudder with longing.

"Stop it." She took a step backward and collided with the table. She wasn't sure where the strength had come from, but she prayed she would be able to maintain it. "Don't do this to me again."

"You think I'm crazy, and maybe I am. Because when I'm around you, my whole world spins. I tell myself one thing, but then I see you again, and everything changes."

"What exactly changes, Ashton?"

"I care about you," he said. "And I feel bad about what I said yesterday. I know you must have felt used. But that wasn't the case. I made love to you because I care for you. No other reason."

"Don't . . . don't say things you don't mean."

Ashton slipped his arm around Kelly's waist and pulled her close. White hot desire shot through her body. "God help me Kelly, that is the truest thing I have ever said in my life. I just want to take you home now . . .

to make up for yesterday. And for ten years ago. Even if you do leave and marry Glenn, I owe you that much."

Why was he saying these things to her? Why was he acting like he really cared?

Did he?

Kelly didn't dare ask. She couldn't. But he was saying all the right things now. And last night after the fiasco with Tony she had sensed that he actually did feel something for her.

"Will you come home with me?"

Her body was on fire. She was hot with need and an all-consuming passion. How come she always felt this way with Ashton?

"Don't . . ."

"I need you, Kelly."

Those words were her undoing. How could she refuse him when her own need was so great? And he was right. She wanted one time with him when things ended in a pleasant way. Maybe she couldn't have his heart, but if they made love again, she wanted to know that afterward, she would always have his friendship.

Yes, things were unresolved. Maybe one more time together would resolve everything.

Closing her eyes, she hesitated for a moment, then said, "I need you, too."

Ashton lowered his head and took Kelly's mouth fiercely, stoking the flame that was burning within her. It was an urgent kiss, one that had her head spinning with passion. Kelly slipped her arms around Ashton's neck and softly moaned.

An erotic growl escaped Ashton's throat, and he ended the kiss with a playful nip on her bottom lip. "Come on." He took Kelly's hand possessively and led her to the dance floor. Approaching Karen, who was dancing with a few of her girlfriends, he kissed her on the cheek.

"Karen, I hope you don't mind if we take off. Kelly and I have to work something out."

Karen raised an inquisitive eyebrow, then smiled. "I don't mind." She took Kelly's free hand in hers and squeezed it. "I guess I'll see you tomorrow." As Ashton led Kelly away, she turned her head and saw Karen wink at her.

Kelly was crazy, she knew it, to be going home with Ashton for one more roll in the hay. She should have said no when they got in the cab, or when they got to the condo, or when they got to Ashton's door. But she didn't. She couldn't.

Because she wanted this.

One more night with Ashton . . . was that too much to ask?

Chapter 24

Kelly clung to Ashton's hand as he led her through his apartment door, still held it as he locked the door behind them. He scooped her into his arms then, forcefully, causing Kelly to gasp. She couldn't describe what she was feeling. Fear . . . delight . . . desire.

One more night.

Ashton carried her into his bedroom, flicking on the light with his shoulder as he stepped inside the large room. Knowing that there was no turning back now, Kelly wrapped her arms tightly around his neck.

And she didn't want to turn back.

"I want you so much," Ashton whispered against her ear as he laid her down on his bed. "I don't know what it is about you, but you make me absolutely crazy."

And then he was kissing her. His lips probed hers slowly at first, tentative, teasing. But then his warm, wet tongue delved into her mouth with urgency, and the kiss became an explosion of passion.

Kelly surrendered to the kiss, to the blinding desire that consumed her. Her tongue danced with Ashton's in a desperate song of love. His mouth was warm and sweet and intoxicating. She moaned against his kiss, enjoying the here and now, not thinking about tomorrow.

Breaking the kiss, Ashton looked deeply into Kelly's eyes. "You want me to get a condom?"

Bereft of speech, Kelly nodded.

Ashton's eyes crinkled as he looked down at her, heated longing evident in their depths. He brought his hand to her lips and softly traced the outline of her mouth with one finger. One finger, yet the light touch was so stimulating, Kelly's entire body tingled with sexual fervor.

With his skilled hands, Ashton trailed a sensuous path down her smooth neck, then pulled the zipper on her shirt downward, just below her breasts. He drew in a deep breath and released it on a moan, then brought his tongue to her searing skin and kissed the smooth, soft flesh between her breasts. Kelly shuddered with delight as Ashton ran his tongue along her skin, up to the hollow of her neck, and back down again.

Pulling the zipper on Kelly's shirt completely down, Ashton gently pushed the material aside. "You're so beautiful," he said, his voice shimmering with husky promise. Bringing both hands to her breasts, he softly stroked and kneaded the silky, supple flesh. Then, with a carnal sigh, he lowered his head and circled his tongue around a hard peak through her white lace bra.

Thrilled with the glorious feel of his tongue, Kelly arched her back seductively, wanting more. She moaned Ashton's name when he slid the silky material of her bra off her breast and took a nipple into his mouth.

Fire soared through Kelly's veins right to her feminine core. Wantonly, she clasped Ashton's head, holding it to her breast as he suckled, as ripples of pleasure coursed through her body.

She was mad with sweet longing, unlike anything she had ever experienced. Both hot and wet, her center of pleasure was throbbing incessantly. And just when she thought she would die of the ecstasy, Ashton slid a hand under her skirt and began daintily caressing her most private part. A rapturous moan escaped Kelly's lips, and between ragged breaths she said, "Oh, Ashton. I need you."

Despite the overpowering, glorious sensations she was feeling, Kelly pulled herself up onto her side and reached for Ashton's shirt. Her fingers were shaking as she undid the first button, then the second. Pinning her with a heated gaze, Ashton pulled his shirt out of his pants, then undid his belt, his button, and his zipper. Hastily, Kelly pushed the unbuttoned shirt off his shoulders, longing to feel his naked chest against her own.

Why was it that every time they were together seemed more urgent than the last?

A sliver of desire skittered down Kelly's spine as her hardened nipples grazed the solid muscles of Ashton's chest. She brought her mouth to his neck and ran her tongue along it, wanting to excite Ashton the way he was exciting her. Ashton gripped her arms, a raw sexual groan emanating from his throat. Feeling a sudden surge of power, Kelly skimmed her tongue down to his chest, across the heated, brawny flesh, then over to one of his small nipples, taking the peak between her teeth.

Ashton shuddered, then pushed Kelly onto her back with a force that thrilled her. She stared up at him from lowered lids, and watched as he brought his hand to her breast, gliding his fingers along the full, soft flesh. Keeping his gaze steadfast on her eyes, Ashton unfastened the clasp of her bra and slipped the flimsy material off her body. Then he stood and slid out of his pants.

Kelly too disrobed, then lay back on Ashton's bed. The significance of this situation hit her with full force. She was offering Ashton more than her body.

She was offering him her heart.

Ashton's breath caught in his throat as he took in Kelly's exquisite beauty. Her soft, flat stomach, her full breasts and their dark, erect tips. "You're perfect, Kelly," he uttered softly. "Absolutely beautiful." He lay beside her and kissed her lightly, then with his fingers trailed a fiery path from her neck to her stomach, stopping just above her lace panties. "Hell, I'd better get the condom."

He rushed to his dresser, found a condom, and rolled it over his erection. Then he hurried back to Kelly.

She reached for him, stroked his face. "Make love to me."

With delicate hands, Ashton skimmed the white lace panties over Kelly's round hips, then over her long, smooth legs. An inferno of passion was burning in his loins as his eyes roamed her body, her beautiful skin, and her tempting curves.

A soft sigh fell from Kelly's lips, and tears threatened to fall as her emotions overwhelmed her. No matter what happened after this, she would always have this moment in time.

She stroked Ashton's inner thigh with feathery fingers. "Love me, Ashton."

Ashton lowered himself onto Kelly's body, gently parting her legs with his own. Slipping a hand between their bodies, he found her throbbing center, then moaned softly when he discovered she was wet and ready for him. He immersed a finger deep inside her, enjoying the way she arched her back at his touch, the way an excited moan escaped her lips. He played with her until she was whimpering and groaning and tossing her head from side to side. Then, capturing her mouth with his, he pulled her hips upward, and thrust deep inside her.

A half moan, half cry fell from Kelly's lips. She dug her nails into Ashton's back, squeezing hard as he filled her completely. Nothing had ever felt as glorious as this. Her body was alive with sensations, wonderful sensations that threatened to take control of her very being. "Oh, yes!" she cried. "Oh Ashton . . . *Oh!*"

Kelly was driving him crazy. She knew just how to touch him, how to meet his wild thrusts. She knew what thrilled him, what turned him on.

Ashton had had other lovers, but it was different with Kelly. Real with Kelly in a way he had never experienced with anyone else. For before Kelly, he had never experienced the feeling of closeness with a woman. Even in high school, he had known there was something special about the night they'd shared. So special that it had scared him to death.

"Ashton!" Kelly squealed, gripping his firm buttocks as the most delightful dizzying sensation swept over her. She let out a loud, ravished moan as her hips bucked savagely, as contractions rippled through her core, one after the other until every ounce of strength drained from her body. As the contractions subsided, she clung to Ashton's slick body, luxuriating in the aftermath of her splendid climax, knowing that what she had just experienced was heaven on earth. She wished she could stay in his arms forever.

Ashton seized Kelly's lips in a short, fierce kiss, just before his head grew light and he was swallowed up by a passionate fire. He plunged into Kelly's sweet warmth one last time, collapsing on top of her as he succumbed to his own release. As sweet sensations rocked his body, he held her to him tightly, knowing that he had never experienced anything as wonderful as this with any other woman.

They stayed there like that, holding each other, their bodies wet, their breathing frantic. And finally, when their breathing returned to normal, Ashton slid off Kelly and lay beside her.

"Are you okay?" he asked, once again concerned that he may have hurt her, may have been too rough.

Turning and draping a leg over Ashton's glistening thigh, Kelly replied, "Yes." Her wanton behavior during their lovemaking now surprised her, but she wasn't embarrassed. "You were right, Ashton. Making love again was a good thing."

Slipping an arm around Kelly's waist, Ashton pulled her close. Her soft breasts grazed his chest. "This is how it should have been before. You and me, lying together like this."

Kelly found herself getting aroused all over again. She glided a finger along Ashton's shoulder, hoping to reignite the fire. "Lying . . . or loving?"

"You haven't had enough?"

Would she ever have enough of Ashton? "Let me know when you're ready for round two."

Ashton's warm laughter filled the room. "Insatiable."

"Only when it comes to you."

Silence passed between them, and Kelly wondered what he was thinking. Had anything changed for them?

If there was any hope for them, if they had a chance, now was the time to find out. Now that they were both in sync.

Inhaling deeply and placing a palm on his chest, she said softly, "Ashton."

"Yes?"

"Will it bother you if I ask you something?"

"I already told you, I feel sorry about how I reacted yesterday. Ask me whatever you like."

Kelly gulped hard. Was she crazy for even daring to broach this subject yet again? Diamond had told her that if Ashton was the man for her, he would step up to the plate and do what was right. "I know things have been up and down for us since I came here, but you said . . . at the restaurant you said that you care about me."

Tracing Kelly's jaw lightly with his forefinger, Ashton replied, "Yes. I do."

"Care about me . . . *how?*"

Ashton's chest rose and fell as he drew in a deep breath and released it slowly. "I care, Kelly. But what you said before was right. I've got a lot of problems. I'm just starting to figure that out."

A tiny knot of fear coiled inside Kelly's stomach as she pondered Ashton's response. It wasn't exactly what she had hoped to hear. Forging ahead, she asked, "Does it bother you that I'm leaving tomorrow night?"

Ashton shrugged. "I know that I don't want you to leave."

"Why not?" *Please Ashton. Please say what I need to hear.*

"I want us to always stay in touch."

Stay in touch. How sweet.

"Kelly, I know you said you were planning on marrying Glenn. I don't know if you were serious about that, but I've realized . . ." He sighed. "As much as I care about you, I've got to work on me, first. Know that I have in my heart to give what you deserve."

Kelly's heart plummeted. Great, so now Ashton was taking the I'm-doing-this-for-you route to dump her!

"So even if my leaving means I'll end up marrying Glenn, you wouldn't try to stop me?"

There was a long pause before Ashton answered. "I want you to be happy. If you'll be happy with Glenn, then I have to accept that."

It had been her last chance, and she had once again laid her heart on the line. And once again, it had all blown up in her face.

"Wow. You're just Mr. Nobility, aren't you?"

Ashton groaned softly. He wished he could tell Kelly what she wanted to hear, wished he could take a chance on love. It was what he had planned to do, but something had stopped him.

Something kept telling him that any hope of a happy, loving relationship with a woman was a stupid pipe dream.

"I'm trying to do the right thing."

Kelly's throat was suddenly dry and tight, aching with suppressed emotion. She rose from the bed and hastily gathered her clothes. "Thanks, Ashton." She slipped into her bra and her shirt. "Thanks for that."

Ashton found his underwear and put it on. "Kelly, this isn't what I wanted. For you to leave like this."

"That's too bad." She fastened her skirt, then slipped into her shoes.

Ashton reached out and softly stroked her face. "I don't know, Kelly. Maybe—"

"I can't settle for *maybe*, Ashton," she retorted. She paused, then added, "I'm leaving tomorrow night. I'm going back to Fort Lauderdale. Back to . . . Glenn."

As she hurried to the door, Ashton was behind her every step of the way. "Don't go like this," he said.

Turning around to face him, she asked, "What reason is there for me to stay?" She looked into Ashton's eyes, into their glistening depths, searching for an answer. She knew he didn't really love her, but it hurt so much to accept that fact. God, she was stupid for believing anything would change between them.

When Ashton remained silent, merely looked at her but gave her no answers, Kelly fought back the tears. "That's what I thought. Good-bye, Ashton."

Kelly pulled the door open and rushed into the hallway. She closed the door behind her with a resounding thud, then gripped her stomach as anguish overwhelmed her. She fought the tears as she ran to Karen's apartment.

What a fool she was! How on earth could she have believed that one more night together would solve anything? Why oh why was she able to lie to herself so easily?

Well, never again.

She had called the airline earlier and learned that there were three flights she could catch to Fort Lauderdale tomorrow. There was space on all of them, so all she had to do was show up at the airport.

Tomorrow, she would be on her way home. And Ashton would be out of her life forever.

The next twenty-four hours were going to be the hardest twenty-four hours of her life.

Chapter 25

"Oh, Kelly," Karen said as she hugged her. "Maybe you should stay a few more days. Try to work it out with him."

"He doesn't love me," Kelly protested. "There's no point."

For the umpteenth time this morning, Karen rubbed Kelly's back tenderly. Kelly knew that Karen was both shocked and confused by the story she had told her. No doubt, Karen had been hoping to hear wonderful news when she had awakened Kelly and, with a wide smile and a gleam in her eyes, asked to hear every romantic detail of her evening with Ashton. Instead of returning her smile, Kelly had burst into tears. Then the two had had a heart-to-heart about what had happened and about how devastated Kelly felt.

Karen asked, "So you're just going to go back to Fort Lauderdale and marry Glenn, and forget about your feelings for Ashton?"

Kelly nodded weakly. "Why not? Since Ashton doesn't love me . . ."

"Oh, Kelly, are you sure? Maybe if you give him more time he'll come around."

Kelly eased out of Karen's embrace. "You're a sweetheart Karen, as always. But what you're saying just isn't true. I wish it were, but it's not. If all Ashton needed was time, he wouldn't have given me that crap about how he wanted what was best for me. God, that was so *pathetic.*"

The annoying sound of the apartment buzzer went off. Karen flashed Kelly a melancholy look. "That's my cab."

Throwing her arms around Karen's neck, Kelly hugged her fiercely. "I'm gonna miss you, Karen." Tears filled her eyes. "Call me as soon as you can."

"You bet I will." Karen pulled back and wiped at the tears that were streaming down her face. Sighing, she rose from the sofa and grabbed her purse, then sauntered to the door.

Kelly followed her. "Break a leg, hon." She smiled at her friend through her tears. "And whatever you do, don't you dare forget me when you become a big star."

Giggling, Karen hugged Kelly one last time. "Never. Good-bye sweetie." She hesitated for a moment before adding, "And before you leave this afternoon, please talk to Ashton. Try and work it out."

Kelly shrugged noncommittally. She didn't want to think about Ashton ever again. "I guess I'll call him to say good-bye."

"I'll be rooting for you two." Karen opened the door, then bent to lift her luggage. Casting Kelly a sidelong glance, Karen stepped into the hallway. "Bye, sweetie."

And then she was gone. A wave of melancholy swept over Kelly. She felt the same kind of dejection she had experienced years ago when she moved to Florida and left Karen behind. But this time it would be different. From now on, she would always stay in touch with

Karen. Never again would she let anything separate them, not even distance.

As she went into the bedroom to pack the rest of her clothes, Kelly wiped her tears. She had another four hours to kill before she caught the bus that would take her to Buffalo. From the bus depot in Buffalo, she would take a taxi to the airport. It was more of a hassle than asking Ashton to drop her back there, but the last thing she wanted to do was see Ashton again.

And she didn't want to sit in the apartment remembering the fleeting passion she and Ashton had shared. When she finished packing, she would go outside and mentally throw her feelings for Ashton in Lake Ontario, and pray that the gentle waves would swallow them up.

Ashton took the short trip down the hallway to Karen's door. Karen, being the dear that she was, had called him earlier from the airport to tell him that Kelly would be leaving by two P.M. It was now one-fifteen.

Inhaling a steadying breath, he raised his hand to the door and knocked.

Kelly's mouth pulled into a tight line as she opened the door and saw Ashton. The sadness in her eyes was unmistakable, and Ashton felt as if someone had kicked him in the gut. "What do you want?" she asked, her voice distant.

Cautiously, Ashton stepped inside, closing the door behind him. Glancing down, he eyed the two small pieces of luggage near the door. "Karen called and told me you were leaving. I thought you might need a ride back to Buffalo."

Kelly crossed her arms over her chest and shook her head. "No. I don't."

Kelly's sweet fragrance filled Ashton's nose as he inhaled. What was it about her that made him dread the thought of losing her? Last night, they had made sweet, passionate love. Tonight, she was leaving town.

He was *letting* her leave. Yesterday, she'd wanted him to give her a reason to stay, but he couldn't. He was afraid of the feelings he had for her, of giving her the power to hurt him. He had too much emotional baggage, and Kelly deserved better than that. If he couldn't offer her his love, then how could he prevent her from marrying a man who *did* love her?

"Kelly, after all that's . . . happened between us, I hope we can at least be friends. Maybe talk once in a—"

"Friends?" Kelly asked sourly, then looked at Ashton as though he were insane. "Look, Ashton, you don't owe me anything, and I don't expect anything. So if it's okay with you, I'd just prefer that we go our separate ways . . . make a clean break." Kelly looked down at her wristwatch. "If you don't mind, I'd like to finish getting ready." She turned hastily, heading for the bedroom.

Ashton grabbed her by her arm, forcing her to turn and face him. "Were you even going to say good-bye?"

"I figured I'd call you from the airport."

Was she lying or telling the truth? It was hard to tell by looking into the soft depths of her brown eyes, eyes that once held warmth but now held coldness and anger. He didn't want her to leave like this, angry with him. "Are you sure you don't want a ride? I'd be happy to take you."

Kelly shook her head. Ashton found it hard to believe that he would never run his fingers over her skin again, nor kiss her luscious lips.

"Let's just say our good-byes now. It's"—she sighed— "easier that way."

What could he do? He knew she was hurting, and he was doing nothing to ease her pain. He took her in his arms and held her close, inhaling her flowery scent.

Why was he letting her go when she felt so good in his arms?

Because he couldn't give her what she needed.

"Good-bye," he said softly, committing the feel and smell of her to memory. "Good luck."

After a few seconds, Kelly jerked away from Ashton and opened the apartment door. "Good-bye." Her gaze focused straight ahead, she held the door open until he walked through it. Turning, Ashton looked back at her, at her rueful eyes. He wished the last memory of her would be of her smiling, but clearly that wasn't to be.

"Good-bye," he whispered one last time, surprised at the sadness he was feeling. Kelly abruptly closed the door, and he heard the lock click shut.

Slowly, Ashton walked down the hallway to his condo unit, trying to block out the painful emotions that flooded him. And when he reached his door, he closed his eyes and tried to block out Kelly's image, determined to forget the woman who had made him care.

Kelly sat quietly looking through the bus's window, feeling an unbearable sense of loss. With each passing moment, the bus was taking her closer to home and farther away from Ashton.

Ashton. The man she loved, but didn't have a future with. She had to let go of the dream now, of her stupid teenage fantasy.

But damn if it wasn't hard. Even as she had boarded the bus, she had hoped that Ashton would stop her from leaving, that he would show up at the bus station and beg her to stay. But he hadn't. He'd just let her go, knowing that he would never see her again.

Well, at least this put to rest Karen's crazy notion that Ashton was in love with her but just couldn't express his feelings. If he did love her, he would never have let her get on this bus and head back to Fort Lauderdale, straight into the arms of another man. It was obvious now, painfully so, that Ashton didn't love her. He never had.

Sure, he cared about her, and they had shared one night of beautiful passion. But love? It was stupid to think that because a man slept with a woman that he was in love with her. After all, this was the twenty-first century. Kelly had to accept reality and get on with her life.

And that life included marrying Glenn. There was no reason not to.

Then why did she feel a heaviness in her chest, a lump in her throat, and an emptiness in her soul?

Because despite her resolve, she had put her heart on the line. Again.

If only he could have loved me, Kelly thought. Then maybe. Just maybe she would have stayed in Toronto and pursued her dream. But there was no point in dwelling on what might have been. She was going back home, to Glenn and to a secure and stable future.

But it wasn't stability Kelly wanted.

She wanted Ashton.

The ride to the Buffalo airport had drained her, but she was finally here.

In a zombielike state, she gathered her luggage from the taxi and started for the terminal.

"Can I help you with your luggage, ma'am?" a skycap asked.

"No, thank you. I'm fine."

It was just after five o'clock, and the sun was shining brightly. Despite the sun's warmth, Kelly shivered, and she knew that she would never truly be warm again.

Without Ashton in her life she would merely survive from day to day, and it would be a pitiful existence.

Kelly drew in a deep breath of the warm summer air, letting it fill her lungs to full capacity. She held it a few seconds before exhaling quickly, then walked through the revolving doors and into the terminal.

"Kelly."

Was that her name she had heard?

Of course not. No one here would be calling out to her.

"Kelly."

It was louder this time. And it sounded like . . . Kelly surveyed the crowd of people before her, but there were so many. She didn't see anyone she recognized.

"Of course not, you fool," she chastised herself. She turned in the direction of the JetBlue counter and started walking.

But then she heard her name again, and when she turned around this time, she saw the face that went along with the voice that had called out to her.

At first, Kelly thought that she must have been dreaming. She had been thinking about Ashton so much, she actually now believed she was seeing him. She had gone and lost her mind.

But her skin began to prickle when the figment of her imagination started to move. He pushed his way through the crowd, making his way toward her.

Good Lord, her mind was not playing tricks on her. It *was* Ashton!

Ashton broke through the crowd and ran toward her. "Kelly."

A dizzying sensation overwhelmed Kelly, making her head light and her knees weak. She still couldn't believe her eyes. Why was Ashton here? What was going on?

"Don't tell me I've left you speechless?" he asked, a

smile playing on his sensuous lips. "That would be a first."

It was only then that Kelly realized she *had* been speechless. Her mind was buzzing with so many questions, she didn't realize she hadn't voiced them.

She managed to find her voice. "Ashton . . . what are you doing here?"

"We've got some unfinished business."

Her mind in a confused haze, Kelly asked, "What? Did I forget something in Toronto?"

Ashton chuckled. "You could say that."

Taking Kelly by the elbow, Ashton gently led her to an unpopulated area near the doors. There was a bench there, and he sat, guiding Kelly down beside him.

His hazel eyes glistened with a smile as he looked at her and lightly stroked her cheek.

Kelly's heart pounded with excitement, and her stomach tightened with apprehension. What would have possessed Ashton to drive all the way here to see her? "Ashton . . . I don't understand."

Ashton's eyes grew serious. "It suddenly hit me that once you got on that plane, I would never see you again. That you would go on with your life and get married, and I would have nothing. I knew that if you were taking the bus it would take you longer to get here. So, I just hopped into my car and drove."

Kelly's brow wrinkled as she scrutinized Ashton carefully. His full mouth was curved in the slightest of smiles, and his eyes held a spark that threatened to ignite her passion for him once again. "Ashton, what are you saying?"

Her eyes focused on his hands as he reached into the pocket of his blue denim shirt. Completely intrigued, she watched him withdraw a small, pink, velvet box. Looking down at her hands, he said, "This is for you."

He placed the velvet box in her hands and closed her fingers around it.

Kelly's heart went wild as her mind considered the possibilities.

"I can't let you marry Bozo, Kelly."

"Excuse me?"

"Sorry. That's my nickname for him." He grinned sheepishly.

Kelly couldn't help laughing. "Bozo?"

Ashton shrugged.

"Glenn really is a nice guy."

"I don't care if he's the pope. I don't want you to marry him."

"Why not?" Kelly asked as her heart fluttered. She needed to hear Ashton say it, needed to know this was real.

"Just open the box."

It was almost cute, the way he fumbled nervously with his fingers as he kept his gaze on the small box in her hands. She smiled. "Not until you tell me why you don't want me to marry Glenn."

"I want you to realize . . . I hope . . . I want you to know . . ."

Her heart full of optimism, Kelly watched as Ashton struggled for words. The suspense was killing her. And thrilling her.

It was just the kind of drama she loved.

"Oh, hell," he spat out. "I'm trying to tell you that I love you."

There. He'd said it. Finally. And it hadn't been so bad. But the look in Kelly's beautiful brown eyes wasn't exactly the one he'd expected to see. Her eyes had widened as though startled, and they were glistening with tears.

"Damnit, Ashton, how could you do this to me?"

Ashton's heart fell to his stomach. Had he been dead wrong? He'd hoped that when he came out here and told Kelly how he felt that she would squeal with delight. He hadn't considered the fact that she might reject him.

It's too late, he thought. Damn, he'd waited too long. She didn't believe his declaration, and how could he blame her? After all, last night he'd been so uncertain of his feelings.

Ashton stood. He rubbed the back of his neck with his hand. "Kelly, I'm sorry."

"You're not getting off that easy," she almost sang. "You'd better explain yourself. And I mean fully."

There was a hopeful glow in Kelly's eyes that hadn't been there last night. Ashton's heart leapt with excitement. Maybe he had a chance. Taking a deep breath to steady his nerves, he sat down and prepared to bare his soul. He felt so out of his element, so unsure of the words that would come to his mouth. Now that he had decided to take a chance on love, he didn't want to blow it.

"You said you loved me, Ashton," Kelly said, more pleadingly than matter-of-factly. "I want to know—I need to know—what you meant by that."

Ashton took the small velvet box from her and opened it. The pear shaped engagement ring sparkled under the sun. Kelly gasped, then put a trembling hand to her mouth. "Oh my God . . ."

"I had just enough time to run to the jewelry store and buy this before I got in my car."

"Ashton . . ."

"I said I love you, Kelly. The way you look. The way you feel. The way you drive me crazy when I'm near you. The way I miss you when you're not around. The way you make me feel . . . complete. I love you the way a man loves a woman."

Kelly's heart fluttered and her knees weakened. "But yesterday . . ."

"Yesterday, I didn't realize that what I felt was love, but now I do." He ran a finger along her smooth forehead. "What did I know about love? My mother walked out on my father and me when I was a boy. And the few times I dated seriously . . . Let's just say that all I ever knew in my life was that women hurt men, and I didn't want to get hurt."

"I would never hurt you."

Ashton gently stroked her cheek. "I know that, Kelly. You're different. You're special. That's why I can't lose you."

Kelly wanted to throw her arms around Ashton and hug him to death. Instead, she flashed him a dejected look. "But what about Glenn? I already called him from the bus terminal . . . and I told him I'd accepted his proposal."

Ashton framed Kelly's face with his hands. "You know as well as I do that you are not going to marry Bozo . . . Glenn. Not when we both know how much we mean to each other. And not after I drove all the way here, determined to find you and tell you how I feel."

Kelly was too stunned to speak. It was just beginning to register in her brain that Ashton had actually said he loved her, and actually sounded like he meant it. Why else would he have come all the way here if he weren't telling the truth?

As if in answer to her unspoken question, Ashton said, "I meant what I said. I'm willing to marry you today. This minute. Because I love you, and I want to spend the rest of my life with you. I know I've got my share of problems, but the bottom line is, your leaving zapped some sense into me. I never forgot you, not even after all these years. I remembered what we shared that graduation night. How special it was . . . and how much it had scared me."

"I wish you hadn't been scared."

"So do I. But maybe we were too young to make it work, then. Too young to appreciate what we had. Maybe we had to take the long way to find our way home."

His words touched her heart.

"I love you, Kelly. Please tell me that you feel the same way."

Her unshed tears couldn't be held back any longer. Ashton really loved her! Her dream had finally come true. "Oh, Ashton! I *do* love you."

A half sigh, half chuckle, burst from Ashton's throat. Taking her in his arms, he held her tightly, held the woman that he loved.

When he heard her soft sobs, he pulled back to look at her face. Although tears streamed down her cheeks, she was smiling. With his thumbs, Ashton wiped away her tears.

And then he kissed her, a deeply passionate kiss, burning with desire and the promise of the future. This was the woman he loved.

Ashton ended the kiss. "It's hard to explain, but now that I've told you how I really feel, a burden's been lifted. This feels right, Kelly. In my heart and in my soul."

"Oh, Ashton. You really are a musician. You make music just with your words."

"But everything I'm saying, I mean. I never wanted to say it if it wasn't true."

And that much she appreciated.

Diamond had been right. So had Karen.

"So what do we do now?" he asked.

"I don't have to leave yet," she told him. "But I will, eventually. My life's in Florida. I'm a Canadian citizen, though, so I can always get a job in Toronto."

"We'll cross that bridge when we come to it," he said. "Right now, I want to take you home. Make up for lost time."

Ashton took the dazzling diamond ring out of the small velvet box and slipped it onto Kelly's finger. Looking down at the ring, Kelly smiled brightly, a smile that tugged on Ashton's heart, a smile that made him feel warm all over.

And then suddenly he rose to his feet and pulled Kelly up with him. Startled, Kelly giggled. "It's official!" Ashton announced, looking around at anyone who would listen. "The lady loves me!" Wrapping his arms around Kelly, he hugged her with all his strength, with all his love.

Passersby stopped and started clapping and cheering. Kelly grinned like a fool as these strangers applauded the promise she and Ashton had just made.

"I don't know what I'm going to do with you," Kelly said, returning her gaze to Ashton. She reached up and playfully squeezed one of his cheeks.

"Oh, I could think of plenty." Ashton raised his eyebrows suggestively.

Slipping her arm around Ashton's neck, Kelly pulled his face down to meet hers. She planted a soft kiss on his lips. On a sigh, she ended the kiss, then took Ashton's hand in hers. "Let's get out of here."

Epilogue

The evening before the wedding, Kelly sat contentedly on Ashton's lap, her head resting on his solid shoulder, his strong arm possessively draped around her waist. The wooden swing in the school playground swayed gently beneath their weight, creaking slightly with each motion. The light evening breeze enveloped them in an aura of peace.

Some brides were nervous wrecks before their weddings, but Kelly was calm and happy. She'd pinched herself several times over the past three months, and she'd ascertained without doubt that she wasn't dreaming.

Kelly was elated that Ashton had decided to relocate to Fort Lauderdale, since she already had a career as a teacher here. But one thing worried her: that Ashton would one day regret his decision. However, Ashton had assured her he could work on his music anywhere, as long as they were together.

"Besides," he'd told her. "You have a great rapport at your school. It doesn't make sense to start from scratch."

"You're sure?"

"Hey, living in Florida where the sun shines all the time is a no brainer."

Kelly thought back to that evening when Ashton had stopped her at the airport. It had been the best day of her life. But on the way back to Toronto, she had dreaded calling Glenn to tell him she wouldn't be marrying him. She didn't like to hurt anyone. But to her surprise, when she'd called Glenn, he'd told her that he was relieved!

"I thought the proposal was a good idea at the time," he'd confessed. "But then I started to get scared. What if things didn't work out? I didn't want to lose my friend. Because first and foremost, you are my friend. And that's what matters to me the most."

Kelly had burst into laughter. She'd agonized over breaking *his* heart, yet he had been second-guessing the proposal altogether.

The memory fading, Kelly concentrated on the love of her life. She fingered his goatee. "Please, Ashton. Tell me what you're going to sing while I walk down the aisle."

Ashton shook his head. "Nope. My lips are sealed."

Kelly frowned. "But Karen's dying to know."

"She'll just have to find out tomorrow along with everyone else."

Even Diamond hadn't been able to crack him. And she was so good at breaking down anybody. People thought they could keep things quiet around her, but Diamond always had them spilling their guts.

Looking toward the setting sun, Kelly smiled. Michael had welcomed Ashton with open arms. So had Diamond. Diamond's cousin, Tara, and her husband, Darren, had thrown a huge celebratory party for them in their backyard.

The only sadness Kelly felt was that her parents wouldn't be here to witness this.

Yes, they will. They'll be here in spirit.

The day she'd lost them, she had been devastated. Her close family had been taken away from her in the blink of an eye. Except for Michael. It had been just the two of them, and Kelly had never imagined that her family would grow again. But it had. With her and Ashton. Michael and Diamond. Tara and Darren. And Tara and Darren were now expecting their first child.

Yeah, her life was more full than she had imagined it could be.

And tomorrow, her lifelong dream was coming true. It was going to be so much more special now that Karen had been able to take the time from her schedule to attend and be her maid of honor.

Kelly softly stroked Ashton's beautiful face. "Are you sure you want to do this?"

"There's no way I'm going to let you back out now."

Kelly chuckled. As if! "But to move out here to be with me . . . Are you sure you won't regret it?"

Ashton planted a soft kiss on Kelly's chin. "Anywhere you are is where I want to be."

"But your music. Opportunities here may not be as good as in Toronto. What if you end up resenting me?"

Raising an eyebrow, Ashton smiled at Kelly. "Are you trying to get out of marrying me?"

Kelly grinned sweetly. "No. I just don't want you to think you gave up your life for me."

Ashton ran seductive fingers up Kelly's back, then kissed her cheek. "I was going to surprise you with the news tomorrow, but since you're so worried about whether or not I'm making the right decision, I'll tell you now."

Instantly sitting upright, Kelly looked down at Ashton, intrigued. "Tell me what?" When he merely flashed her a sexy smile, Kelly frantically asked, "What? What is it?

You have to go back to Toronto? You got a recording contract?"

Ashton chuckled softly. "You don't have to worry about my music career. I've landed a gig at *Tiffany's* by the marina, doing a two-hour show Thursdays and Saturdays. If it's successful, I could be booked for more time."

Kelly let out a high-pitched squeal and hugged Ashton with all her strength. "*Tiffany's!* That's the hottest entertainment spot in Fort Lauderdale! Oh my God, Ashton!"

Tightening his arm around her waist, Ashton brushed his nose against Kelly's cheek. "So you see, there's nothing to worry about."

Elated, Kelly drew in a lungful of the tantalizing evening air. "You're right. Everything's perfect." She snuggled her head against Ashton's shoulder, gratified with the thought that he really loved her and that she was really going to be happy. If Karen hadn't gotten that part in the musical, if Ashton hadn't called and invited her to Toronto, if she hadn't gone to celebrate her friend's success . . .

If schmiff. This was here. This was now. This was reality.

"Pinch me," she said.

"How about I do this instead?"

Ashton seized her mouth with his. Kelly wrapped her arms around his broad shoulders and gave in to the sweetness of his lips.

And as the swing swayed beneath them, their lips danced in an age-old ritual. And she knew, just *knew*, that they would be together—forever.

Dear Readers,

I was really happy to hear all your responses to *In An Instant* and *In a Heartbeat,* my novels featuring Tara and Diamond, the Montgomery cousins. Thanks so much for your feedback. It's always wonderful to hear that my stories are touching you in some way.

As promised, I gave you Kelly's story. I hope you enjoyed it. She and Ashton are proof that true love never dies, even if you don't know you're in love in the first place! It was a blast writing their journey.

I'd love to hear from you regarding whom you'd like to see next in a book. I'm thinking of something for Karen. After all, she needs to find her Mr. Right, too—doesn't she?

Keep your letters coming. You can reach me by snail mail or e-mail.

E-mail me at: kayla@kaylaperrin.com

Or, send regular mail to:

Kayla Perrin
1405 Upper Ottawa Street
Suite #10-121
Hamilton, ON Canada
L8W 3Y4

If you would like a reply, please include a SASE.

Until next time, happy reading!

Kayla

ABOUT THE AUTHOR

Kayla Perrin spends her time between Toronto and Miami. She has a Bachelor of Arts in english and sociology and a Bachelor of Education, having entertained the idea of becoming a teacher—but she always knew she wanted to be a writer.

A romantic at heart, Kayla is happy to be writing romances for a living. In five years, she has had seventeen original releases published. An Essence bestselling author, she has received many awards for her writing, including twice winning the Romance Writers of America's Top Ten Favorite Books of the Year award. Recently she also won a Career Achievement Award from Romantic Times Magazine for multicultural romance.

You can visit Kayla's Web site at www.kaylaperrin.com

DO YOU KNOW AN ARABESQUE MAN?

CHARLES HORTON, JR.
ARABESQUE MAN 2002
featured on the cover of
One Sure Thing by Celeste O. Norfleet / Published Sept. 2003

Arabesque Man 2001 — PAUL HANEY
Holding Out for a Hero by Deirdre Savoy / Published Sept 2002
Arabesque Man 2000 — EDMAN REID
Love Lessons by Leslie Esdaile / Published Sept 2001
Arabesque Man 1999 — HAROLD JACKSON
Endless Love by Carmen Green / Published Sept 2000

WILL YOUR "ARABESQUE" MAN BE NEXT?

ONE GRAND PRIZE WINNER WILL WIN:
- 2 Day Trip to New York City
- Professional NYC Photo Shoot
- Picture on the Cover of an Arabesque Romance Novel
- Prize Pack & Profile on Arabesque Website and Newsletter
- $250.00

YOU WIN TOO!
- The Nominator of the Grand Prize Winner Receives a Prize Pack & Profile on Arabesque Website
- $250.00

To Enter: Simply complete the following items to enter your "Arabesque Man": (1) Compose an original essay that describes in 75 words or less why you think your nominee should win. (2) Include two recent photographs of him (head shot and one full length shot). Write the following information for both you and your nominee on the back of each photo: name, address, telephone number and the nominee's age, height, weight, and clothing sizes. (3) Include signature and date of nominee granting permission to nominator to enter photographs in contest. (4) Include a proof of purchase from an Arabesque romance novel—write the book title, author, ISBN number, and purchase location and price on a 3-1/2 x 5" card. (5) Entrants should keep a copy of all submissions. Submissions will not be returned and will be destroyed after the judging.

ARABESQUE regrets that no return or acknowledgment of receipt can be made because of the anticipated volume of responses. Arabesque is not responsible for late, lost, incomplete, inaccurate or misdirected entries. The Grand Prize Trip includes round trip air transportation from a major airport nearest the winner's home, 2-day (1-night) hotel accommodations and ground transportation between the airport, hotel and Arabesque offices in New York. The Grand Prize Winner will be required to sign and return an affidavit of eligibility and publicity and liability release in order to receive the prize. The Grand Prize Winner will receive no additional compensation for the use of his image on an Arabesque novel, Website, or for any other promotional purpose. The entries will be judged by a panel of BET Arabesque personnel whose decisions regarding the winner and all other matters pertaining to the Contest are final and binding. By entering this Contest, entrants agree to comply with all rules and regulations. Contest ends October 31, 2003. Entries must be postmarked by October 31, 2003, and received no later than November 6, 2003.

SEND ENTRIES TO: The Arabesque Man Cover Model Contest, BET Books, One BET Plaza, 1235 W Street, NE, Washington, DC 20018. Open to legal residents of the U.S., 21 years of age or older. Illegible entries will be disqualified. Limit one entry per envelope. Odds of winning depend, in part, on the number of entries received. Void in Puerto Rico and where prohibited by law.

More Sizzling Romance From
Francine Craft

Put a Little Romance in Your Life With
Louré Bussey

The Arabesque At Your Service Series

Four superb romances with engaging characters and dynamic story lines featuring heroes whose destiny is intertwined with women of equal courage who confront their passionate—and unpredictable—futures.

__TOP-SECRET RENDEZVOUS – *Air Force*
by Linda Hudson-Smith   1-58314-397-1 $6.99US/$9.99CAN
Sparks fly when officer Hailey Douglas meets Air Force Major Zurich Kingdom. Military code forbids fraternization between an officer and an NCO, so the pair find themselves involved in a top-secret rendezvous.

__COURAGE UNDER FIRE – *Army*
by Candice Poarch   1-58314-350-5 $6.99US/$9.99CAN
Nurse Arlene Taft is assigned to care for the seriously injured Colonel Neal Allen. She remembers him as an obnoxious young neighbor at her father's military base, but now he looks nothing like she remembers. Will time give them courage under fire?

__THE GLORY OF LOVE – *Navy*
by Kim Louise   1-58314-411-0 $6.99US/$9.99CAN
When pilot Roxanne Allgood is kidnapped, Navy Seal Col. Haughton Storm sets out on a mission to find the only person who has ever mattered to him—a lost love he hasn't seen in ten years.

__FLYING HIGH – *Marines*
by Gwynne Forster   1-58314-427-7 $6.99US/$9.99CAN
Colonel Nelson Wainwright must recover from his injuries if he is to attain his goal of becoming a four-star general. Audrey Powers, a specialist in sports medicine, enters his world to get him back on track. Will their love find a way to endure his rise to the top?

Now Available in Bookstores!

Visit our website at **www.arabesquebooks.com**.